CLUE®
CANDLESTICK

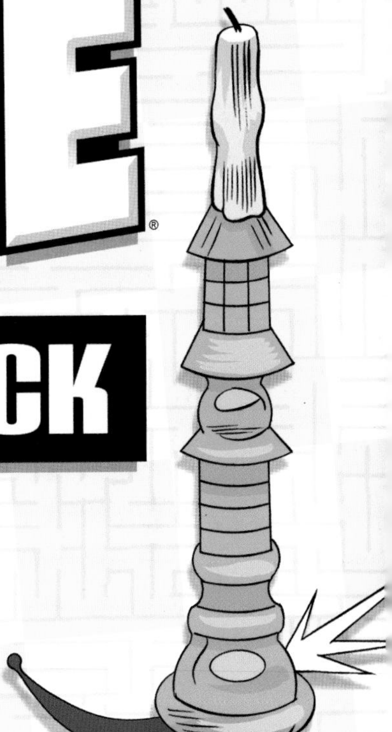

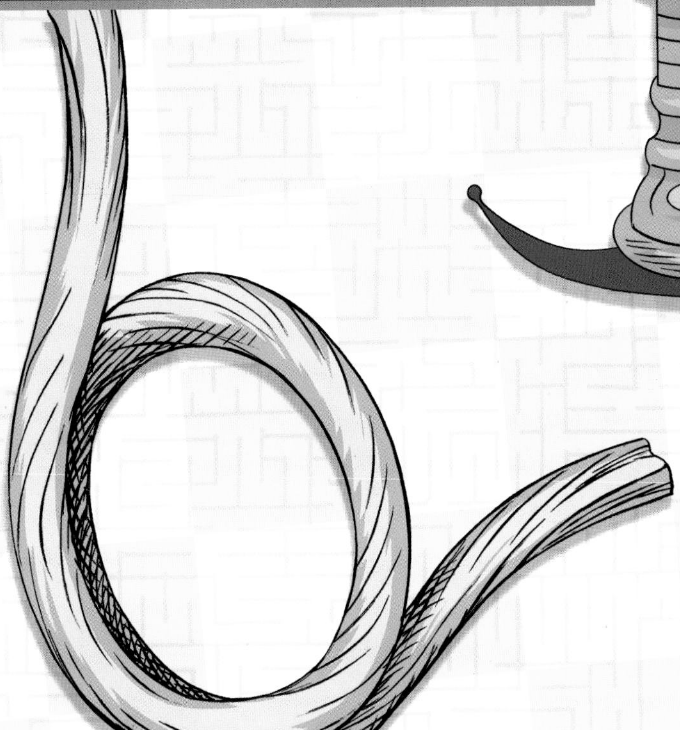

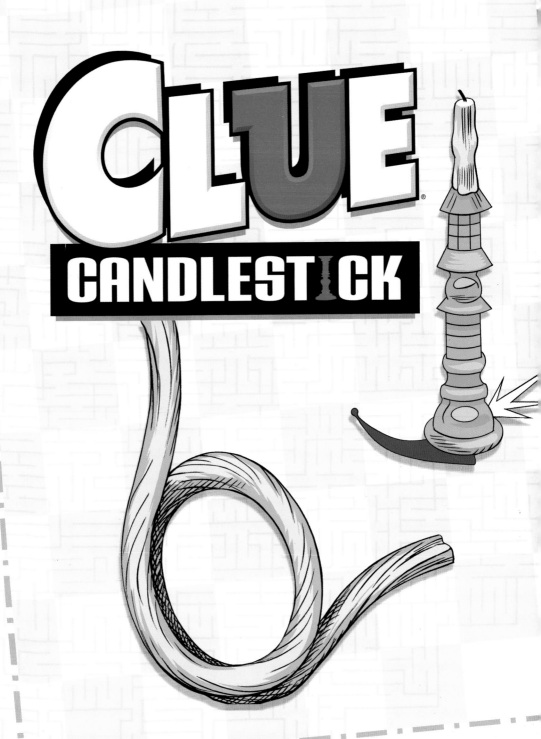

Become our fan on Facebook **facebook.com/idwpublishing**
Follow us on Twitter **@idwpublishing**
Subscribe to us on YouTube **youtube.com/idwpublishing**
See what's new on Tumblr **tumblr.idwpublishing.com**
Check us out on Instagram **instagram.com/idwpublishing**

Chris Ryall, President, Publisher, & CCO
John Barber, Editor-In-Chief
Cara Morrison, Chief Financial Officer
Matthew Ruzicka, Chief Accounting Officer
David Hedgecock, Associate Publisher
Jerry Bennington, VP of New Product Development
Lorelei Bunjes, VP of Digital Services
Justin Eisinger, Editorial Director, Graphic Novels & Collections
Eric Moss, Sr. Director, Licensing & Business Development

Ted Adams and Robbie Robbins, IDW Founders

ISBN: 978-1-68405-611-8   23 22 21 20   1 2 3 4

Originally published as CLUE: CANDLESTICK issues #1–3.

Shaw would like to thank Michelle Dominado, Sophie Franz, David
Hedgecock, Tim Hodler, Kevin Huizenga, Jed McGowan, Jane Samborski,
Tom Scioli, Suzette Smith, Matthew Thurber, Emily Wolver, Mac Wood, and
his parents.

For international rights, contact licensing@idwpublishing.com

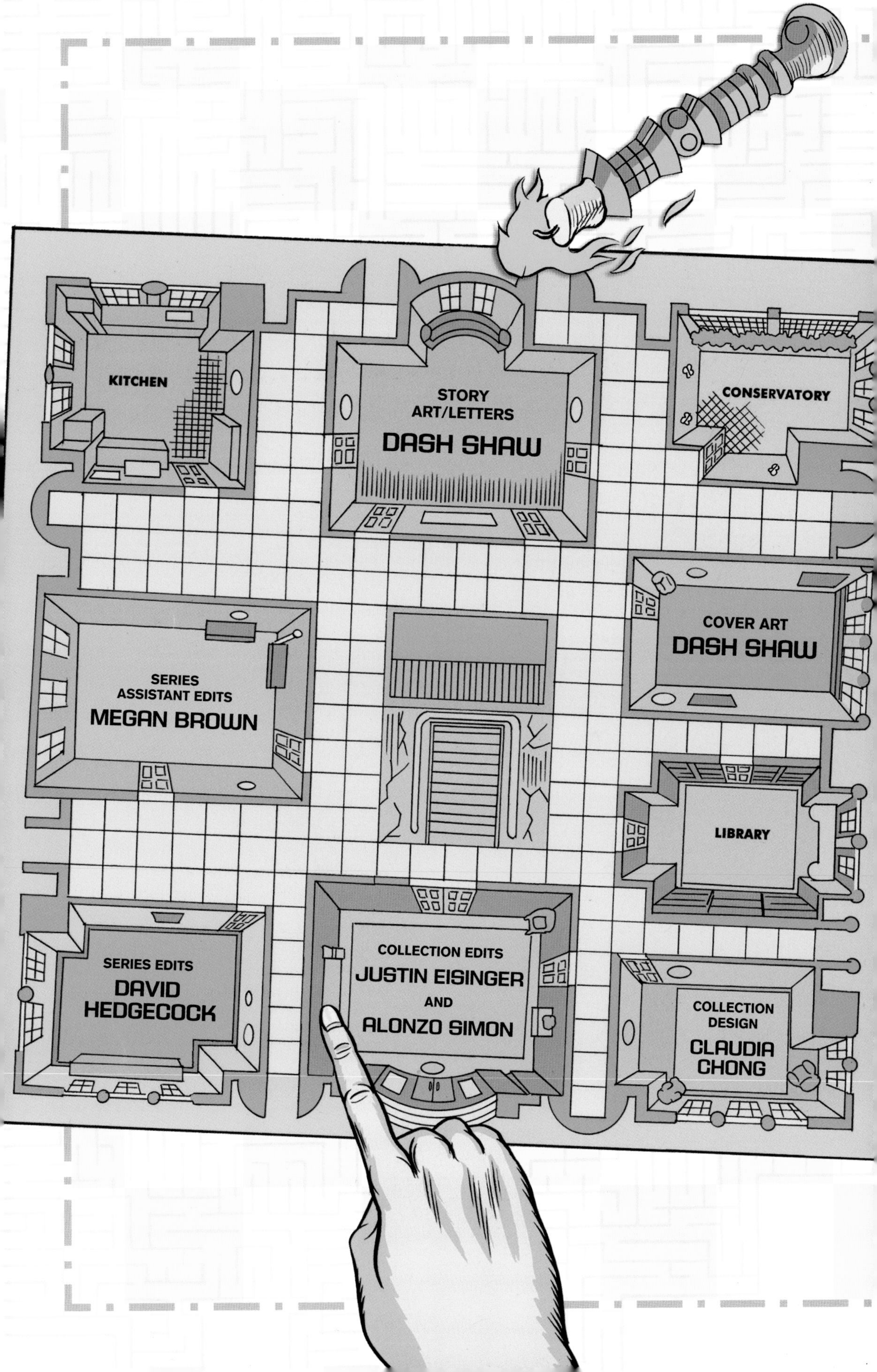
KITCHEN
STORY
ART/LETTERS
DASH SHAW
CONSERVATORY
COVER ART
DASH SHAW
SERIES
ASSISTANT EDITS
MEGAN BROWN
LIBRARY
SERIES EDITS
DAVID
HEDGECOCK
COLLECTION EDITS
JUSTIN EISINGER
AND
ALONZO SIMON
COLLECTION
DESIGN
CLAUDIA
CHONG

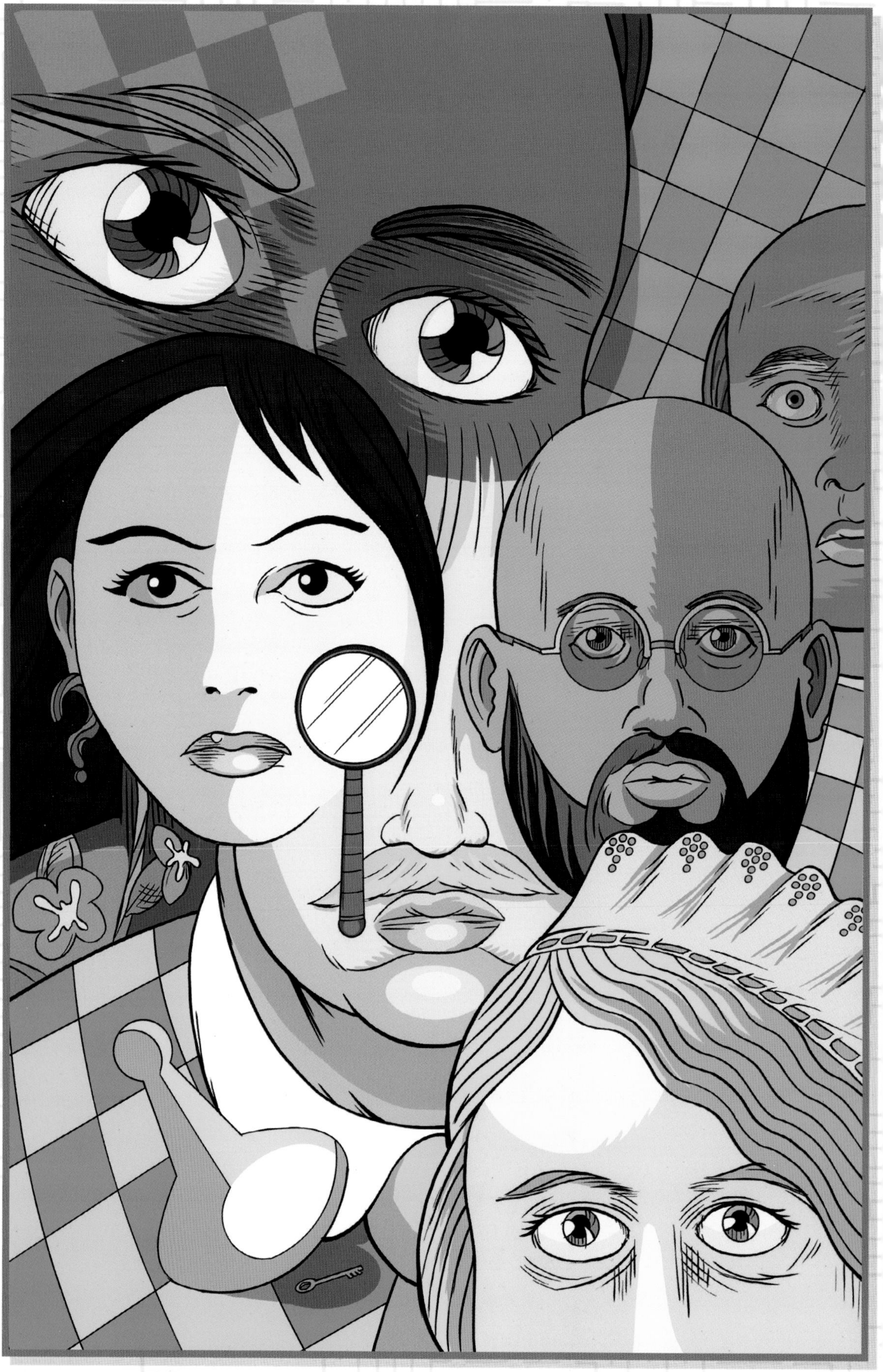

ART BY
DASH SHAW

WIND BLOWS THROUGH THE WINDOWSILL, CREATING AN EERIE WHISTLE.

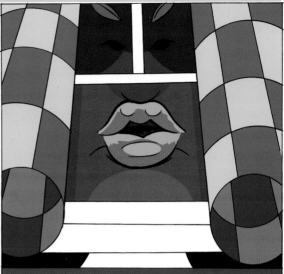

LYING IN BED, AWAKE, I IMAGINE THE PATH THE WIND TAKES THROUGH MY BEDROOM.

THE WHISTLE GROWS SHARPER— SHRILLER— NOW IT'S A POLICEMAN'S WHISTLE— WARNING ME—THERE'S DANGER AHEAD—

DING DONG

NOT A WHISTLE. A DOORBELL. THE POSTMAN.

ANOTHER SLEEPLESS NIGHT, PROFESSOR?

REGRETTABLY SO... I JUST CAN'T TURN MY BRAIN OFF — MY DOCTOR CALLS IT A CASE OF "RACING THOUGHTS."

TRY A TALL GLASS OF MALTED MILK WITH A DROP OF HONEY BEFORE BED... IT KNOCKS ME OUT... KEEPS MY MIND OFF THE DAY'S MAIL.

THANKS, OLLIE... DO YOU HAVE ANYTHING FOR ME?

A PACK OF COUPONS. I'VE CUT OUT ONES THAT MAY BE OF INTEREST. PLEASE DON'T READ INTO ANY PRESUMPTIONS ON MY PART. I HAVE NOTHING BUT NOBLE INTENT.

BLESS YOU.

ANOTHER FROM THE ACADEMY. NOT A CHECK, I'M AFRAID.

IT FEELS AS THOUGH IT NEVER IS.

AND THIS — A MOST CURIOUS PARCEL.

NO RETURN ADDRESS.

HUH

DO TELL ME WHAT IT IS TOMORROW?

THANK YOU, OLLIE. I WILL.

ENVELOPE BACK

THROAT

CONTENTS

SEAM

SIDE FLAP

SALIVA, CAREFULLY APPLIED.

FAINT PEACH MATTE LIPSTICK. SEALED BY MRS. WHITE?

CREAM 1960 ENVELOPE. NEAR MINT CONDITION.

A 1940 STAMP. ONLY A COLLECTOR WOULD HAVE THIS. MR. BODDY?

prof plum
210 Baker St.
Marylebone, london
NW1 6XE

SPACED WRITING. SMALL. ANGLED. THE HANDWRITING OF A LONELY, ISOLATED MAN. IT MUST BE MR. BODDY.

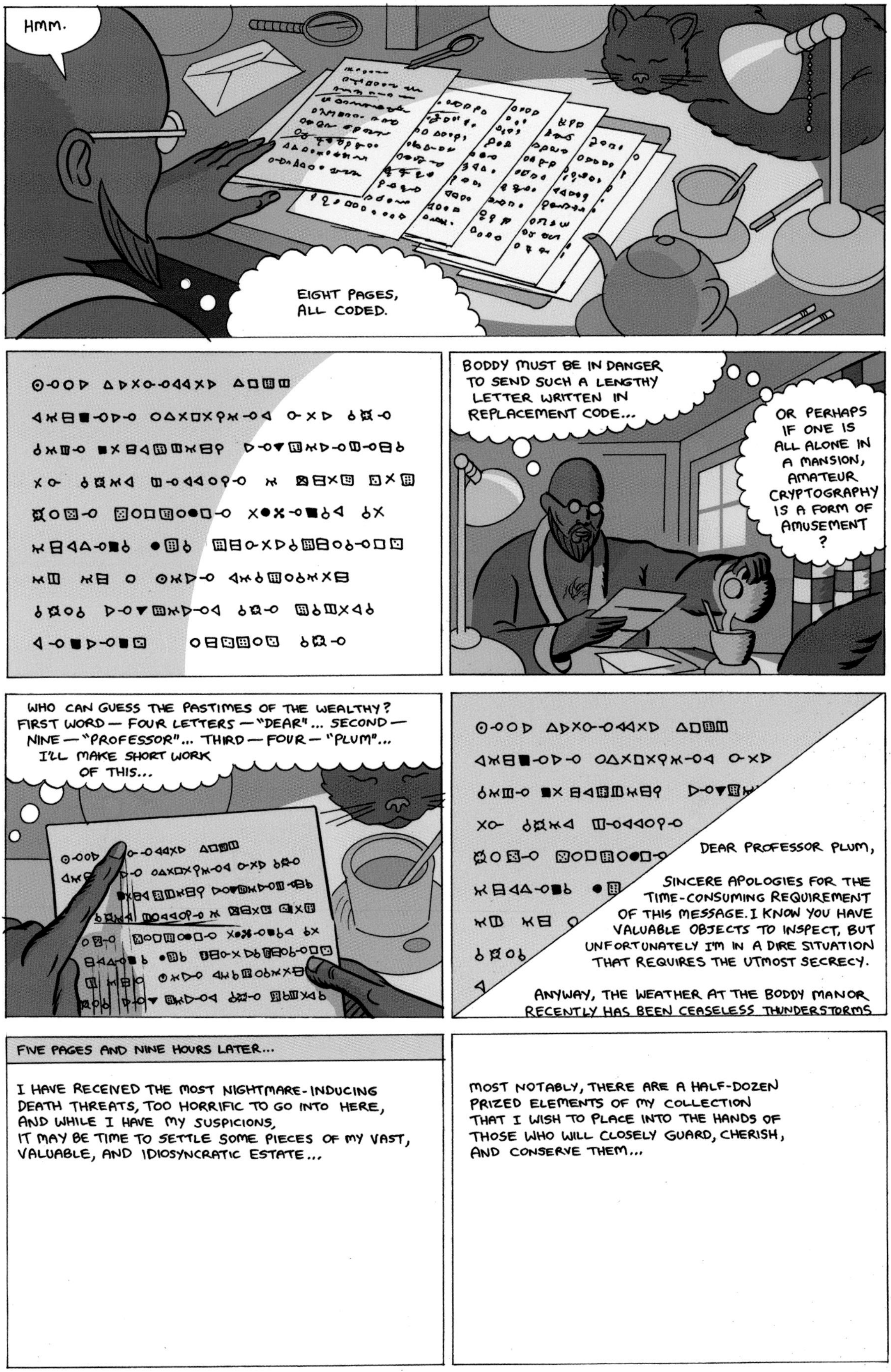
HMM.
EIGHT PAGES, ALL CODED.
BODDY MUST BE IN DANGER TO SEND SUCH A LENGTHY LETTER WRITTEN IN REPLACEMENT CODE...
OR PERHAPS IF ONE IS ALL ALONE IN A MANSION, AMATEUR CRYPTOGRAPHY IS A FORM OF AMUSEMENT?
WHO CAN GUESS THE PASTIMES OF THE WEALTHY? FIRST WORD — FOUR LETTERS — "DEAR"... SECOND — NINE — "PROFESSOR"... THIRD — FOUR — "PLUM"... I'LL MAKE SHORT WORK OF THIS...
DEAR PROFESSOR PLUM,
SINCERE APOLOGIES FOR THE TIME-CONSUMING REQUIREMENT OF THIS MESSAGE. I KNOW YOU HAVE VALUABLE OBJECTS TO INSPECT, BUT UNFORTUNATELY I'M IN A DIRE SITUATION THAT REQUIRES THE UTMOST SECRECY.
ANYWAY, THE WEATHER AT THE BODDY MANOR RECENTLY HAS BEEN CEASELESS THUNDERSTORMS
FIVE PAGES AND NINE HOURS LATER...
I HAVE RECEIVED THE MOST NIGHTMARE-INDUCING DEATH THREATS, TOO HORRIFIC TO GO INTO HERE, AND WHILE I HAVE MY SUSPICIONS, IT MAY BE TIME TO SETTLE SOME PIECES OF MY VAST, VALUABLE, AND IDIOSYNCRATIC ESTATE...
MOST NOTABLY, THERE ARE A HALF-DOZEN PRIZED ELEMENTS OF MY COLLECTION THAT I WISH TO PLACE INTO THE HANDS OF THOSE WHO WILL CLOSELY GUARD, CHERISH, AND CONSERVE THEM...

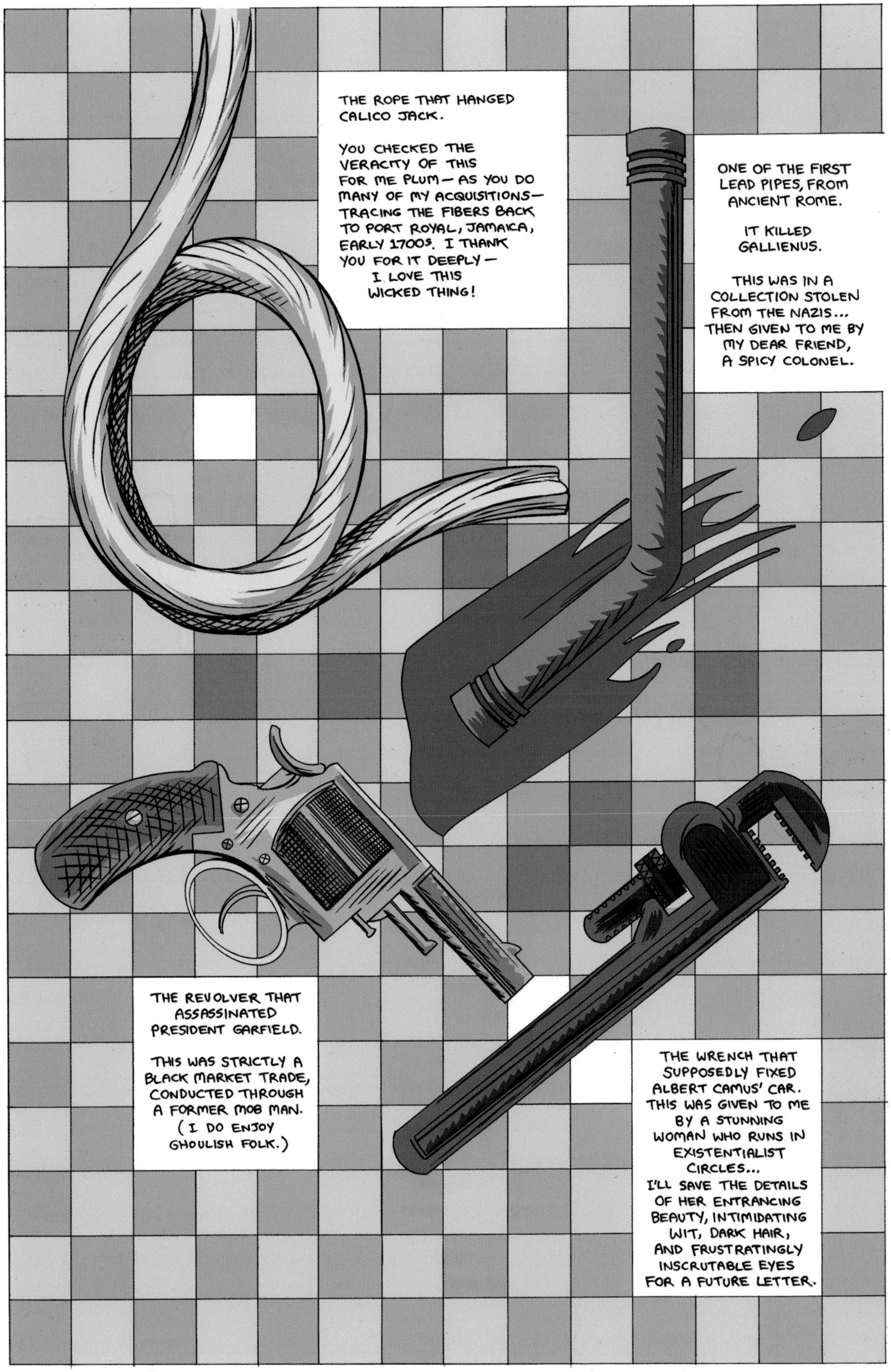
THE ROPE THAT HANGED CALICO JACK.
YOU CHECKED THE VERACITY OF THIS FOR ME PLUM — AS YOU DO MANY OF MY ACQUISITIONS — TRACING THE FIBERS BACK TO PORT ROYAL, JAMAICA, EARLY 1700S. I THANK YOU FOR IT DEEPLY — I LOVE THIS WICKED THING!
ONE OF THE FIRST LEAD PIPES, FROM ANCIENT ROME.
IT KILLED GALLIENUS.
THIS WAS IN A COLLECTION STOLEN FROM THE NAZIS... THEN GIVEN TO ME BY MY DEAR FRIEND, A SPICY COLONEL.
THE REVOLVER THAT ASSASSINATED PRESIDENT GARFIELD.
THIS WAS STRICTLY A BLACK MARKET TRADE, CONDUCTED THROUGH A FORMER MOB MAN. (I DO ENJOY GHOULISH FOLK.)
THE WRENCH THAT SUPPOSEDLY FIXED ALBERT CAMUS' CAR. THIS WAS GIVEN TO ME BY A STUNNING WOMAN WHO RUNS IN EXISTENTIALIST CIRCLES...
I'LL SAVE THE DETAILS OF HER ENTRANCING BEAUTY, INTIMIDATING WIT, DARK HAIR, AND FRUSTRATINGLY INSCRUTABLE EYES FOR A FUTURE LETTER.

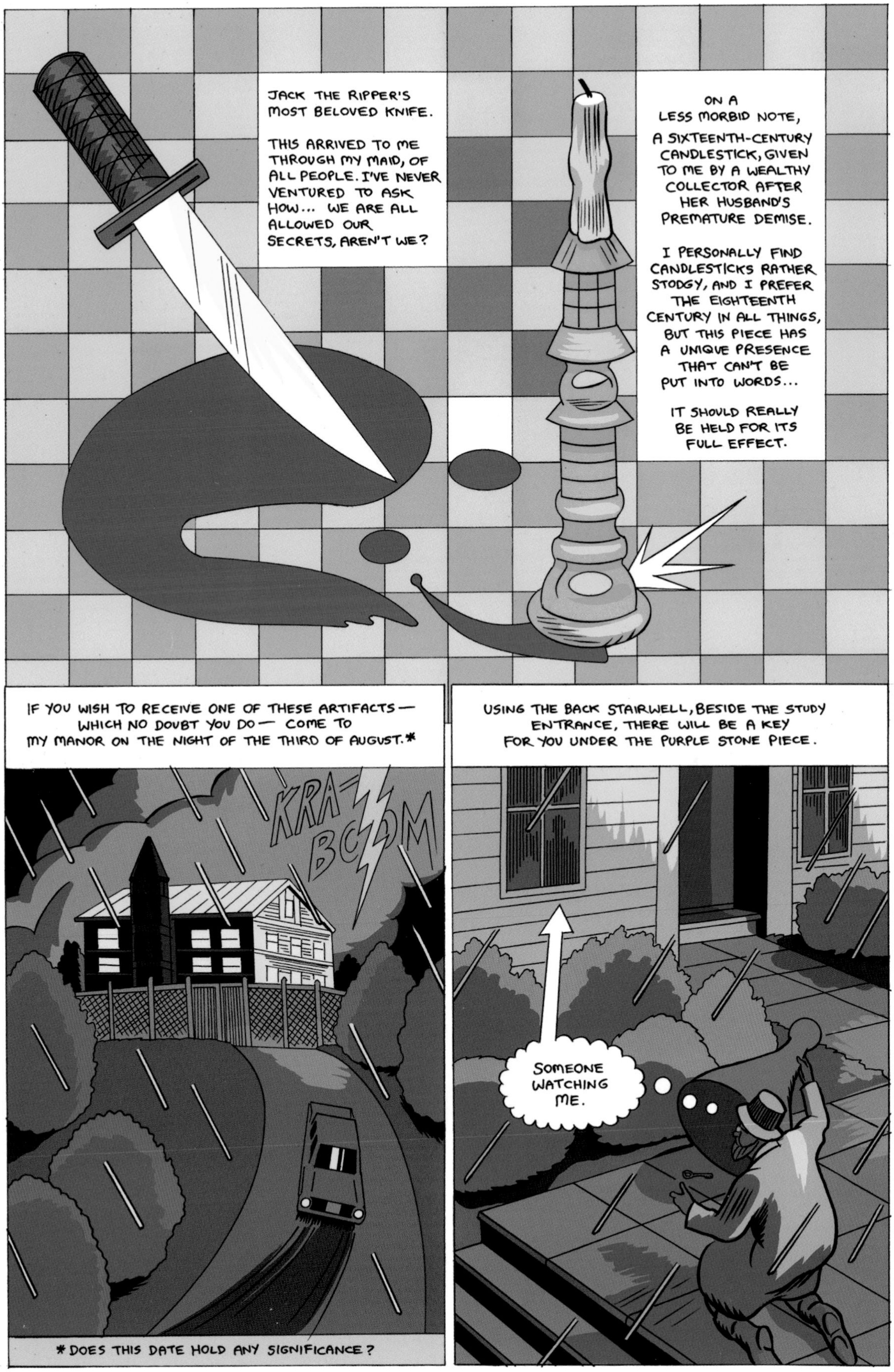
JACK THE RIPPER'S MOST BELOVED KNIFE.
THIS ARRIVED TO ME THROUGH MY MAID, OF ALL PEOPLE. I'VE NEVER VENTURED TO ASK HOW... WE ARE ALL ALLOWED OUR SECRETS, AREN'T WE?
ON A LESS MORBID NOTE, A SIXTEENTH-CENTURY CANDLESTICK, GIVEN TO ME BY A WEALTHY COLLECTOR AFTER HER HUSBAND'S PREMATURE DEMISE.
I PERSONALLY FIND CANDLESTICKS RATHER STODGY, AND I PREFER THE EIGHTEENTH CENTURY IN ALL THINGS, BUT THIS PIECE HAS A UNIQUE PRESENCE THAT CAN'T BE PUT INTO WORDS...
IT SHOULD REALLY BE HELD FOR ITS FULL EFFECT.
IF YOU WISH TO RECEIVE ONE OF THESE ARTIFACTS— WHICH NO DOUBT YOU DO— COME TO MY MANOR ON THE NIGHT OF THE THIRD OF AUGUST.*
KRA-BOOM
*DOES THIS DATE HOLD ANY SIGNIFICANCE?
USING THE BACK STAIRWELL, BESIDE THE STUDY ENTRANCE, THERE WILL BE A KEY FOR YOU UNDER THE PURPLE STONE PIECE.
SOMEONE WATCHING ME.

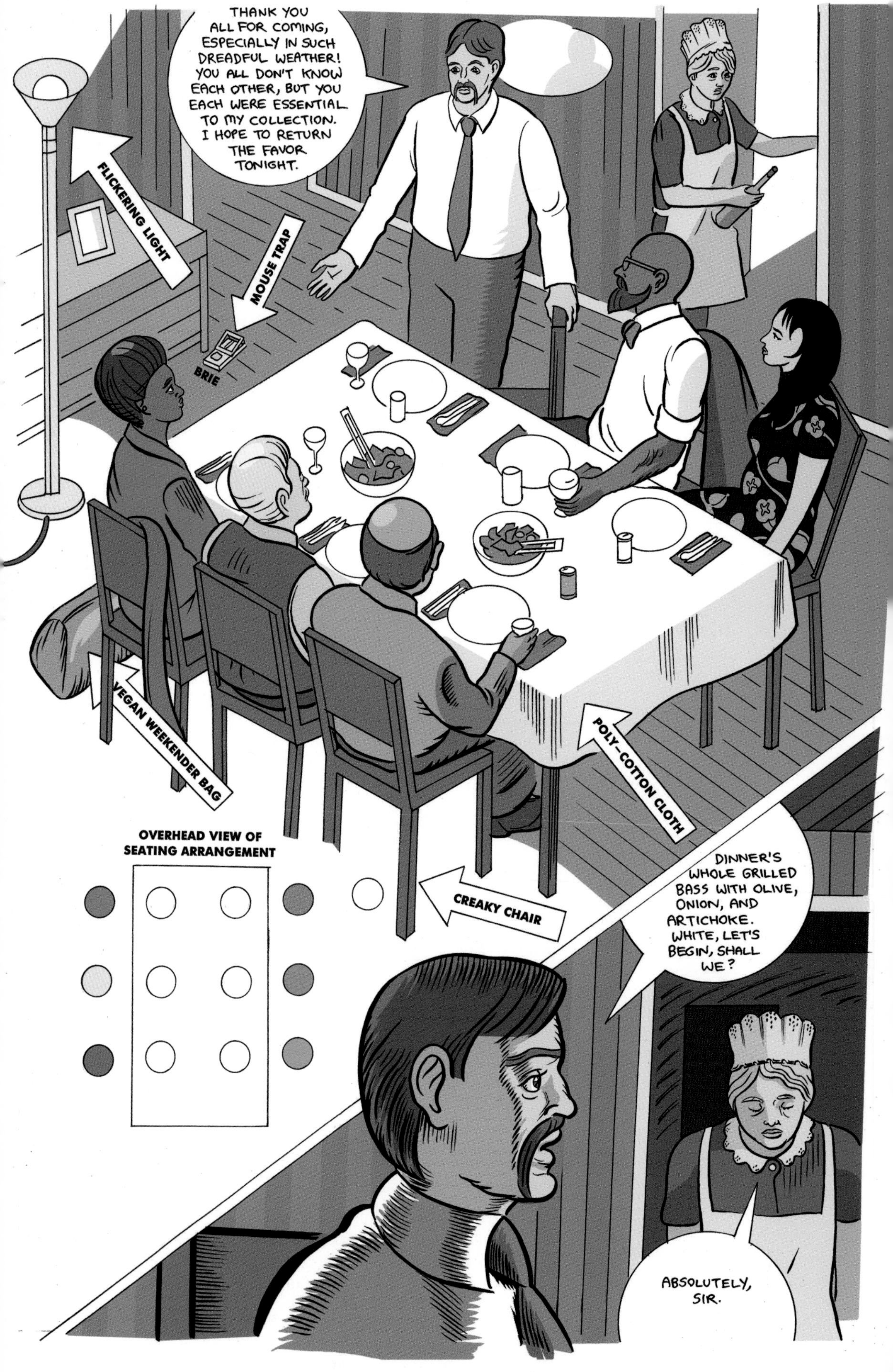
THANK YOU ALL FOR COMING, ESPECIALLY IN SUCH DREADFUL WEATHER! YOU ALL DON'T KNOW EACH OTHER, BUT YOU EACH WERE ESSENTIAL TO MY COLLECTION. I HOPE TO RETURN THE FAVOR TONIGHT.
FLICKERING LIGHT
MOUSE TRAP
BRIE
VEGAN WEEKENDER BAG
POLY-COTTON CLOTH
OVERHEAD VIEW OF SEATING ARRANGEMENT
CREAKY CHAIR
DINNER'S WHOLE GRILLED BASS WITH OLIVE, ONION, AND ARTICHOKE. WHITE, LET'S BEGIN, SHALL WE?
ABSOLUTELY, SIR.

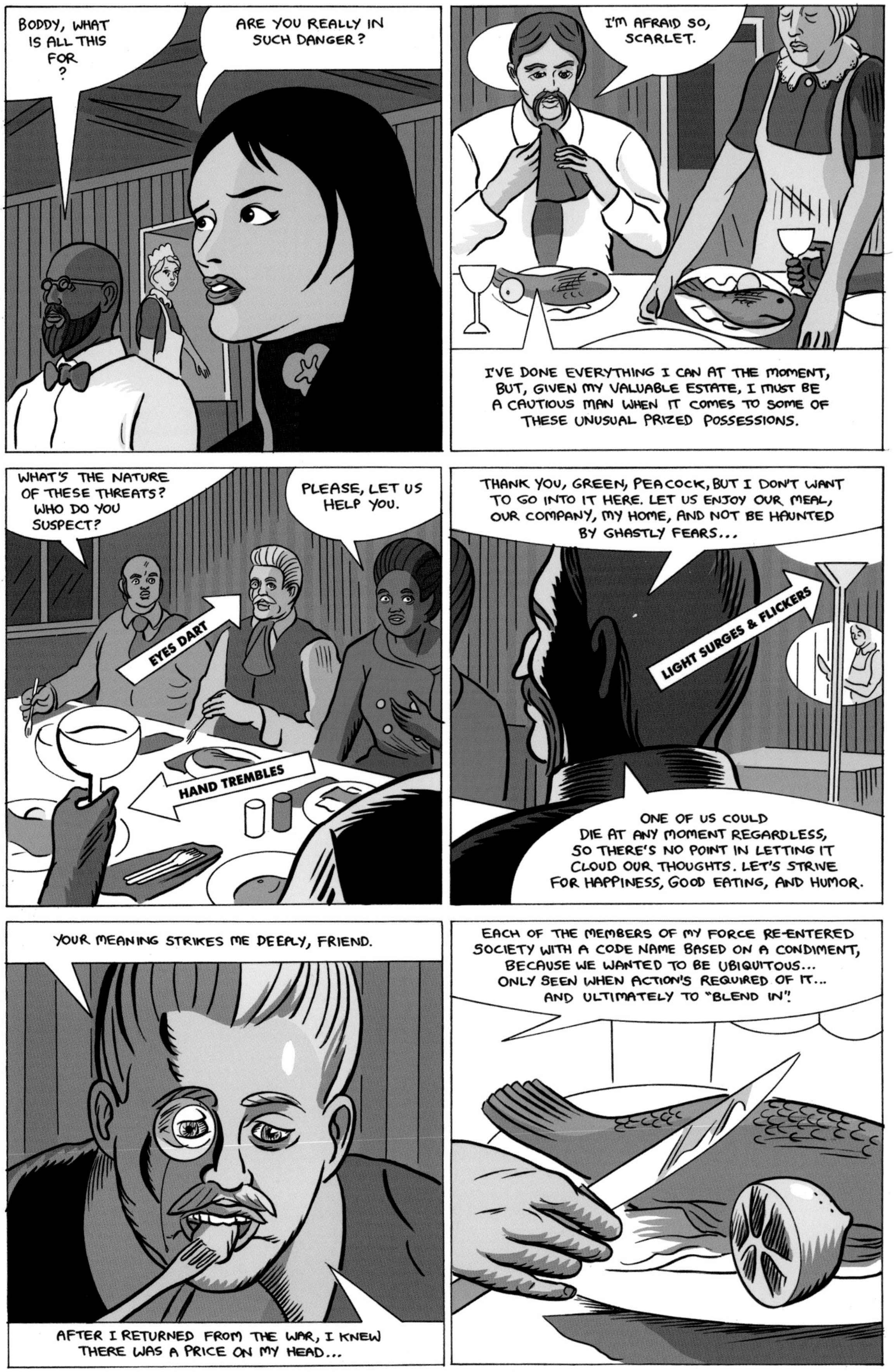
BODDY, WHAT IS ALL THIS FOR ?
ARE YOU REALLY IN SUCH DANGER?
I'M AFRAID SO, SCARLET.
I'VE DONE EVERYTHING I CAN AT THE MOMENT, BUT, GIVEN MY VALUABLE ESTATE, I MUST BE A CAUTIOUS MAN WHEN IT COMES TO SOME OF THESE UNUSUAL PRIZED POSSESSIONS.
WHAT'S THE NATURE OF THESE THREATS? WHO DO YOU SUSPECT?
PLEASE, LET US HELP YOU.
EYES DART
HAND TREMBLES
THANK YOU, GREEN, PEACOCK, BUT I DON'T WANT TO GO INTO IT HERE. LET US ENJOY OUR MEAL, OUR COMPANY, MY HOME, AND NOT BE HAUNTED BY GHASTLY FEARS...
LIGHT SURGES & FLICKERS
ONE OF US COULD DIE AT ANY MOMENT REGARDLESS, SO THERE'S NO POINT IN LETTING IT CLOUD OUR THOUGHTS. LET'S STRIVE FOR HAPPINESS, GOOD EATING, AND HUMOR.
YOUR MEANING STRIKES ME DEEPLY, FRIEND.
AFTER I RETURNED FROM THE WAR, I KNEW THERE WAS A PRICE ON MY HEAD...
EACH OF THE MEMBERS OF MY FORCE RE-ENTERED SOCIETY WITH A CODE NAME BASED ON A CONDIMENT, BECAUSE WE WANTED TO BE UBIQUITOUS... ONLY SEEN WHEN ACTION'S REQUIRED OF IT... AND ULTIMATELY TO "BLEND IN".

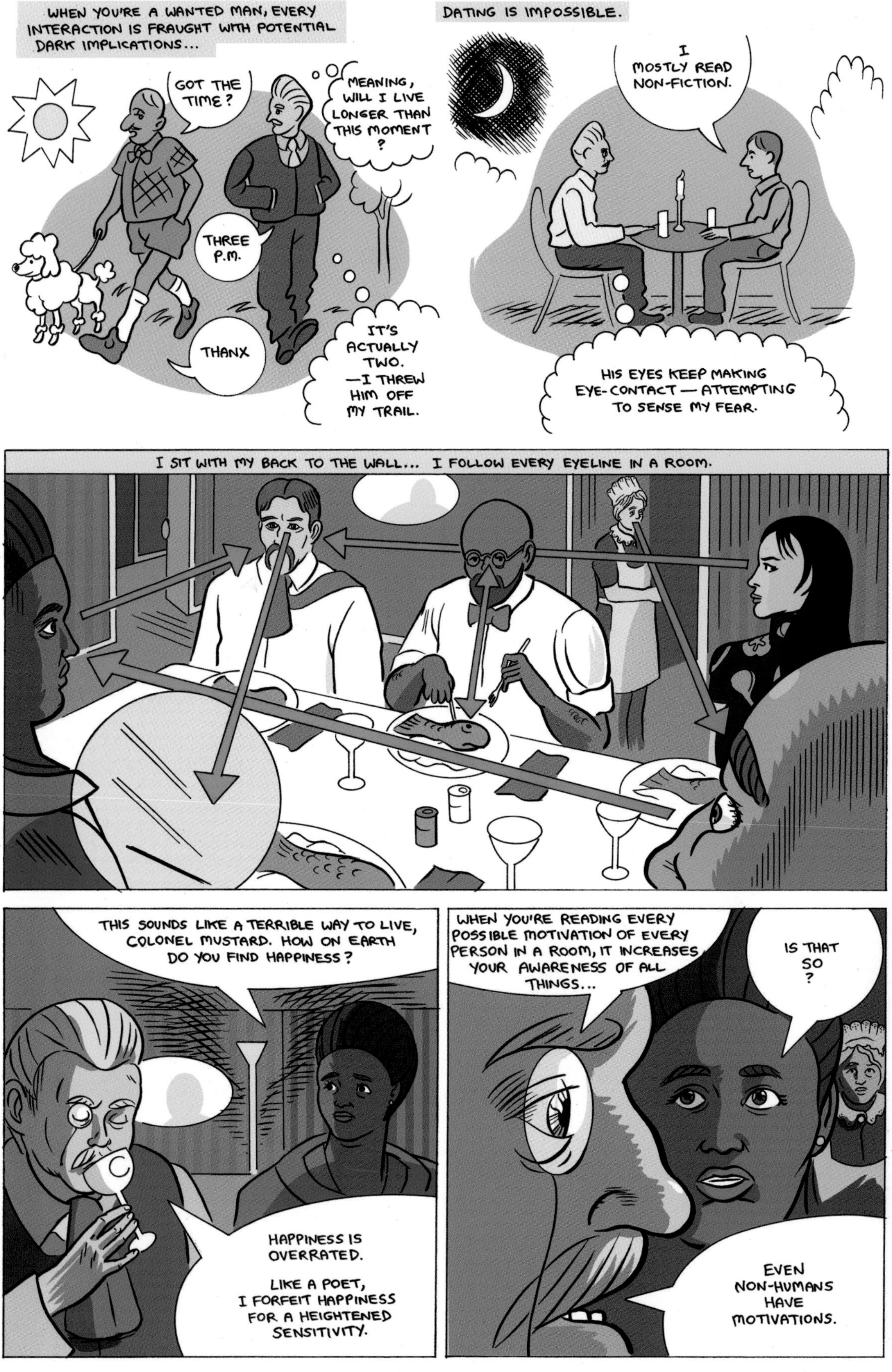
WHEN YOU'RE A WANTED MAN, EVERY INTERACTION IS FRAUGHT WITH POTENTIAL DARK IMPLICATIONS...
GOT THE TIME?
MEANING, WILL I LIVE LONGER THAN THIS MOMENT ?
THREE P.M.
THANX
IT'S ACTUALLY TWO. —I THREW HIM OFF MY TRAIL.
DATING IS IMPOSSIBLE.
I MOSTLY READ NON-FICTION.
HIS EYES KEEP MAKING EYE-CONTACT — ATTEMPTING TO SENSE MY FEAR.
I SIT WITH MY BACK TO THE WALL... I FOLLOW EVERY EYELINE IN A ROOM.
THIS SOUNDS LIKE A TERRIBLE WAY TO LIVE, COLONEL MUSTARD. HOW ON EARTH DO YOU FIND HAPPINESS?
HAPPINESS IS OVERRATED.
LIKE A POET, I FORFEIT HAPPINESS FOR A HEIGHTENED SENSITIVITY.
WHEN YOU'RE READING EVERY POSSIBLE MOTIVATION OF EVERY PERSON IN A ROOM, IT INCREASES YOUR AWARENESS OF ALL THINGS...
IS THAT SO ?
EVEN NON-HUMANS HAVE MOTIVATIONS.

A PLANT, OF COURSE, WANTS TO GROW.

AN INSECT WANTS TO EAT.

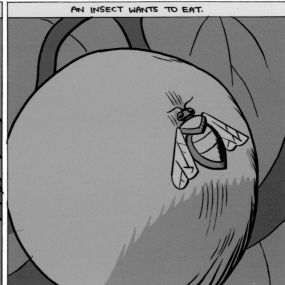

NOT ONLY DO LIVING BEINGS HAVE MOTIVATIONS, BUT INANIMATE ONES DO AS WELL.

KRA-BOOM

ABSURD!

NOT AT ALL... FOR INSTANCE, THIS KNIFE WANTS TO CUT.

ANY-ONE CAN SENSE THAT.

BRING IN THE CHEST.

YES, SIR.

IT IS THE MOTIVE OF A ROLLING PIN TO ROLL, AND OF A PEELER TO PEEL.

A BALL WANTS TO BOUNCE.

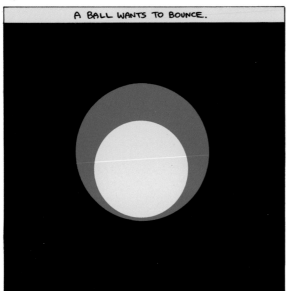

A DIE WANTS TO CHOOSE FATE.

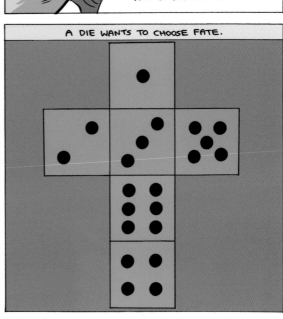

OTHER OBJECTS ARE EVEN MORE SUBTLE OR MISCHEVIOUS IN THEIR DESIRES...

OH?

HEH

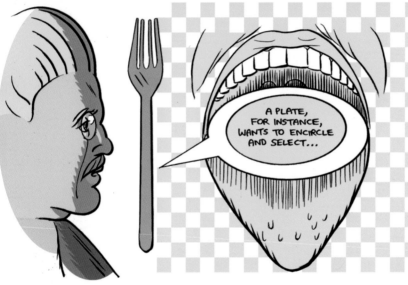

A PLATE, FOR INSTANCE, WANTS TO ENCIRCLE AND SELECT...

IT CONTROLS WHAT IS EATEN AND WHAT IS NOT.

THINGS OUTSIDE THE PLATE ARE ALLOWED TO GO UNCONSIDERED FOR CONSUMPTION.

AND THE CONTENTS OF THE PLATE COULD EASILY BE POISONOUS OR ILL-CHOSEN.

THAT WOULD OBVIOUSLY BE THE MOTIVE OF THE SERVERS OF THE PLATE — NOT THE PLATE ITSELF!

YES, BUT CERTAIN PLATES ATTRACT CERTAIN SERVERS —

WHAT ABOUT YOU, MUSTARD?!

WHAT'S THE MOTIVE BEHIND YOU TELLING US THIS RIDICULOUSNESS?!

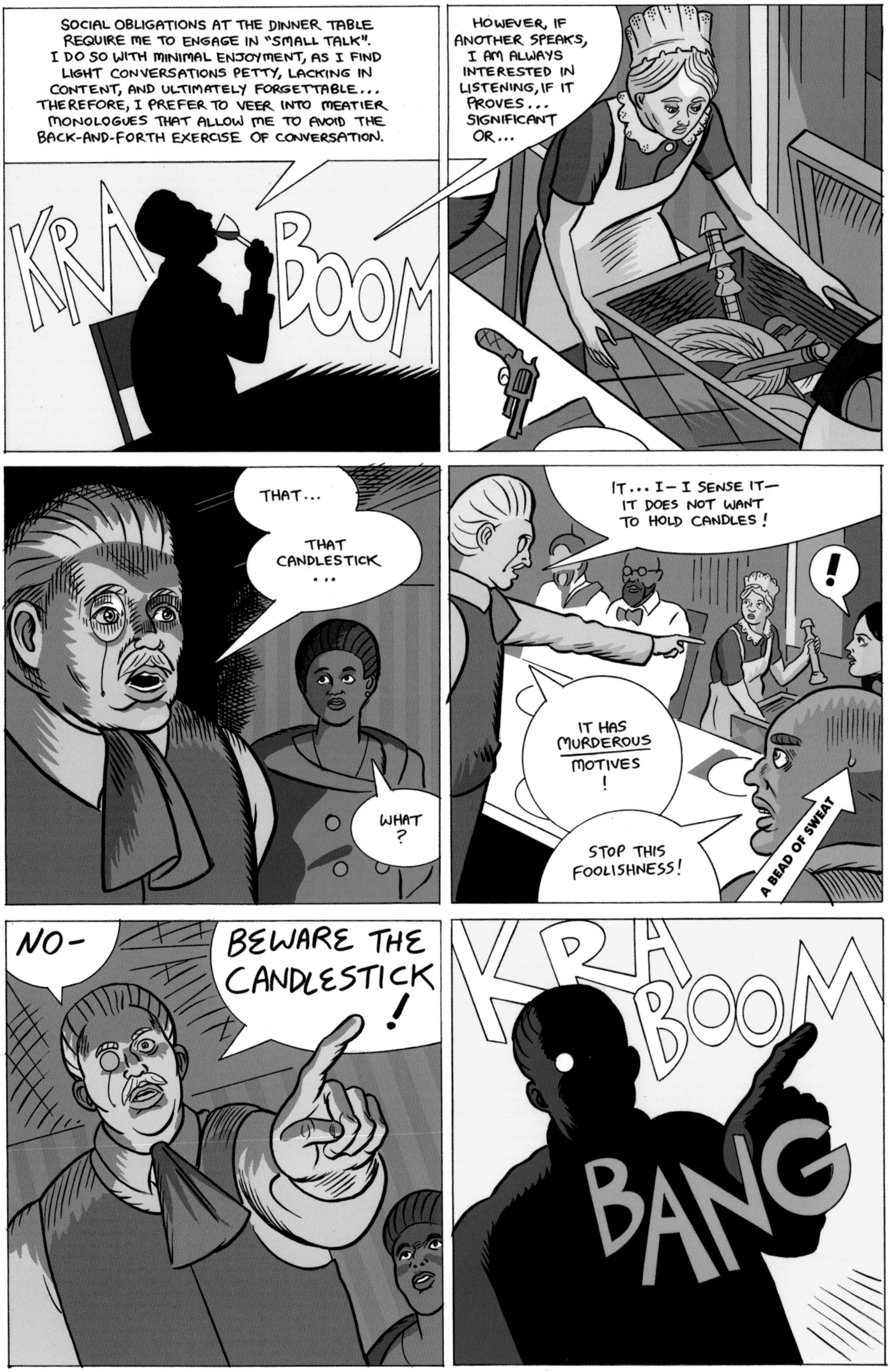
SOCIAL OBLIGATIONS AT THE DINNER TABLE REQUIRE ME TO ENGAGE IN "SMALL TALK". I DO SO WITH MINIMAL ENJOYMENT, AS I FIND LIGHT CONVERSATIONS PETTY, LACKING IN CONTENT, AND ULTIMATELY FORGETTABLE... THEREFORE, I PREFER TO VEER INTO MEATIER MONOLOGUES THAT ALLOW ME TO AVOID THE BACK-AND-FORTH EXERCISE OF CONVERSATION.
KRA BOOM
HOWEVER, IF ANOTHER SPEAKS, I AM ALWAYS INTERESTED IN LISTENING, IF IT PROVES... SIGNIFICANT OR...
THAT...
THAT CANDLESTICK...
WHAT?
IT... I— I SENSE IT— IT DOES NOT WANT TO HOLD CANDLES!
!
IT HAS MURDEROUS MOTIVES!
STOP THIS FOOLISHNESS!
A BEAD OF SWEAT
NO-
BEWARE THE CANDLESTICK!
KRA BOOM
BANG

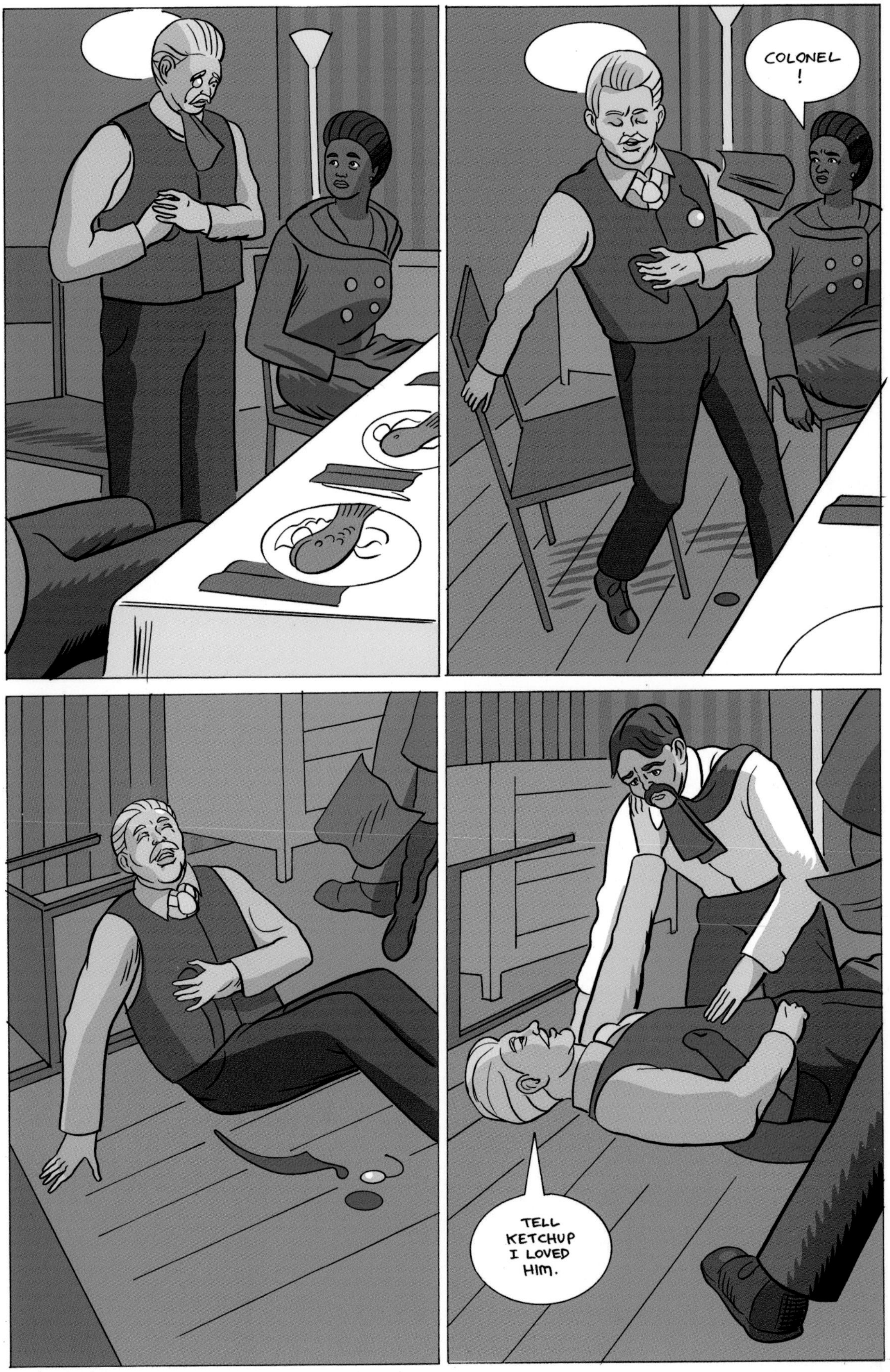
COLONEL !
TELL KETCHUP I LOVED HIM.

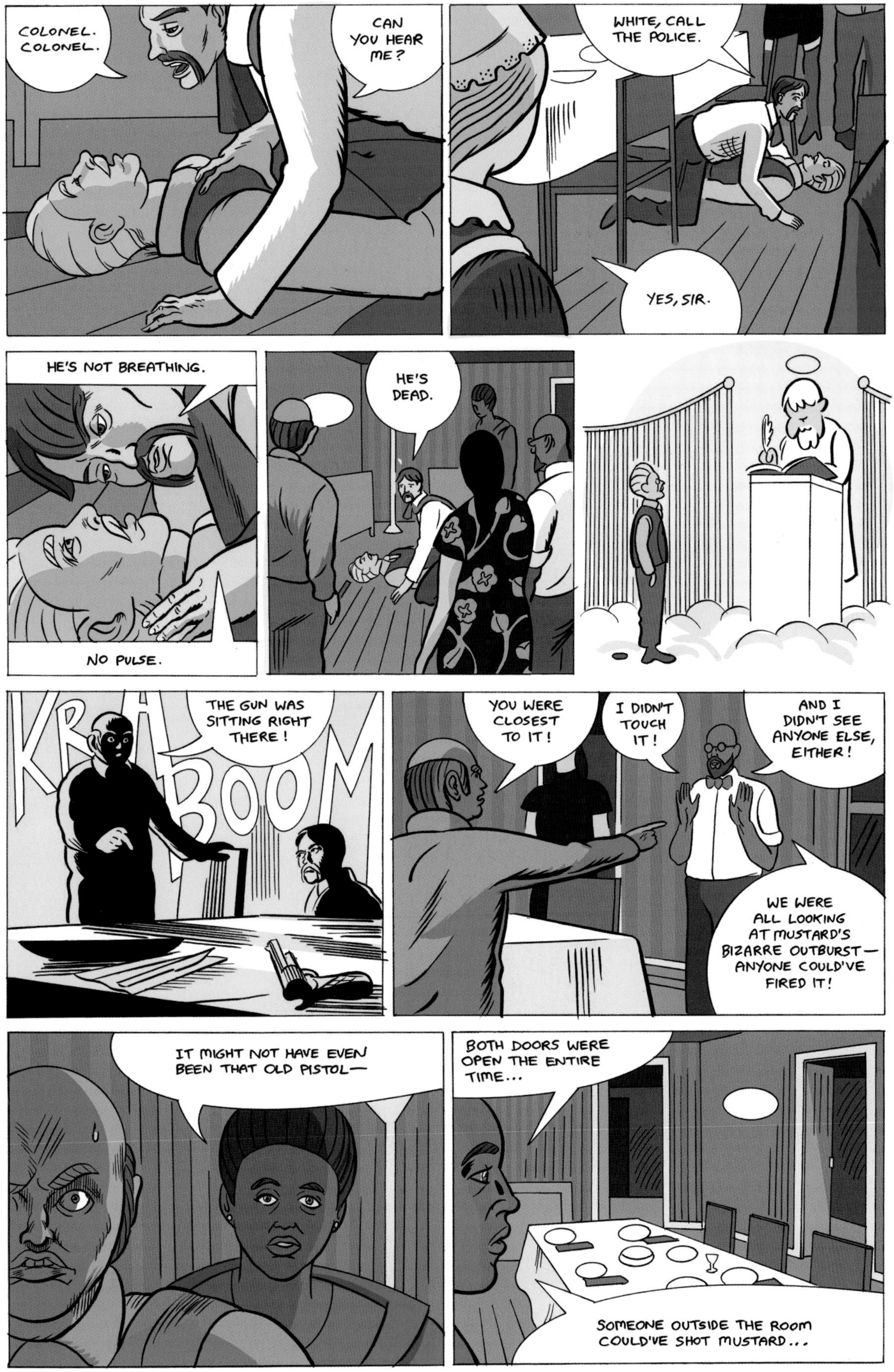
COLONEL. COLONEL.
CAN YOU HEAR ME?
WHITE, CALL THE POLICE.
YES, SIR.
HE'S NOT BREATHING.
NO PULSE.
HE'S DEAD.
KRA BOOM
THE GUN WAS SITTING RIGHT THERE!
YOU WERE CLOSEST TO IT!
I DIDN'T TOUCH IT!
AND I DIDN'T SEE ANYONE ELSE, EITHER!
WE WERE ALL LOOKING AT MUSTARD'S BIZARRE OUTBURST— ANYONE COULD'VE FIRED IT!
IT MIGHT NOT HAVE EVEN BEEN THAT OLD PISTOL—
BOTH DOORS WERE OPEN THE ENTIRE TIME...
SOMEONE OUTSIDE THE ROOM COULD'VE SHOT MUSTARD...

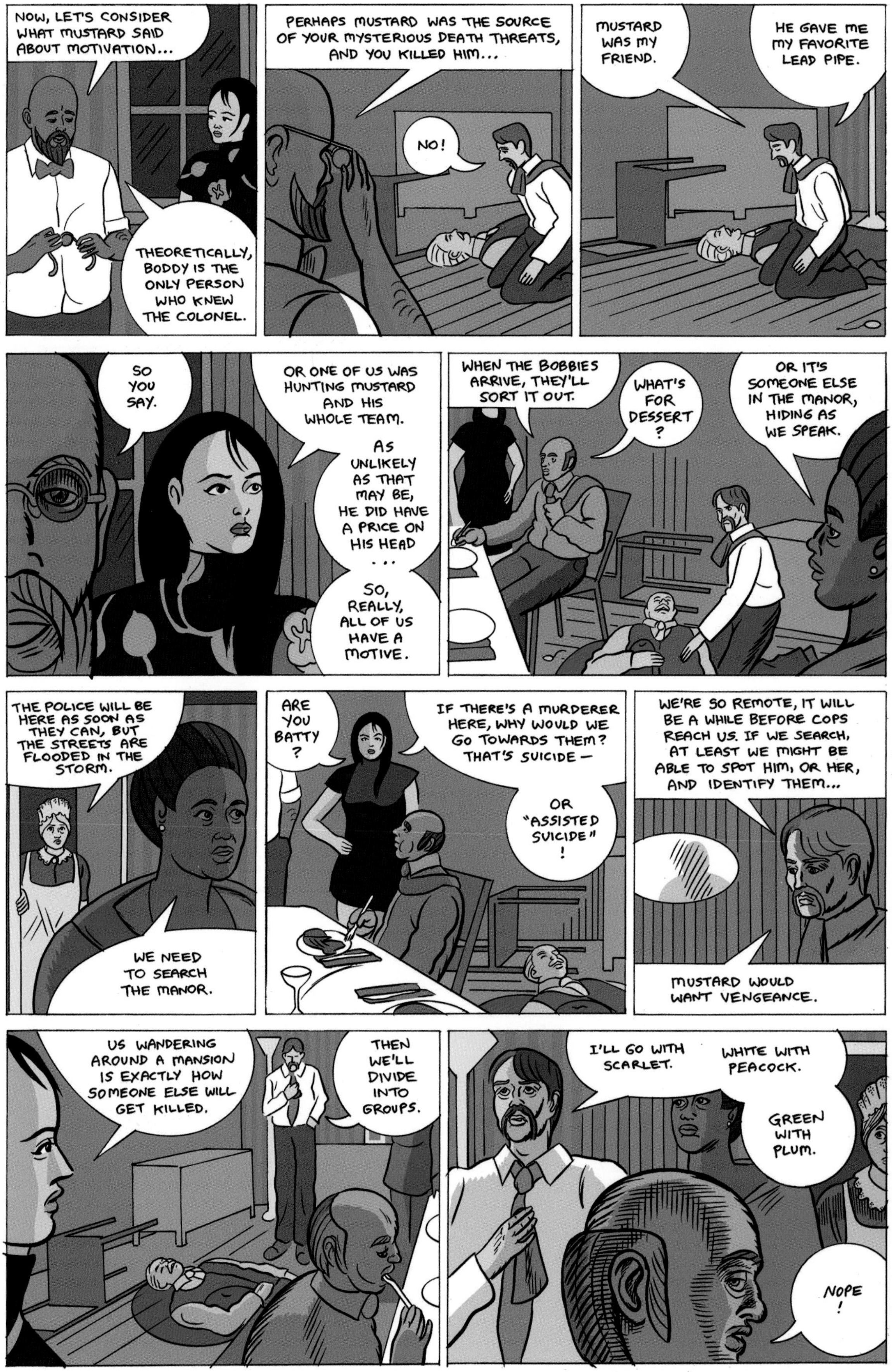
NOW, LET'S CONSIDER WHAT MUSTARD SAID ABOUT MOTIVATION...
THEORETICALLY, BODDY IS THE ONLY PERSON WHO KNEW THE COLONEL.
PERHAPS MUSTARD WAS THE SOURCE OF YOUR MYSTERIOUS DEATH THREATS, AND YOU KILLED HIM...
NO!
MUSTARD WAS MY FRIEND.
HE GAVE ME MY FAVORITE LEAD PIPE.
SO YOU SAY.
OR ONE OF US WAS HUNTING MUSTARD AND HIS WHOLE TEAM.
AS UNLIKELY AS THAT MAY BE, HE DID HAVE A PRICE ON HIS HEAD . . .
SO, REALLY, ALL OF US HAVE A MOTIVE.
WHEN THE BOBBIES ARRIVE, THEY'LL SORT IT OUT.
WHAT'S FOR DESSERT?
OR IT'S SOMEONE ELSE IN THE MANOR, HIDING AS WE SPEAK.
THE POLICE WILL BE HERE AS SOON AS THEY CAN, BUT THE STREETS ARE FLOODED IN THE STORM.
WE NEED TO SEARCH THE MANOR.
ARE YOU BATTY?
IF THERE'S A MURDERER HERE, WHY WOULD WE GO TOWARDS THEM? THAT'S SUICIDE—
OR "ASSISTED SUICIDE"!
WE'RE SO REMOTE, IT WILL BE A WHILE BEFORE COPS REACH US. IF WE SEARCH, AT LEAST WE MIGHT BE ABLE TO SPOT HIM, OR HER, AND IDENTIFY THEM...
MUSTARD WOULD WANT VENGEANCE.
US WANDERING AROUND A MANSION IS EXACTLY HOW SOMEONE ELSE WILL GET KILLED.
THEN WE'LL DIVIDE INTO GROUPS.
I'LL GO WITH SCARLET.
WHITE WITH PEACOCK.
GREEN WITH PLUM.
NOPE!

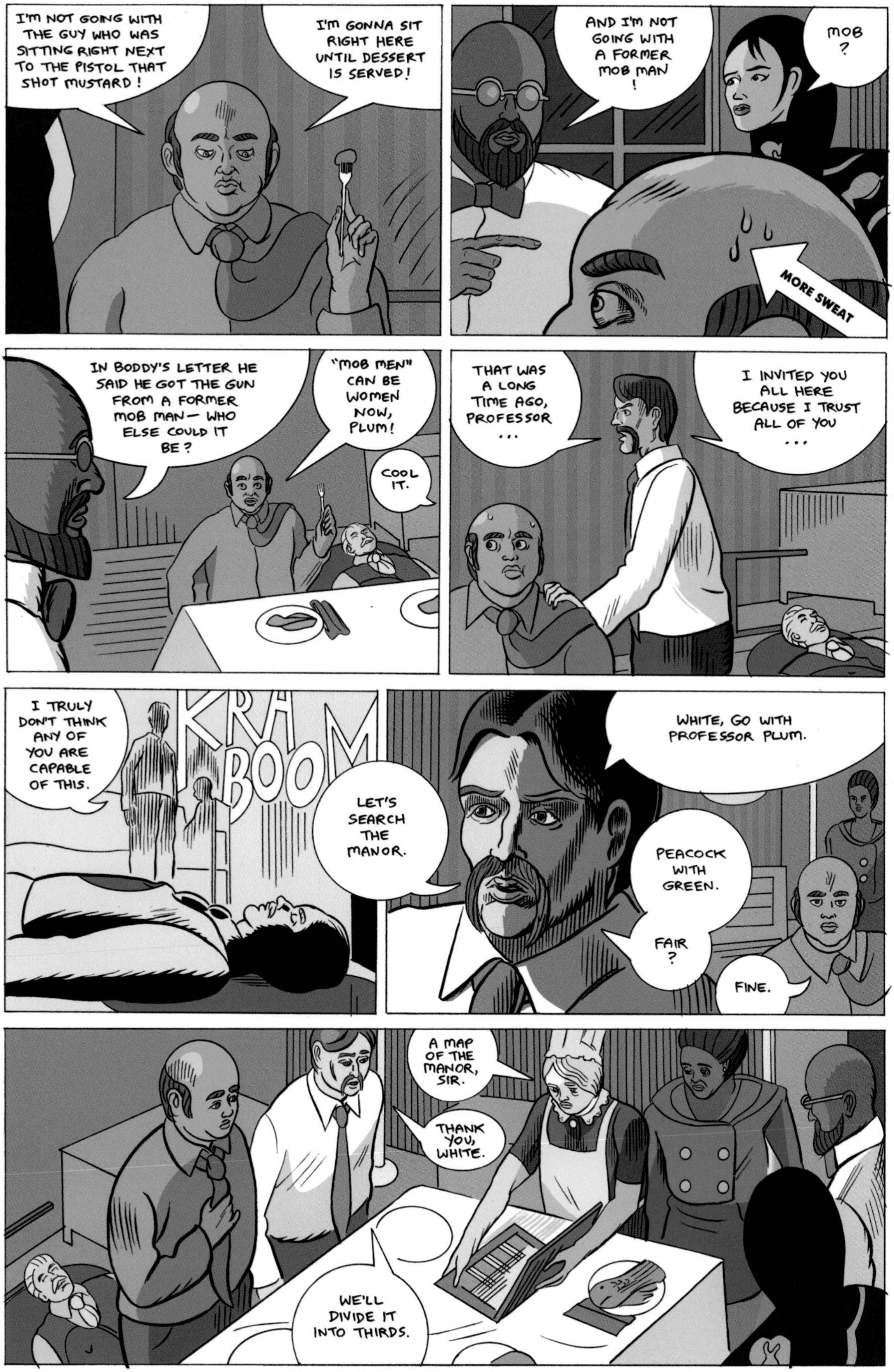
I'M NOT GOING WITH THE GUY WHO WAS SITTING RIGHT NEXT TO THE PISTOL THAT SHOT MUSTARD!
I'M GONNA SIT RIGHT HERE UNTIL DESSERT IS SERVED!
AND I'M NOT GOING WITH A FORMER MOB MAN!
MOB?
MORE SWEAT
IN BODDY'S LETTER HE SAID HE GOT THE GUN FROM A FORMER MOB MAN— WHO ELSE COULD IT BE?
"MOB MEN" CAN BE WOMEN NOW, PLUM!
COOL IT.
THAT WAS A LONG TIME AGO, PROFESSOR...
I INVITED YOU ALL HERE BECAUSE I TRUST ALL OF YOU...
I TRULY DON'T THINK ANY OF YOU ARE CAPABLE OF THIS.
KRA BOOM
LET'S SEARCH THE MANOR.
WHITE, GO WITH PROFESSOR PLUM.
PEACOCK WITH GREEN.
FAIR?
FINE.
A MAP OF THE MANOR, SIR.
THANK YOU, WHITE.
WE'LL DIVIDE IT INTO THIRDS.

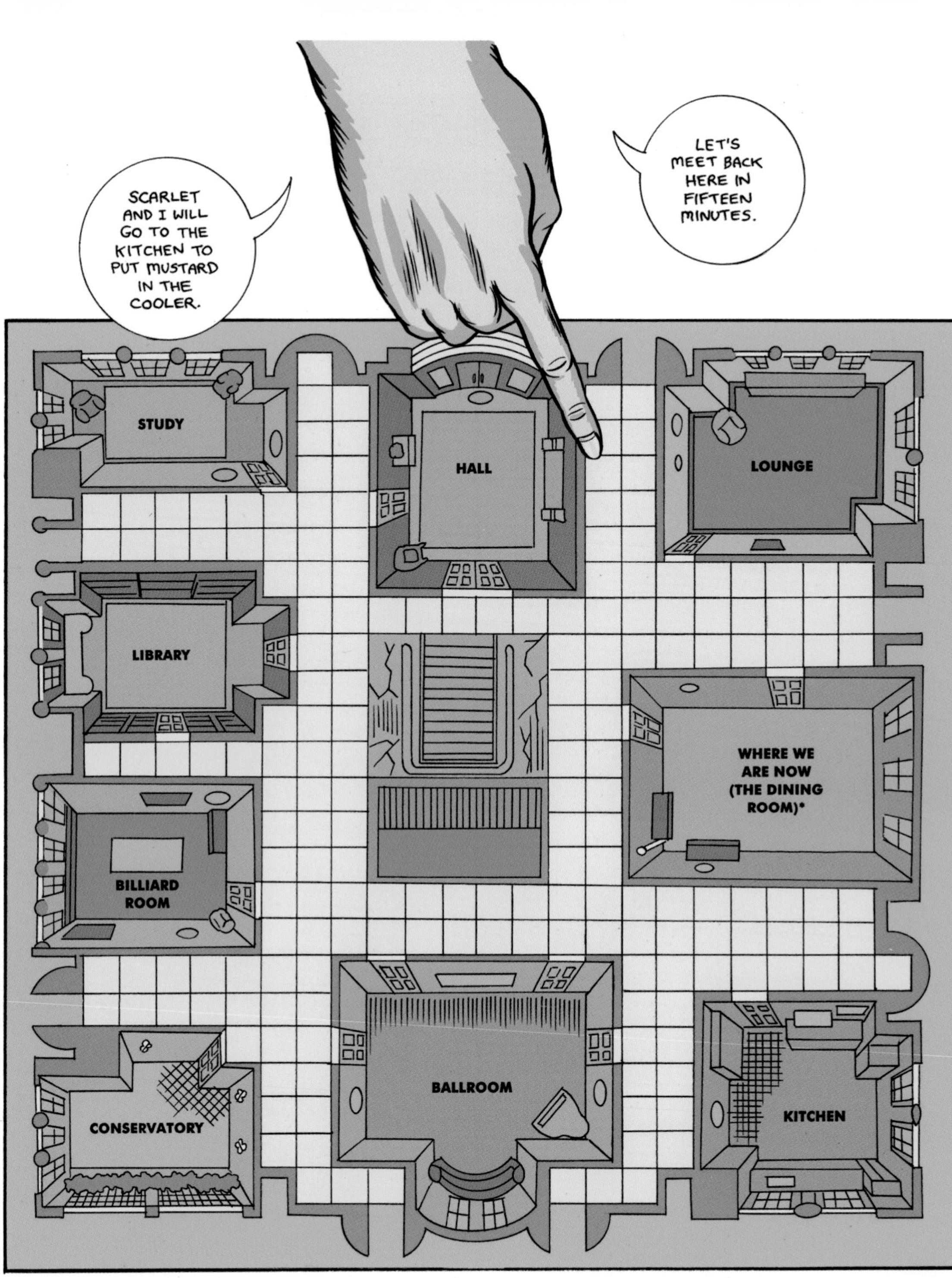
SCARLET AND I WILL GO TO THE KITCHEN TO PUT MUSTARD IN THE COOLER.
LET'S MEET BACK HERE IN FIFTEEN MINUTES.
STUDY
HALL
LOUNGE
LIBRARY
WHERE WE ARE NOW (THE DINING ROOM)*
BILLIARD ROOM
BALLROOM
CONSERVATORY
KITCHEN

EACH PAIR SEARCHES A SET OF CONTINUOUS ROOMS WITHOUT BACKTRACKING.

THE PAIR THAT STARTS IN THE HALL SEARCHES ONE LESS ROOM THAN THE OTHER PAIRS.

PLUM AND WHITE ARE THE ONLY PAIR THAT MOVE COUNTER CLOCKWISE AROUND THE MANOR.

***THE DINING ROOM HAS ALREADY BEEN SEARCHED.**

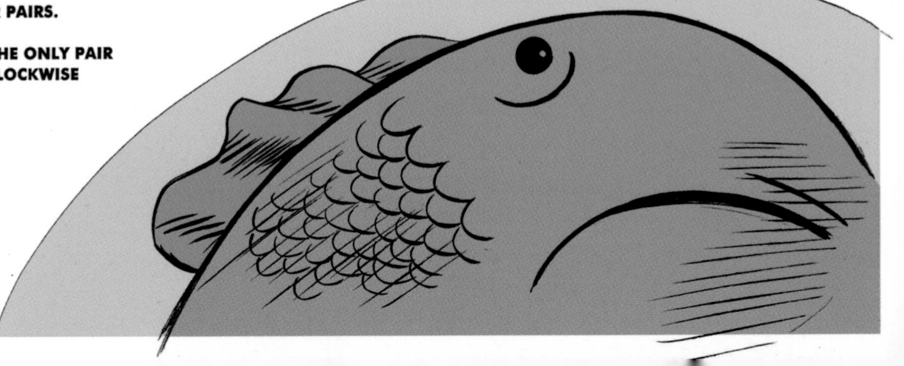

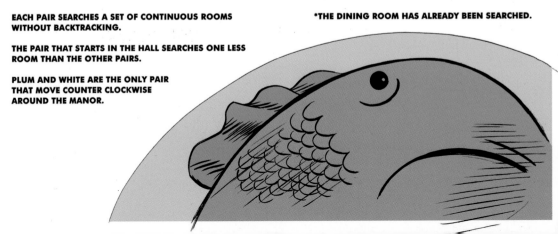

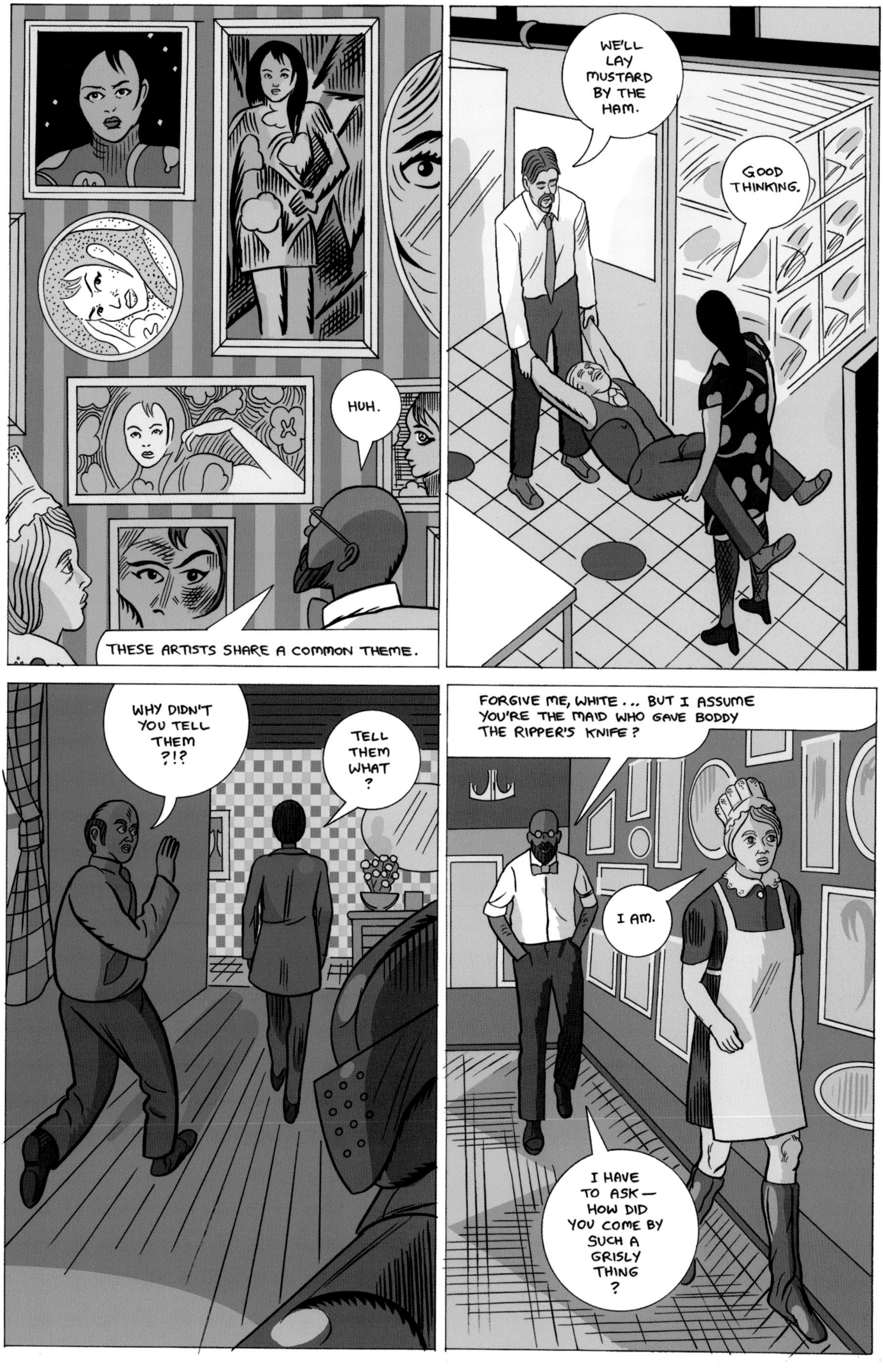
HUH.
THESE ARTISTS SHARE A COMMON THEME.
WE'LL LAY MUSTARD BY THE HAM.
GOOD THINKING.
WHY DIDN'T YOU TELL THEM ?!?
TELL THEM WHAT ?
FORGIVE ME, WHITE... BUT I ASSUME YOU'RE THE MAID WHO GAVE BODDY THE RIPPER'S KNIFE?
I AM.
I HAVE TO ASK— HOW DID YOU COME BY SUCH A GRISLY THING ?

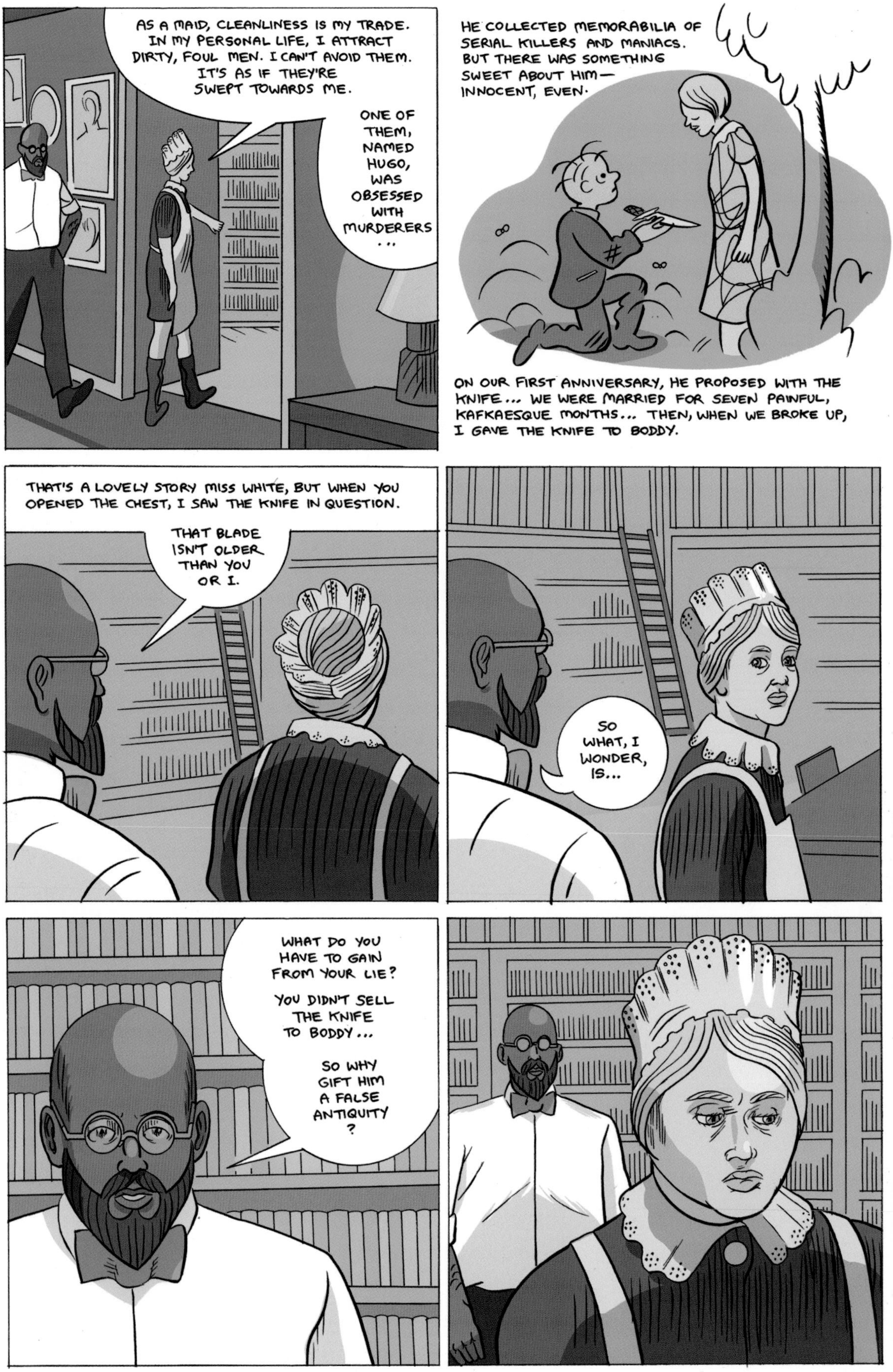
AS A MAID, CLEANLINESS IS MY TRADE. IN MY PERSONAL LIFE, I ATTRACT DIRTY, FOUL MEN. I CAN'T AVOID THEM. IT'S AS IF THEY'RE SWEPT TOWARDS ME.
ONE OF THEM, NAMED HUGO, WAS OBSESSED WITH MURDERERS . . .
HE COLLECTED MEMORABILIA OF SERIAL KILLERS AND MANIACS. BUT THERE WAS SOMETHING SWEET ABOUT HIM— INNOCENT, EVEN.
ON OUR FIRST ANNIVERSARY, HE PROPOSED WITH THE KNIFE... WE WERE MARRIED FOR SEVEN PAINFUL, KAFKAESQUE MONTHS... THEN, WHEN WE BROKE UP, I GAVE THE KNIFE TO BODDY.
THAT'S A LOVELY STORY MISS WHITE, BUT WHEN YOU OPENED THE CHEST, I SAW THE KNIFE IN QUESTION.
THAT BLADE ISN'T OLDER THAN YOU OR I.
SO WHAT, I WONDER, IS...
WHAT DO YOU HAVE TO GAIN FROM YOUR LIE?
YOU DIDN'T SELL THE KNIFE TO BODDY...
SO WHY GIFT HIM A FALSE ANTIQUITY ?

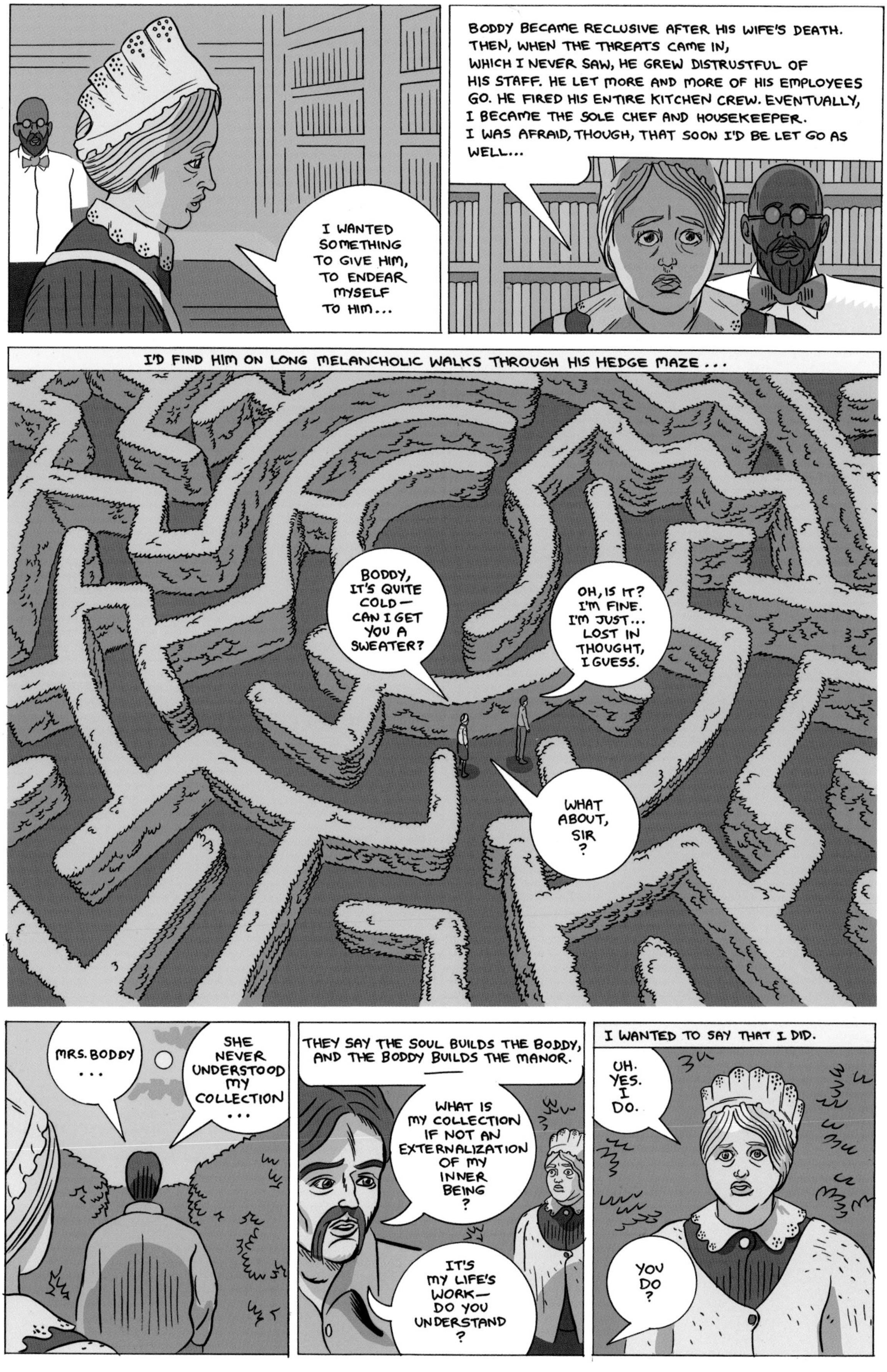
I WANTED SOMETHING TO GIVE HIM, TO ENDEAR MYSELF TO HIM...
BODDY BECAME RECLUSIVE AFTER HIS WIFE'S DEATH. THEN, WHEN THE THREATS CAME IN, WHICH I NEVER SAW, HE GREW DISTRUSTFUL OF HIS STAFF. HE LET MORE AND MORE OF HIS EMPLOYEES GO. HE FIRED HIS ENTIRE KITCHEN CREW. EVENTUALLY, I BECAME THE SOLE CHEF AND HOUSEKEEPER. I WAS AFRAID, THOUGH, THAT SOON I'D BE LET GO AS WELL...
I'D FIND HIM ON LONG MELANCHOLIC WALKS THROUGH HIS HEDGE MAZE...
BODDY, IT'S QUITE COLD— CAN I GET YOU A SWEATER?
OH, IS IT? I'M FINE. I'M JUST... LOST IN THOUGHT, I GUESS.
WHAT ABOUT, SIR?
MRS. BODDY...
SHE NEVER UNDERSTOOD MY COLLECTION...
THEY SAY THE SOUL BUILDS THE BODDY, AND THE BODDY BUILDS THE MANOR.
WHAT IS MY COLLECTION IF NOT AN EXTERNALIZATION OF MY INNER BEING?
IT'S MY LIFE'S WORK— DO YOU UNDERSTAND?
I WANTED TO SAY THAT I DID.
UH. YES. I DO.
YOU DO?

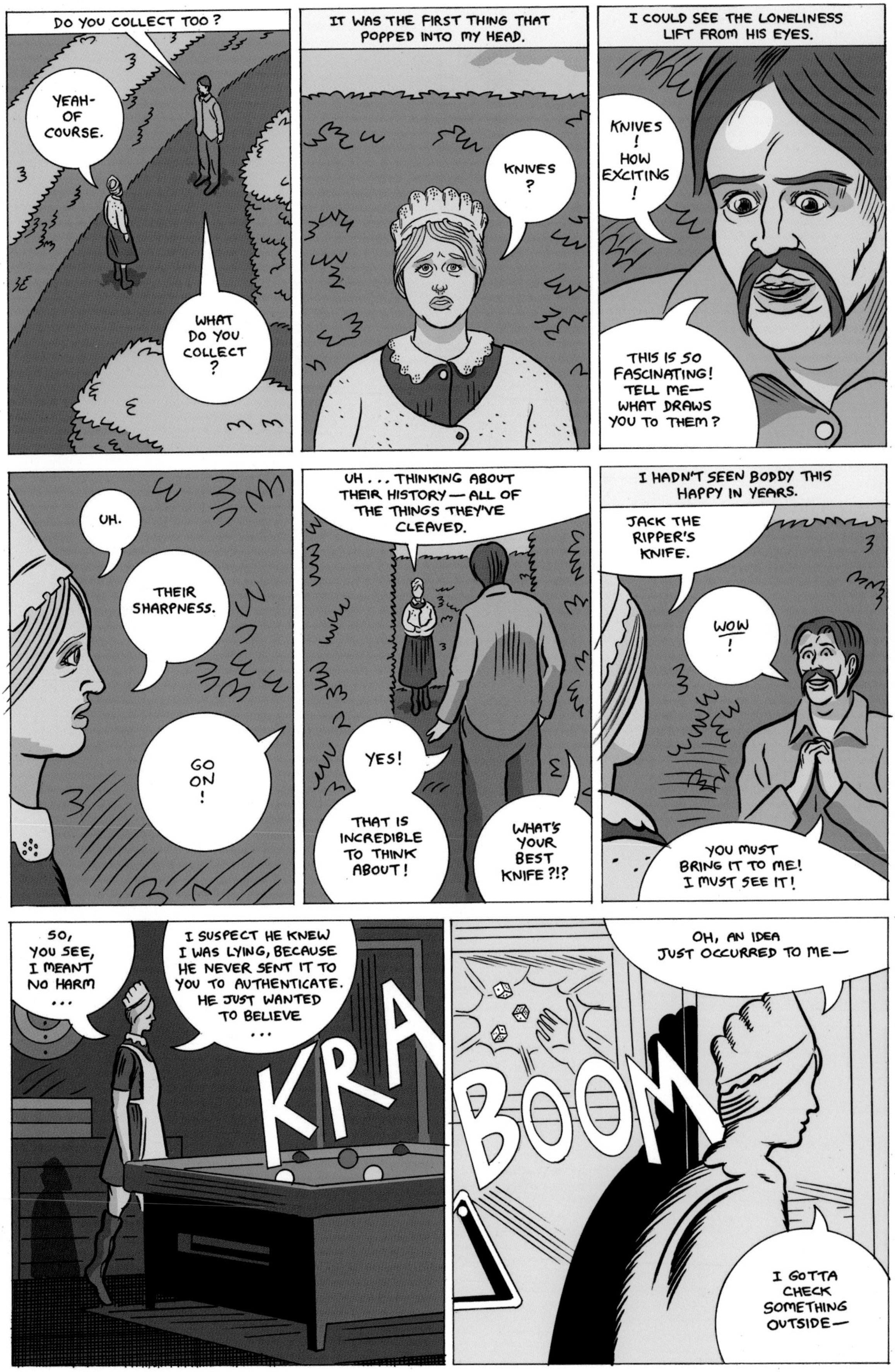
DO YOU COLLECT TOO?
YEAH-OF COURSE.
WHAT DO YOU COLLECT ?
IT WAS THE FIRST THING THAT POPPED INTO MY HEAD.
KNIVES ?
I COULD SEE THE LONELINESS LIFT FROM HIS EYES.
KNIVES ! HOW EXCITING !
THIS IS SO FASCINATING! TELL ME— WHAT DRAWS YOU TO THEM?
UH.
THEIR SHARPNESS.
GO ON !
UH . . . THINKING ABOUT THEIR HISTORY — ALL OF THE THINGS THEY'VE CLEAVED.
YES!
THAT IS INCREDIBLE TO THINK ABOUT!
WHAT'S YOUR BEST KNIFE ?!?
I HADN'T SEEN BODDY THIS HAPPY IN YEARS.
JACK THE RIPPER'S KNIFE.
WOW !
YOU MUST BRING IT TO ME! I MUST SEE IT!
SO, YOU SEE, I MEANT NO HARM . . .
I SUSPECT HE KNEW I WAS LYING, BECAUSE HE NEVER SENT IT TO YOU TO AUTHENTICATE. HE JUST WANTED TO BELIEVE . . .
KRA
BOOM
OH, AN IDEA JUST OCCURRED TO ME—
I GOTTA CHECK SOMETHING OUTSIDE—

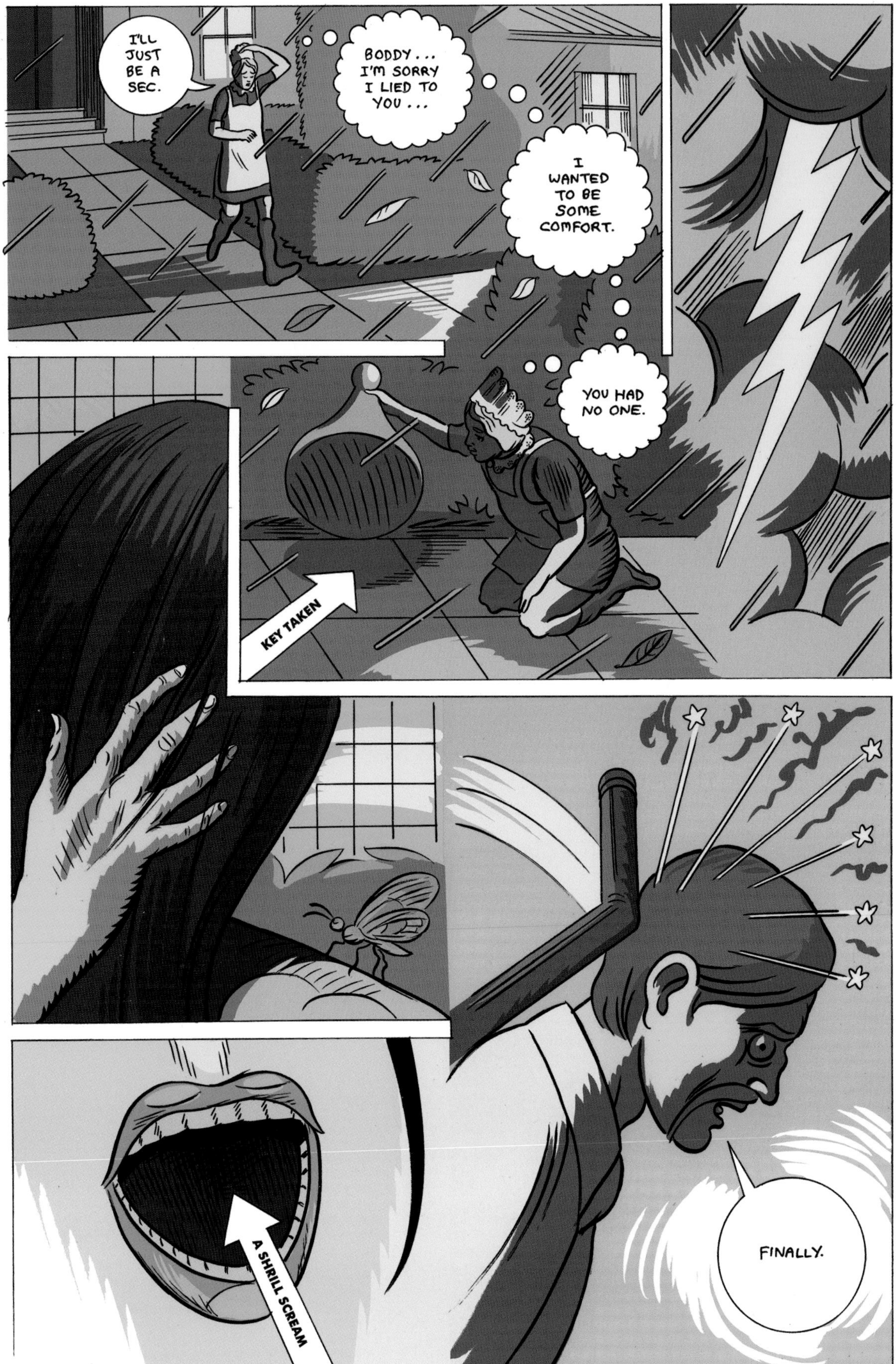
I'LL JUST BE A SEC.
BODDY... I'M SORRY I LIED TO YOU...
I WANTED TO BE SOME COMFORT.
YOU HAD NO ONE.
KEY TAKEN
A SHRILL SCREAM
FINALLY.

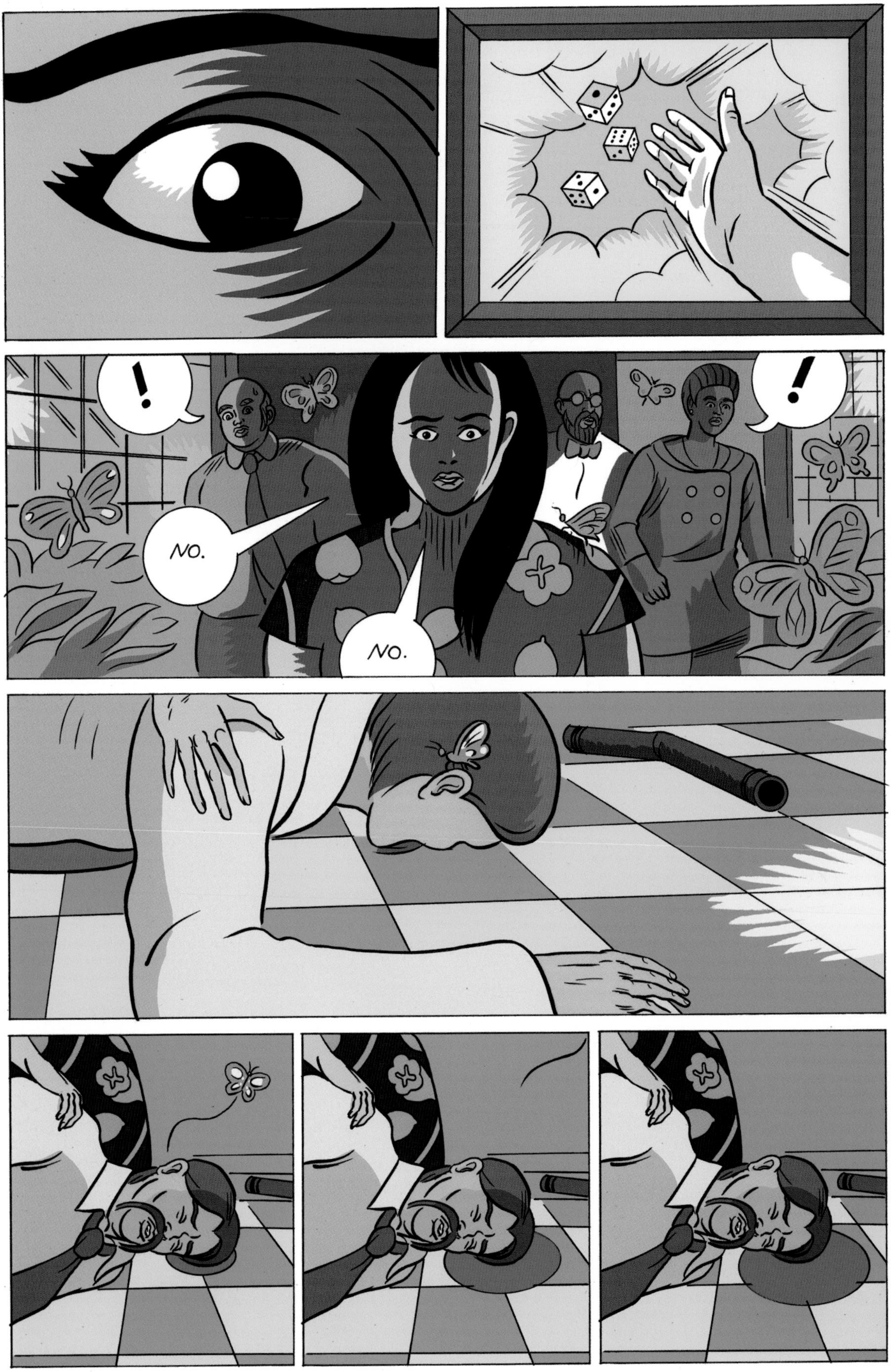
!
!
NO.
NO.

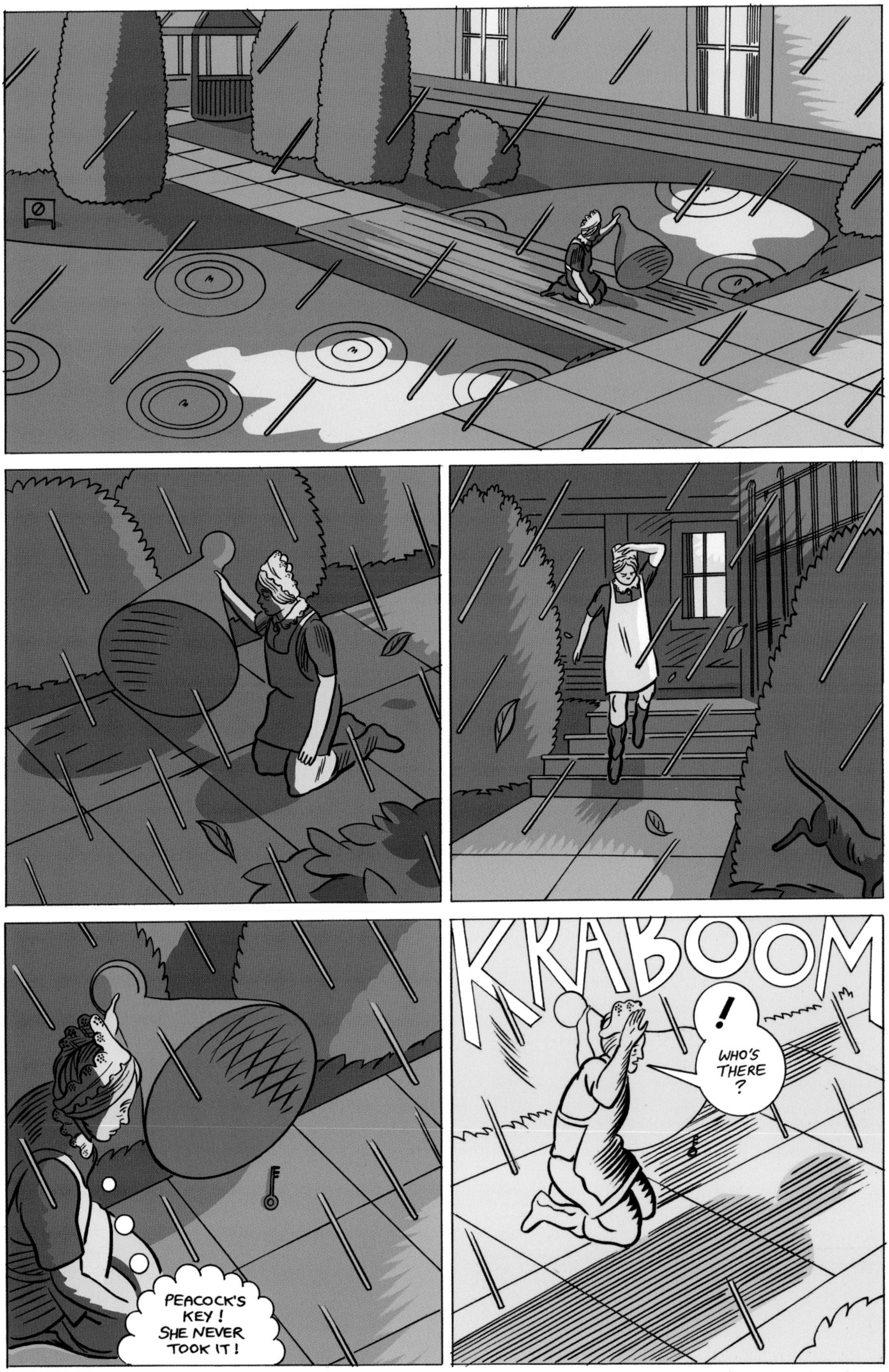
PEACOCK'S KEY! SHE NEVER TOOK IT!
KRABOOM
!
WHO'S THERE ?

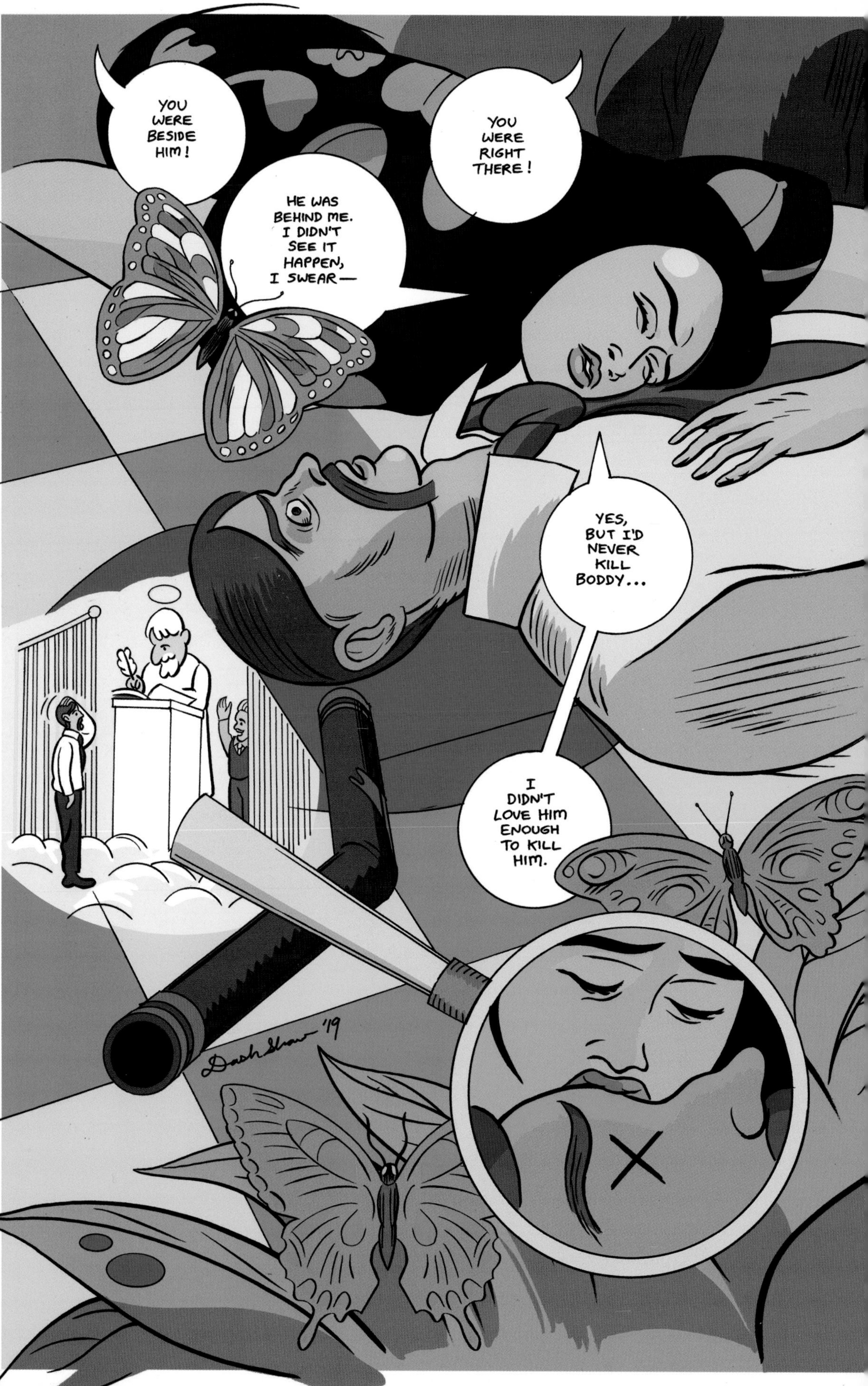
YOU WERE BESIDE HIM!
YOU WERE RIGHT THERE!
HE WAS BEHIND ME. I DIDN'T SEE IT HAPPEN, I SWEAR—
YES, BUT I'D NEVER KILL BODDY...
I DIDN'T LOVE HIM ENOUGH TO KILL HIM.
Dash Shaw '19

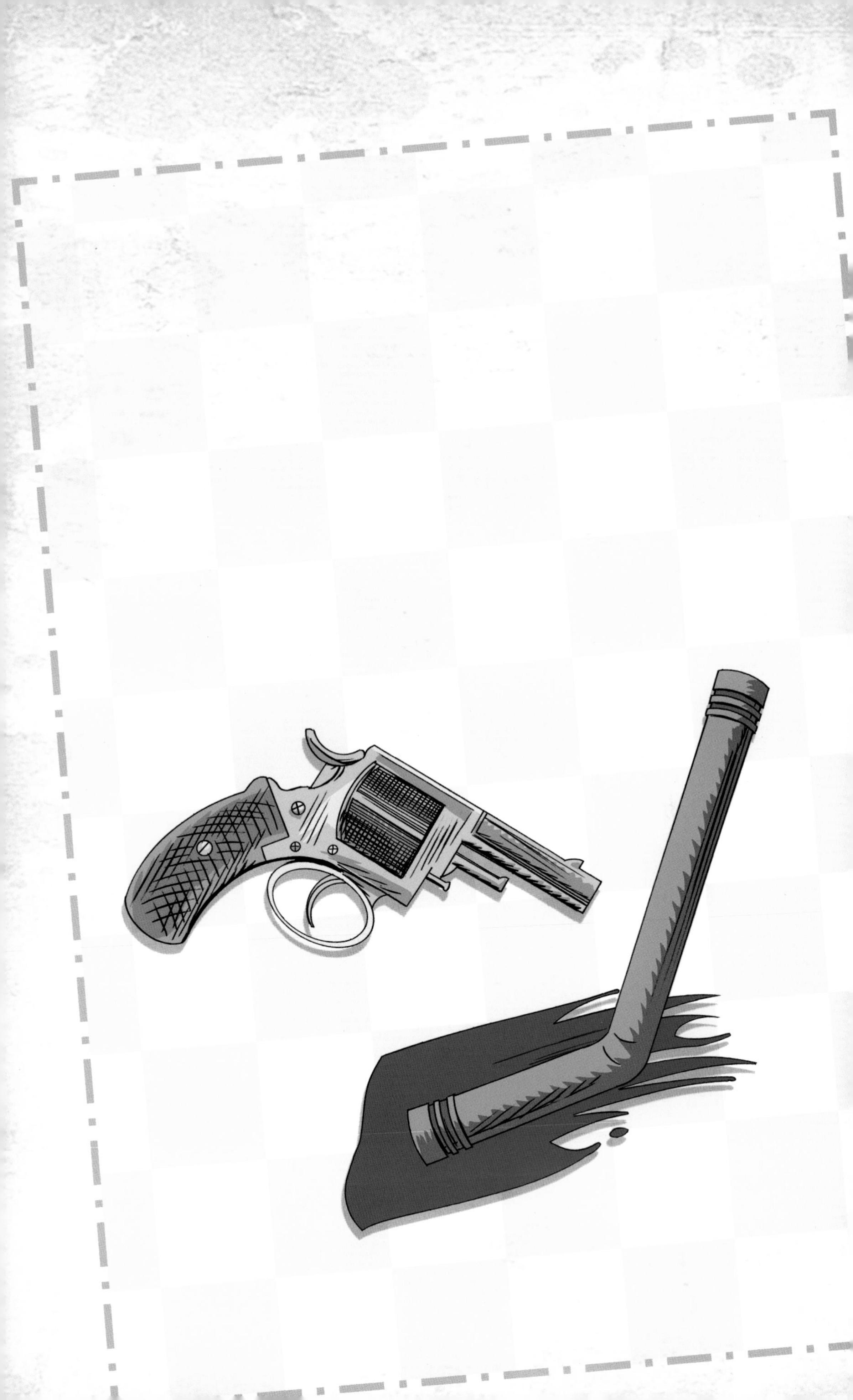

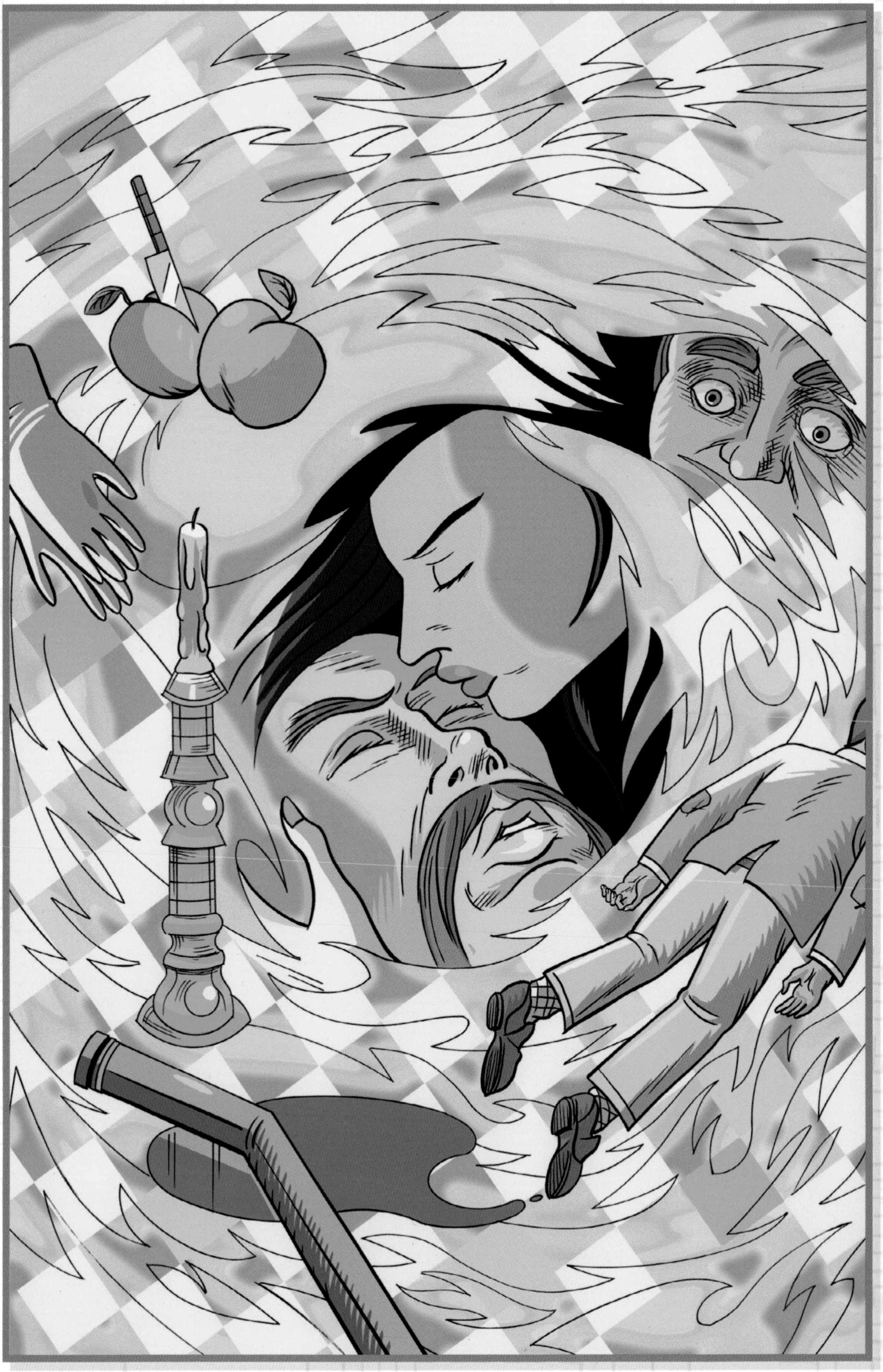

ART BY
DASH SHAW

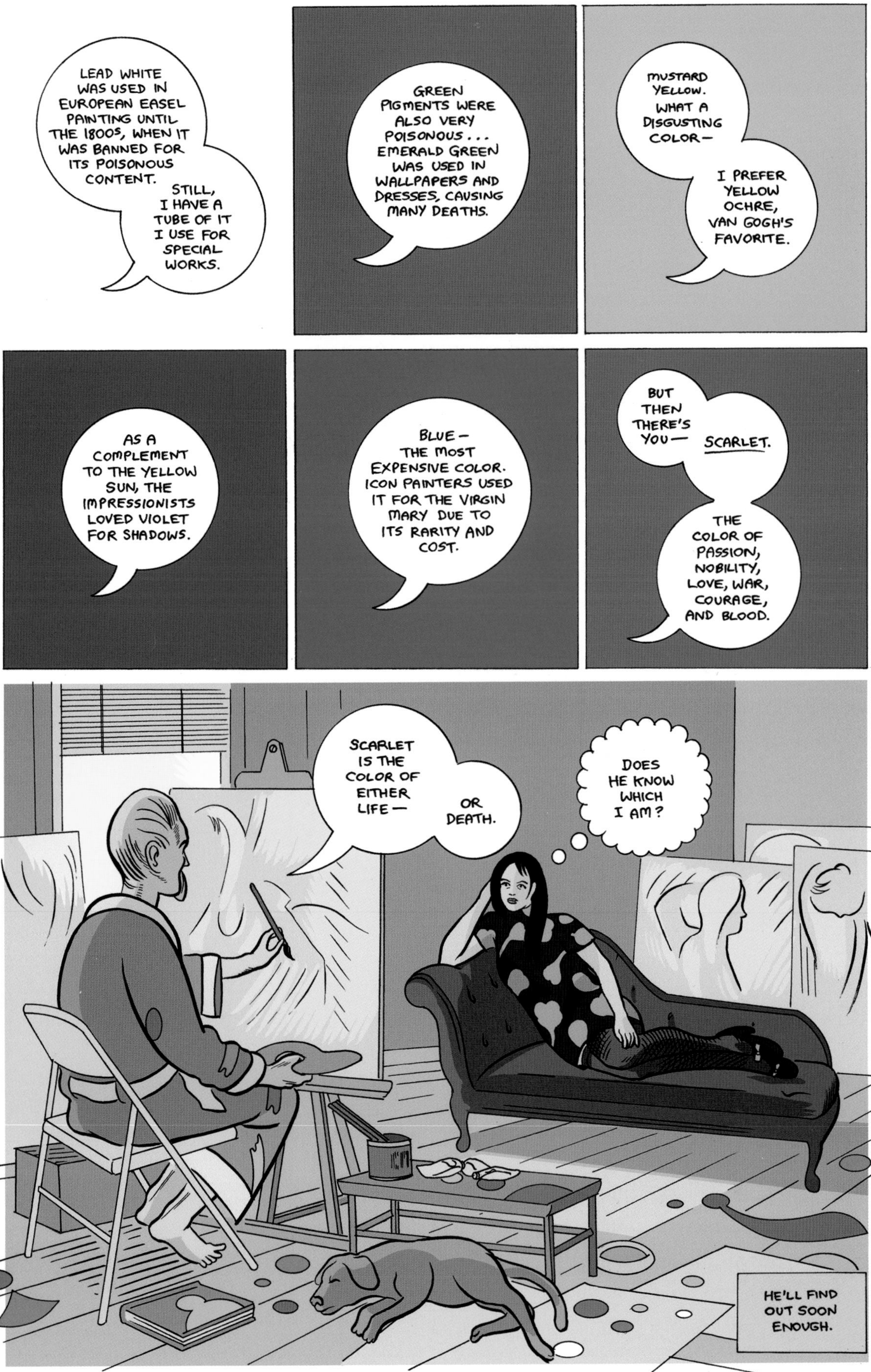
LEAD WHITE WAS USED IN EUROPEAN EASEL PAINTING UNTIL THE 1800s, WHEN IT WAS BANNED FOR ITS POISONOUS CONTENT.
STILL, I HAVE A TUBE OF IT I USE FOR SPECIAL WORKS.
GREEN PIGMENTS WERE ALSO VERY POISONOUS... EMERALD GREEN WAS USED IN WALLPAPERS AND DRESSES, CAUSING MANY DEATHS.
MUSTARD YELLOW. WHAT A DISGUSTING COLOR—
I PREFER YELLOW OCHRE, VAN GOGH'S FAVORITE.
AS A COMPLEMENT TO THE YELLOW SUN, THE IMPRESSIONISTS LOVED VIOLET FOR SHADOWS.
BLUE— THE MOST EXPENSIVE COLOR. ICON PAINTERS USED IT FOR THE VIRGIN MARY DUE TO ITS RARITY AND COST.
BUT THEN THERE'S YOU— SCARLET.
THE COLOR OF PASSION, NOBILITY, LOVE, WAR, COURAGE, AND BLOOD.
SCARLET IS THE COLOR OF EITHER LIFE—
OR DEATH.
DOES HE KNOW WHICH I AM?
HE'LL FIND OUT SOON ENOUGH.

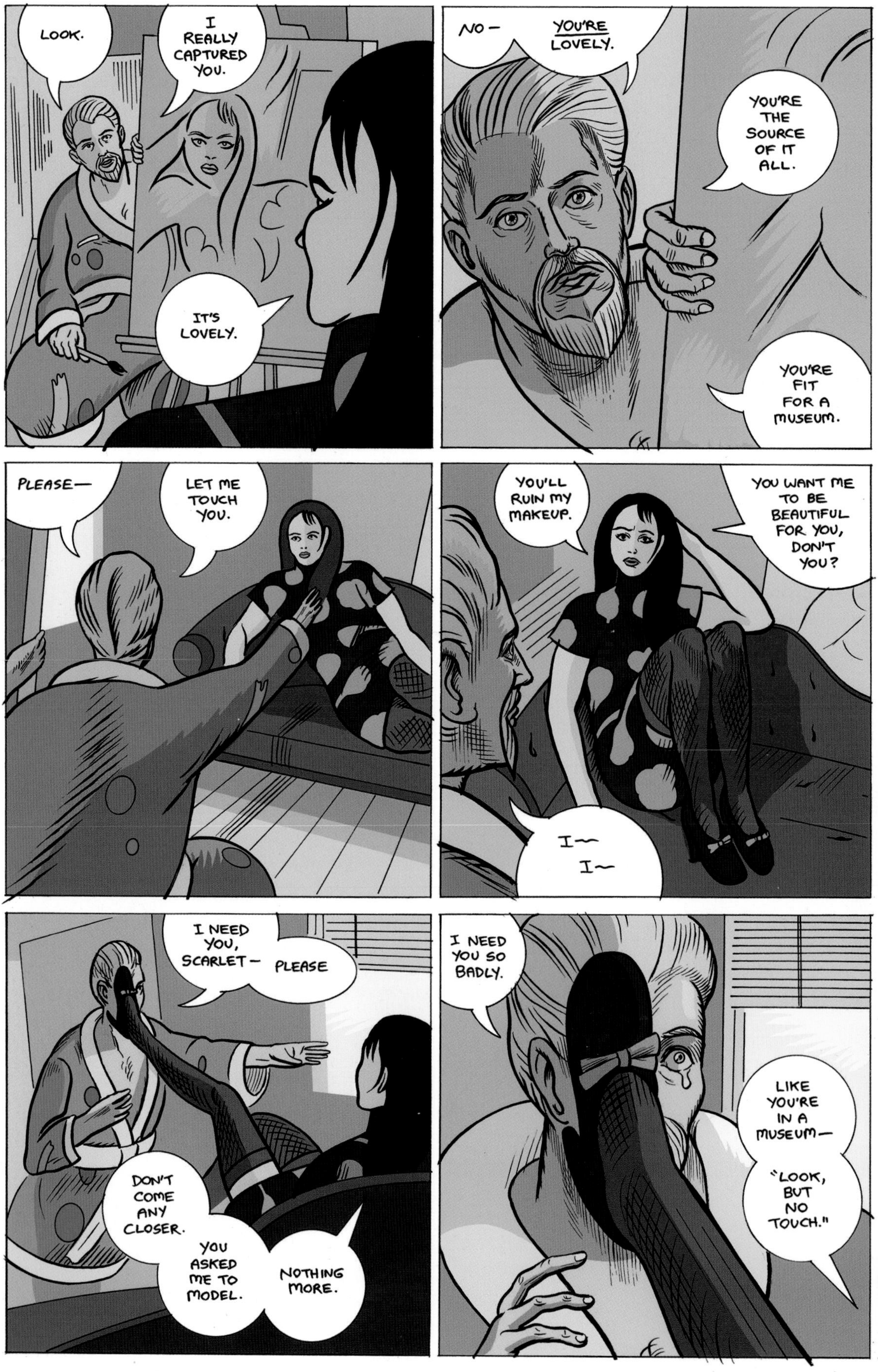
LOOK.
I REALLY CAPTURED YOU.
IT'S LOVELY.
NO— YOU'RE LOVELY.
YOU'RE THE SOURCE OF IT ALL.
YOU'RE FIT FOR A MUSEUM.
PLEASE—
LET ME TOUCH YOU.
YOU'LL RUIN MY MAKEUP.
YOU WANT ME TO BE BEAUTIFUL FOR YOU, DON'T YOU?
I— I—
I NEED YOU, SCARLET—
PLEASE
DON'T COME ANY CLOSER.
YOU ASKED ME TO MODEL.
NOTHING MORE.
I NEED YOU SO BADLY.
LIKE YOU'RE IN A MUSEUM—
"LOOK, BUT NO TOUCH."

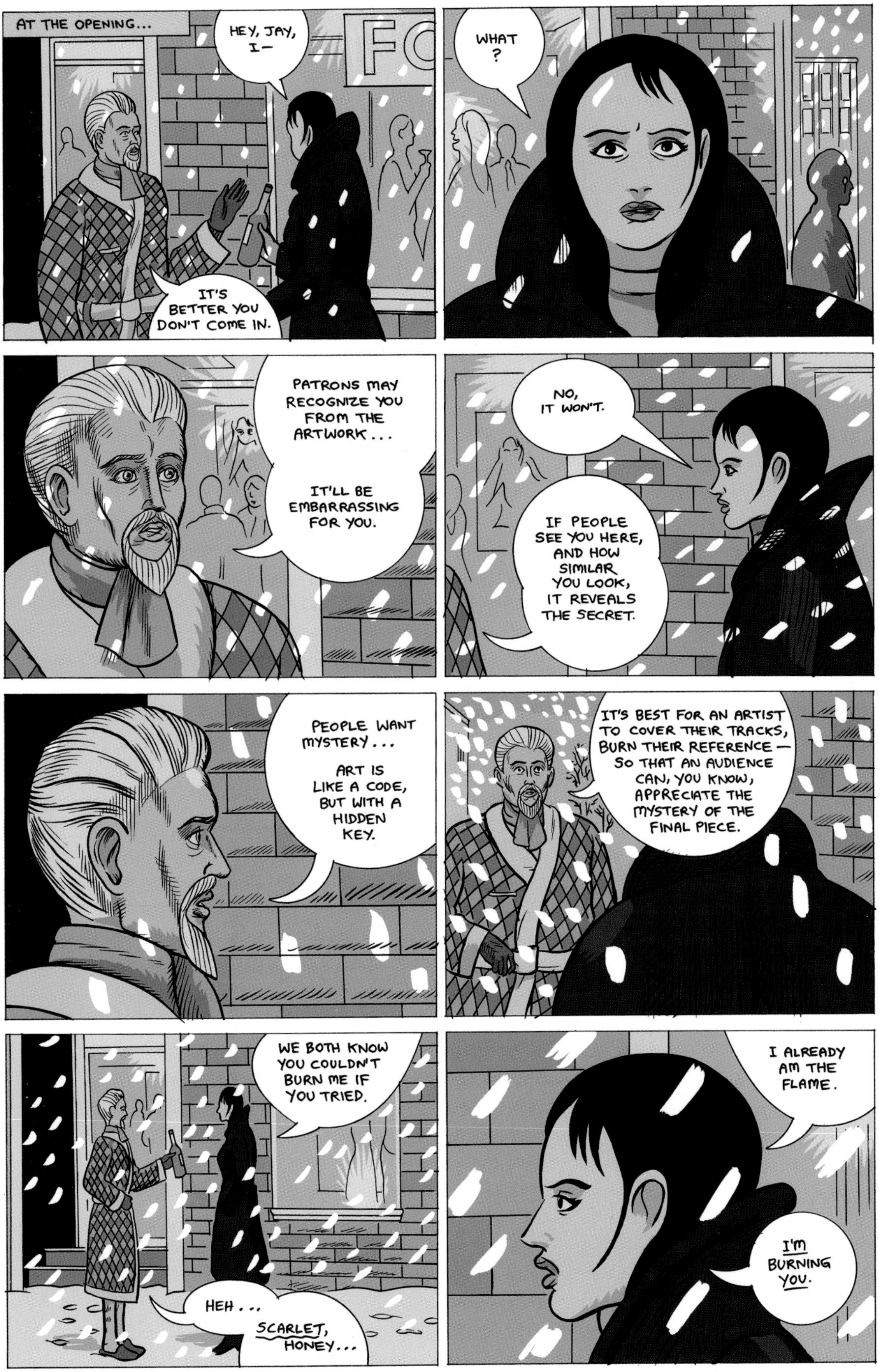
AT THE OPENING...
HEY, JAY, I—
IT'S BETTER YOU DON'T COME IN.
WHAT ?
PATRONS MAY RECOGNIZE YOU FROM THE ARTWORK...
IT'LL BE EMBARRASSING FOR YOU.
NO, IT WON'T.
IF PEOPLE SEE YOU HERE, AND HOW SIMILAR YOU LOOK, IT REVEALS THE SECRET.
PEOPLE WANT MYSTERY...
ART IS LIKE A CODE, BUT WITH A HIDDEN KEY.
IT'S BEST FOR AN ARTIST TO COVER THEIR TRACKS, BURN THEIR REFERENCE — SO THAT AN AUDIENCE CAN, YOU KNOW, APPRECIATE THE MYSTERY OF THE FINAL PIECE.
WE BOTH KNOW YOU COULDN'T BURN ME IF YOU TRIED.
HEH... SCARLET, HONEY...
I ALREADY AM THE FLAME.
I'M BURNING YOU.

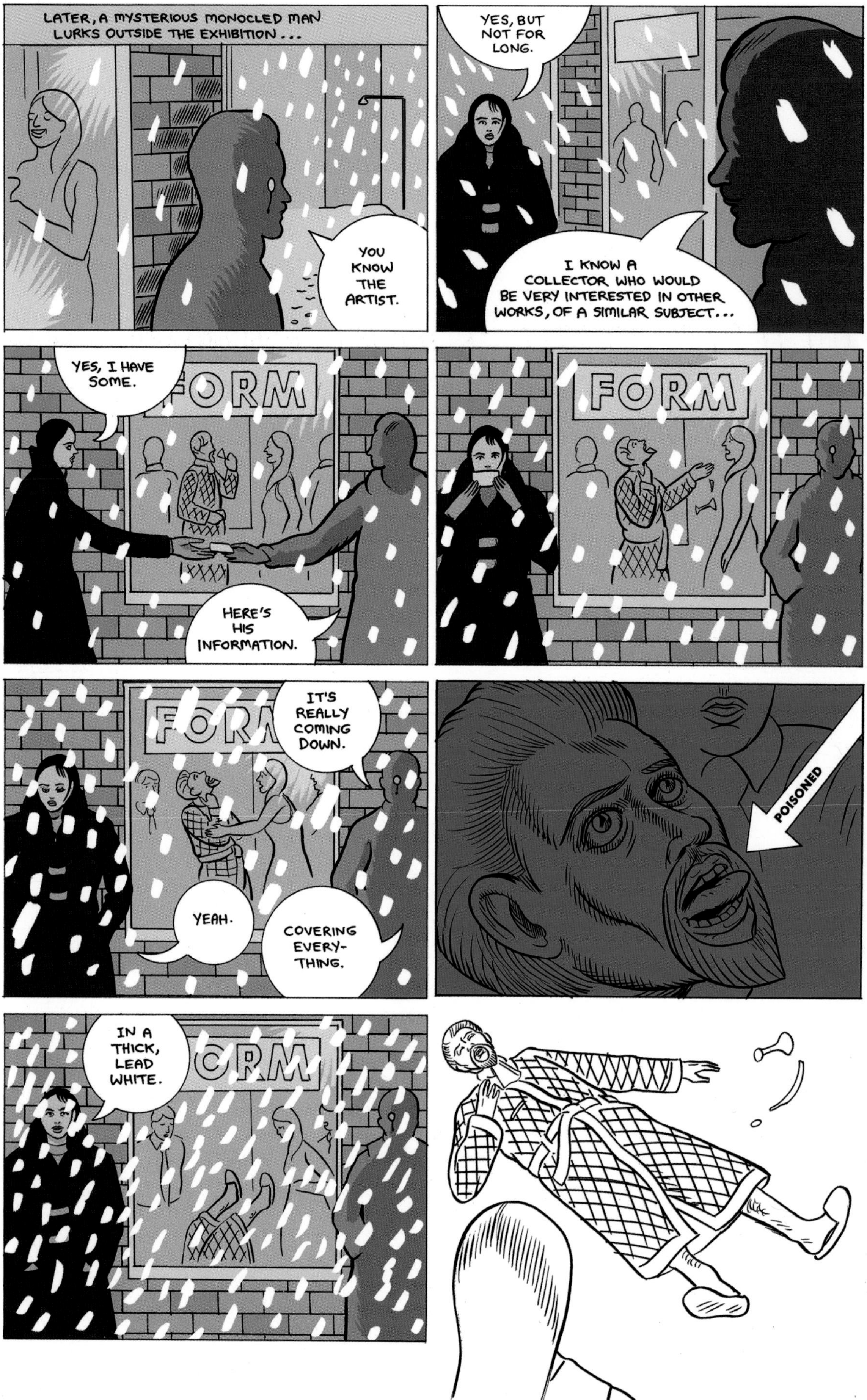
LATER, A MYSTERIOUS MONOCLED MAN LURKS OUTSIDE THE EXHIBITION...
YOU KNOW THE ARTIST.
YES, BUT NOT FOR LONG.
I KNOW A COLLECTOR WHO WOULD BE VERY INTERESTED IN OTHER WORKS, OF A SIMILAR SUBJECT...
YES, I HAVE SOME.
FORM
HERE'S HIS INFORMATION.
FORM
IT'S REALLY COMING DOWN.
YEAH.
COVERING EVERY-THING.
POISONED
IN A THICK, LEAD WHITE.
FORM

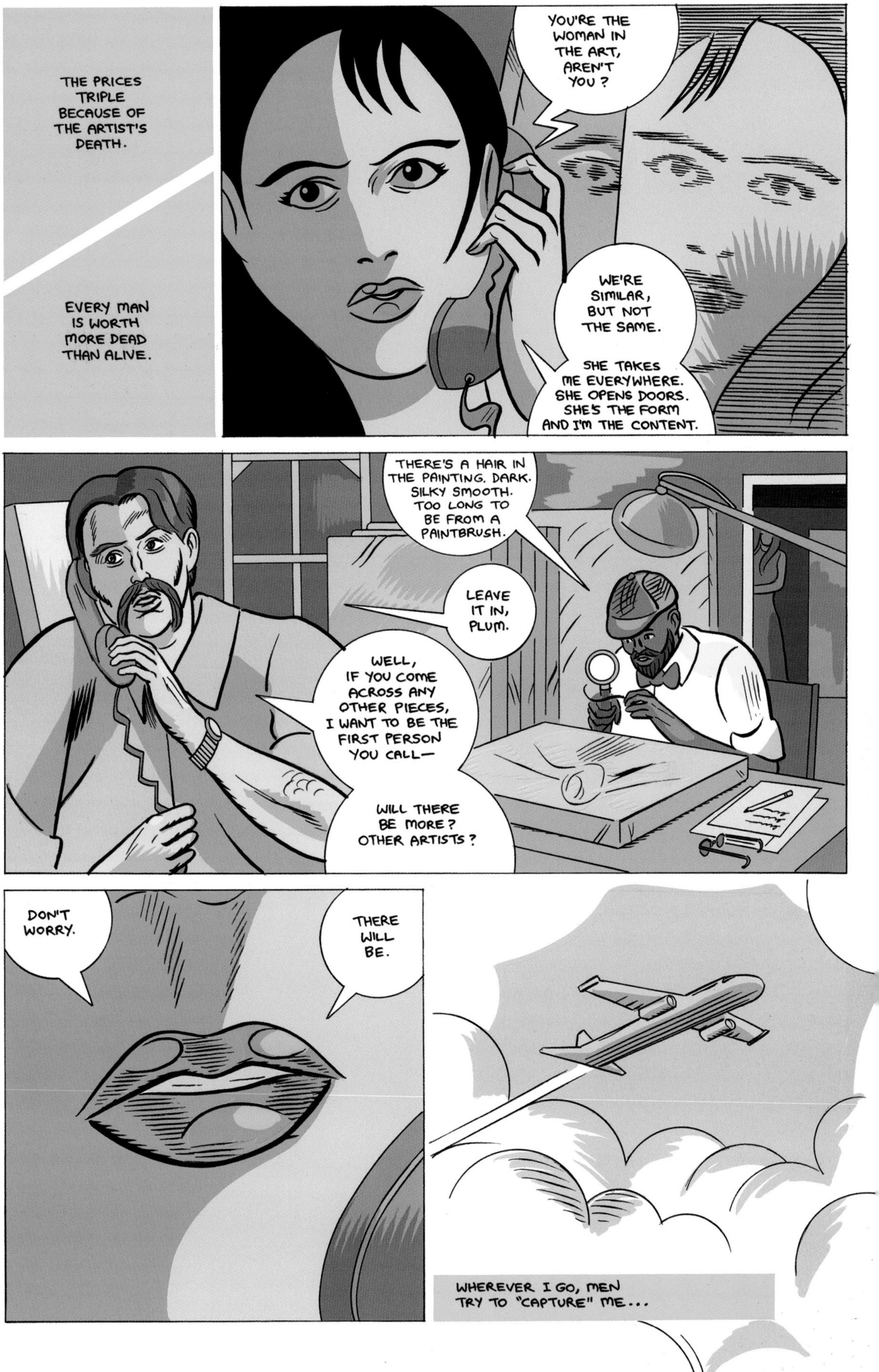
THE PRICES TRIPLE BECAUSE OF THE ARTIST'S DEATH.
EVERY MAN IS WORTH MORE DEAD THAN ALIVE.
YOU'RE THE WOMAN IN THE ART, AREN'T YOU ?
WE'RE SIMILAR, BUT NOT THE SAME.
SHE TAKES ME EVERYWHERE. SHE OPENS DOORS. SHE'S THE FORM AND I'M THE CONTENT.
THERE'S A HAIR IN THE PAINTING. DARK. SILKY SMOOTH. TOO LONG TO BE FROM A PAINTBRUSH.
LEAVE IT IN, PLUM.
WELL, IF YOU COME ACROSS ANY OTHER PIECES, I WANT TO BE THE FIRST PERSON YOU CALL—
WILL THERE BE MORE ? OTHER ARTISTS ?
DON'T WORRY.
THERE WILL BE.
WHEREVER I GO, MEN TRY TO "CAPTURE" ME...

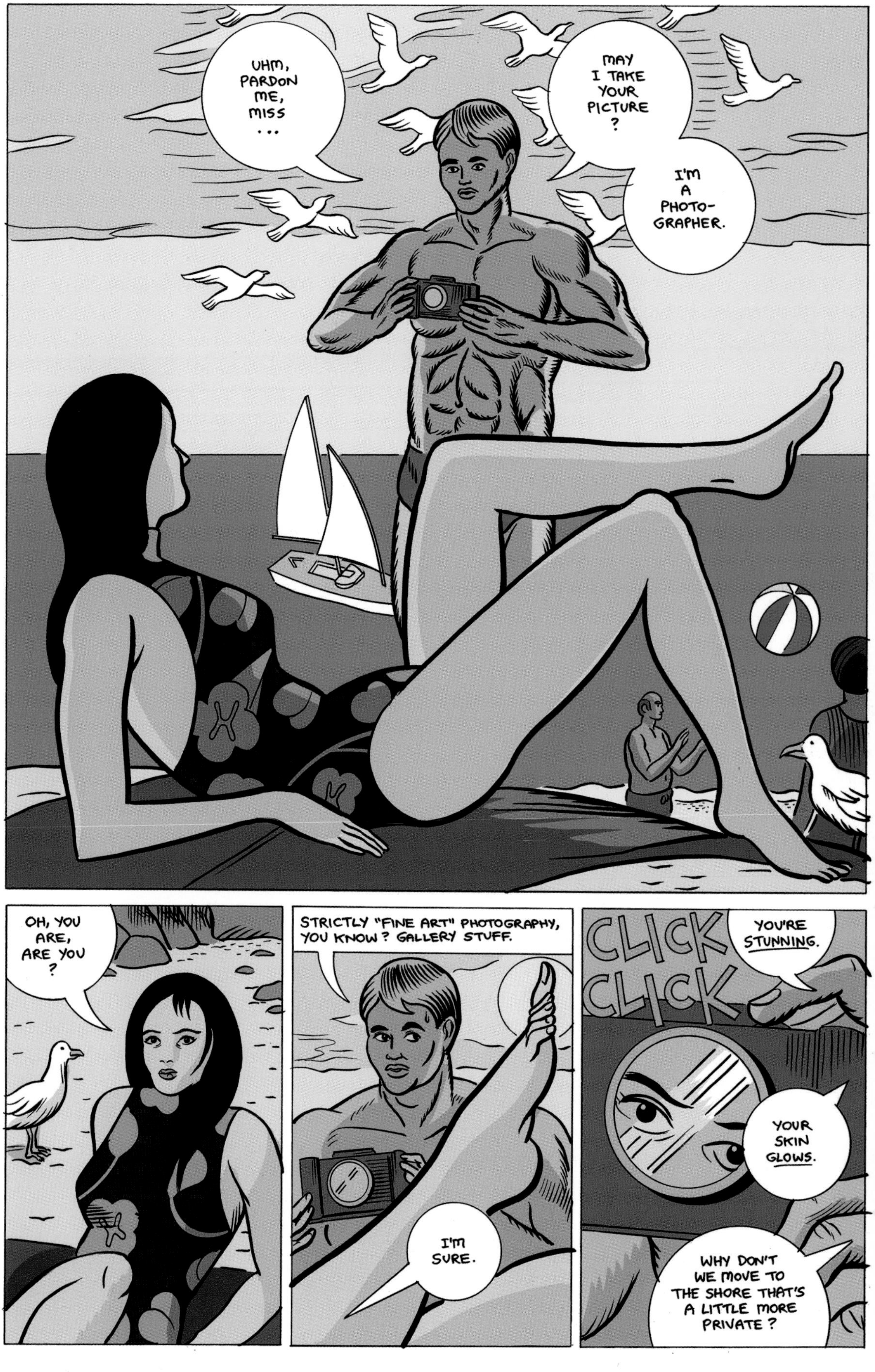
UHM, PARDON ME, MISS . . .
MAY I TAKE YOUR PICTURE ?
I'M A PHOTO-GRAPHER.
OH, YOU ARE, ARE YOU ?
STRICTLY "FINE ART" PHOTOGRAPHY, YOU KNOW? GALLERY STUFF.
I'M SURE.
CLICK CLICK
YOU'RE STUNNING.
YOUR SKIN GLOWS.
WHY DON'T WE MOVE TO THE SHORE THAT'S A LITTLE MORE PRIVATE ?

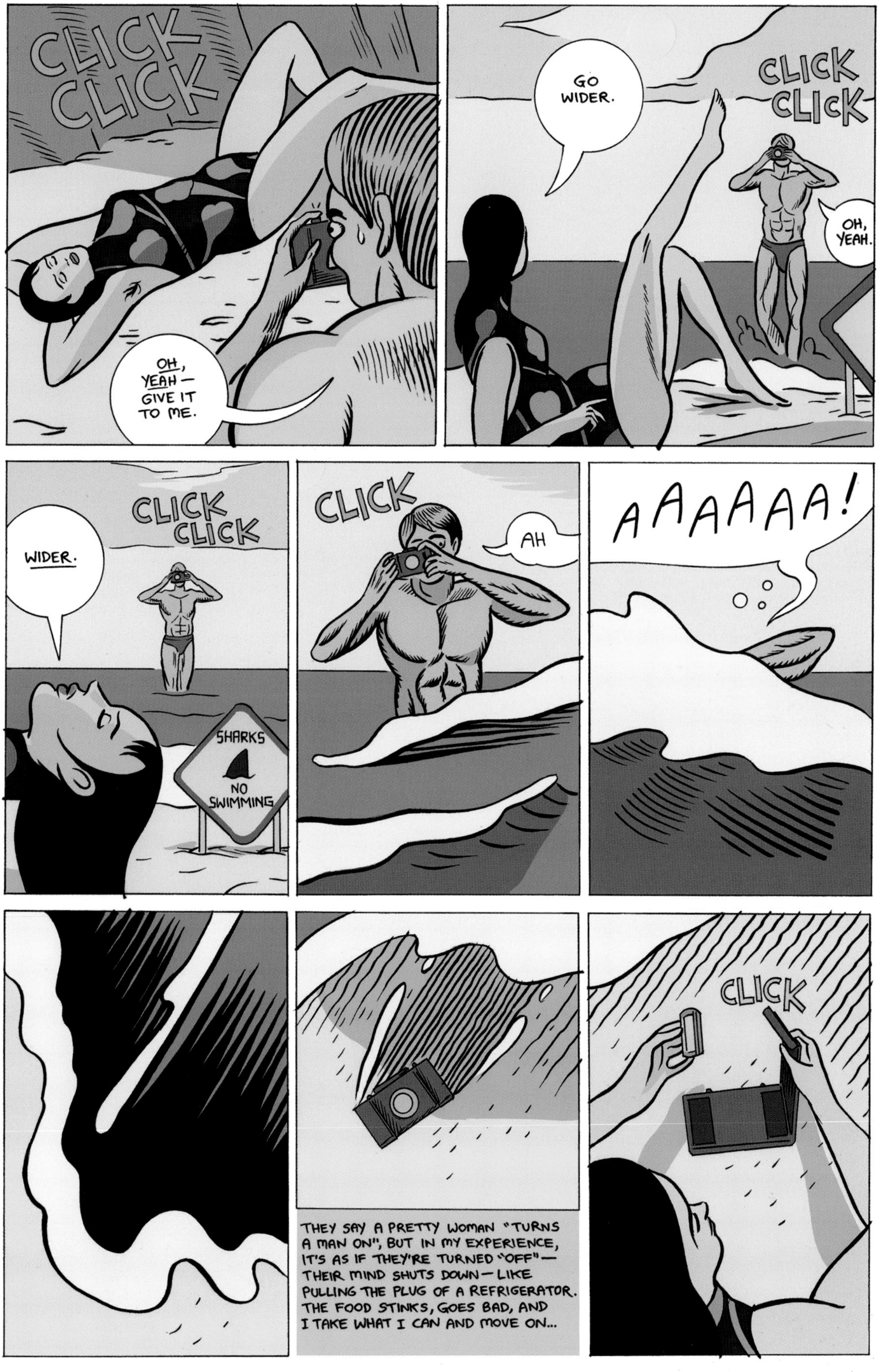
CLICK CLICK
OH, YEAH— GIVE IT TO ME.
GO WIDER.
CLICK CLICK
OH, YEAH.
WIDER.
CLICK CLICK
SHARKS NO SWIMMING
CLICK
AH
AAAAAA!
THEY SAY A PRETTY WOMAN "TURNS A MAN ON", BUT IN MY EXPERIENCE, IT'S AS IF THEY'RE TURNED "OFF"— THEIR MIND SHUTS DOWN—LIKE PULLING THE PLUG OF A REFRIGERATOR. THE FOOD STINKS, GOES BAD, AND I TAKE WHAT I CAN AND MOVE ON...
CLICK

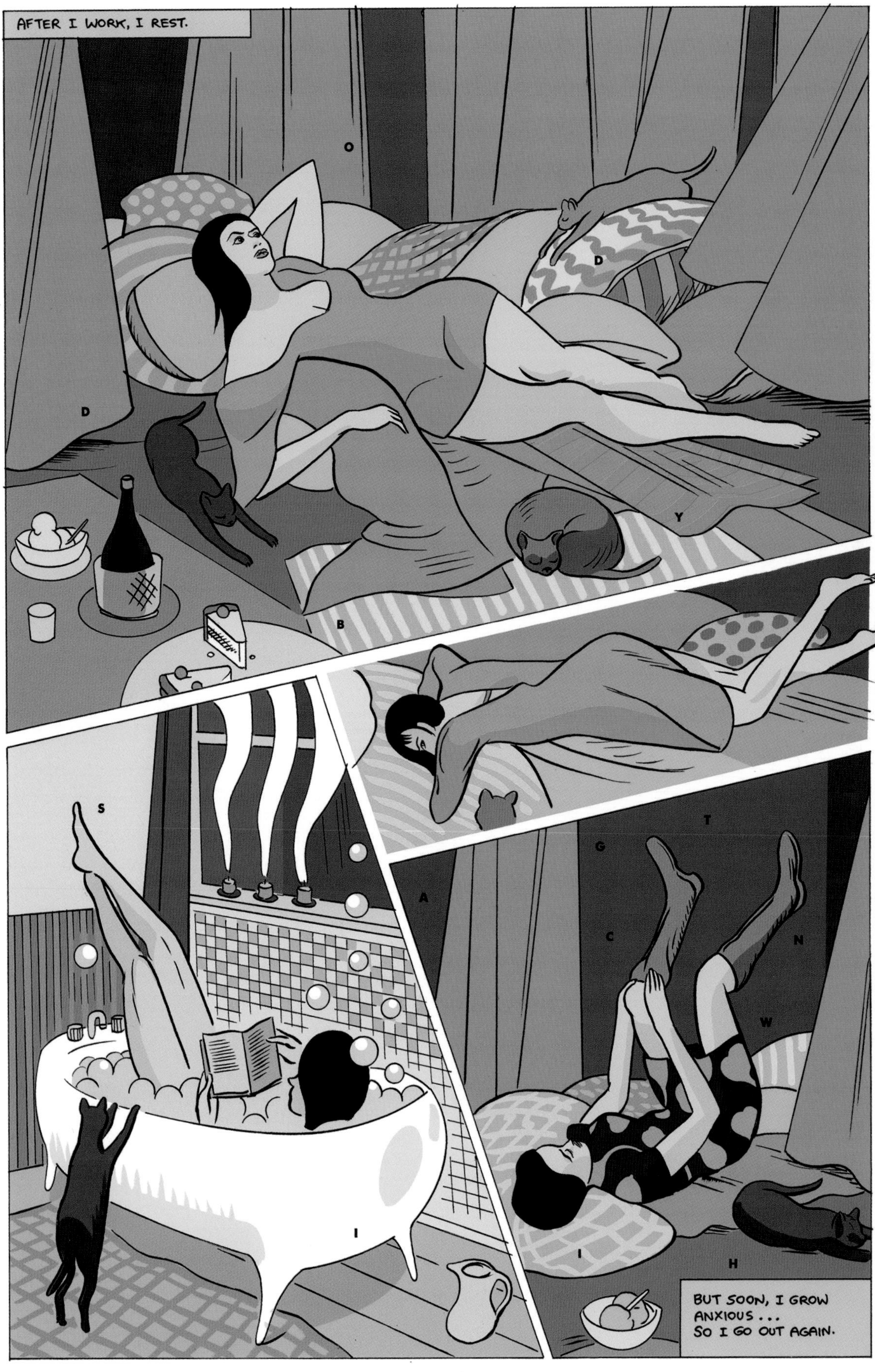
AFTER I WORK, I REST.
BUT SOON, I GROW ANXIOUS...
SO I GO OUT AGAIN.

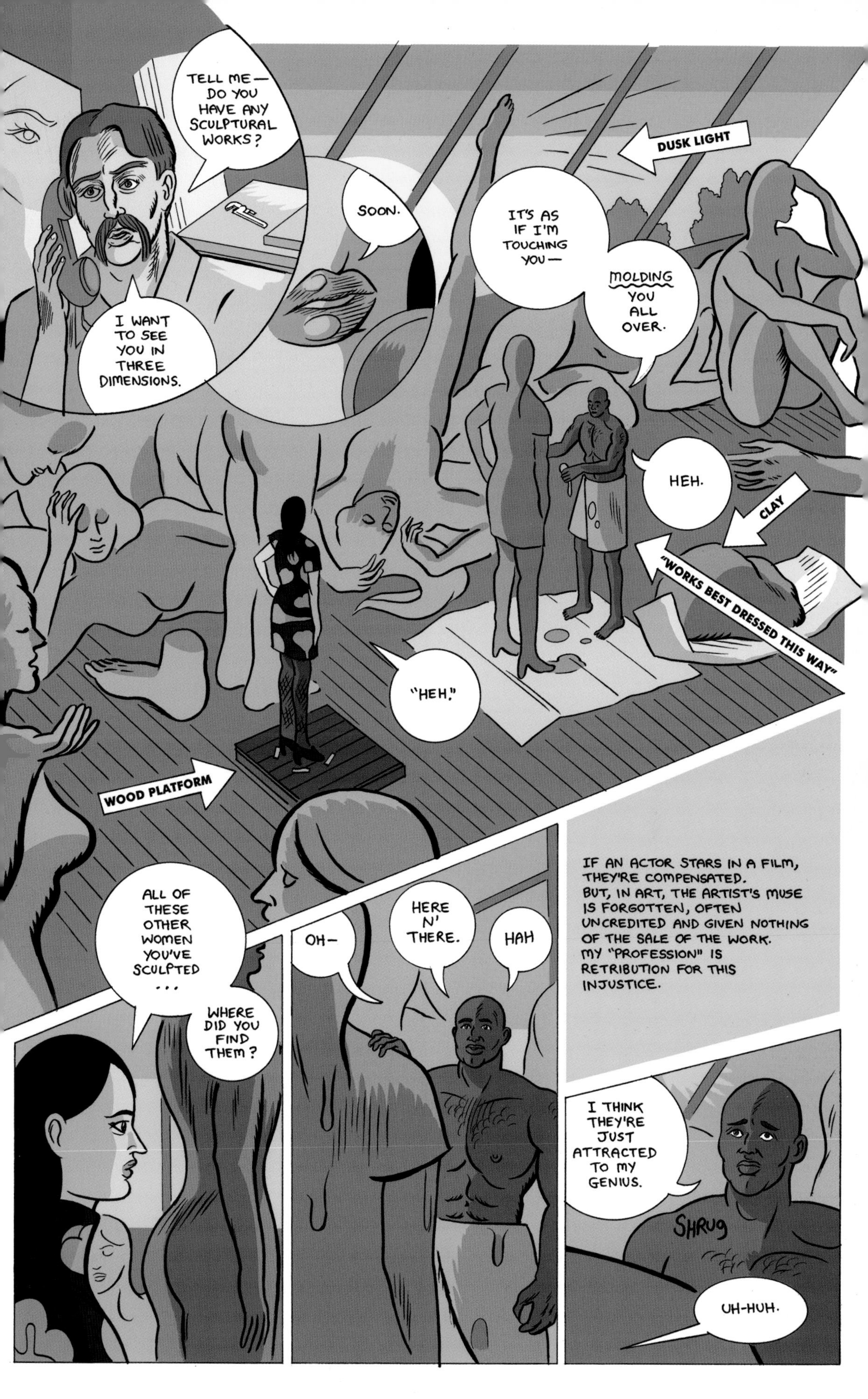
TELL ME— DO YOU HAVE ANY SCULPTURAL WORKS?
I WANT TO SEE YOU IN THREE DIMENSIONS.
SOON.
IT'S AS IF I'M TOUCHING YOU—
MOLDING YOU ALL OVER.
DUSK LIGHT
HEH.
CLAY
"WORKS BEST DRESSED THIS WAY"
"HEH."
WOOD PLATFORM
ALL OF THESE OTHER WOMEN YOU'VE SCULPTED . . .
WHERE DID YOU FIND THEM?
OH—
HERE N' THERE.
HAH
IF AN ACTOR STARS IN A FILM, THEY'RE COMPENSATED. BUT, IN ART, THE ARTIST'S MUSE IS FORGOTTEN, OFTEN UNCREDITED AND GIVEN NOTHING OF THE SALE OF THE WORK. MY "PROFESSION" IS RETRIBUTION FOR THIS INJUSTICE.
I THINK THEY'RE JUST ATTRACTED TO MY GENIUS.
SHRUG
UH-HUH.

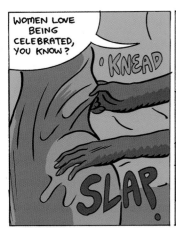

WOMEN LOVE BEING CELEBRATED, YOU KNOW?
KNEAD
SLAP
THAT'S WHAT ART HISTORY IS: A CELEBRATION OF THE FEMALE FORM.
IT'S CLASSICAL. TIMELESS.
"MUSEUM" COMES FROM "MUSE"— "MUSES" ARE WOMEN...
IT'S HARD TO CARRY THE WEIGHT OF HISTORY ON MY BACK ...
THERE'S SUCH A GREAT LINEAGE ... IT'S A STRUGGLE TO GET OUT OF ITS SHADOW... SIGH
IT FEELS IMPOSSIBLE.
YEAH.
IT SOUNDS HARD FOR YOU.
YOU HAVE IT SO EASY... I'M SURE YOU LOVE BEING THE CENTER OF ATTENTION..
AND YOUR BEAUTY IS BEING FROZEN IN TIME, FOREVER.
AH!
CRASH!
AGGHH!
DO YOU LOVE IT ?
PLEASE
BEING FROZEN IN TIME ?
WHAT AN HONOR IT IS FOR YOU.
TO BE THE OBJECT OF MY ATTENTION.

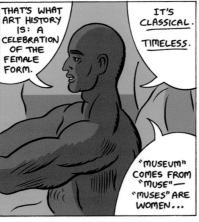

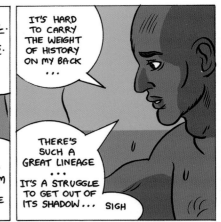

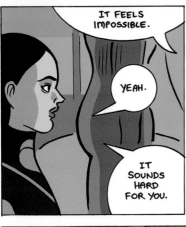

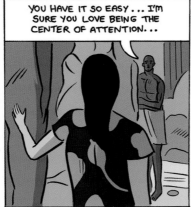

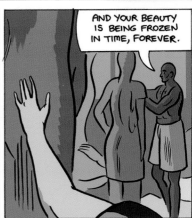

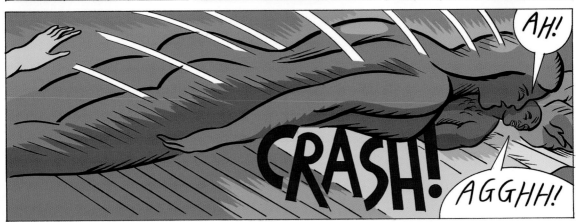

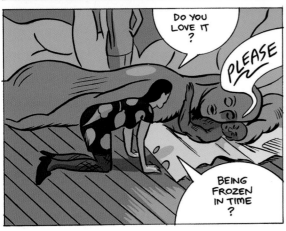

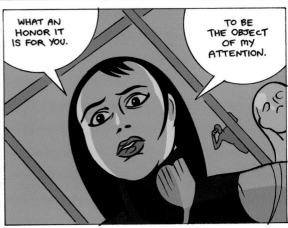

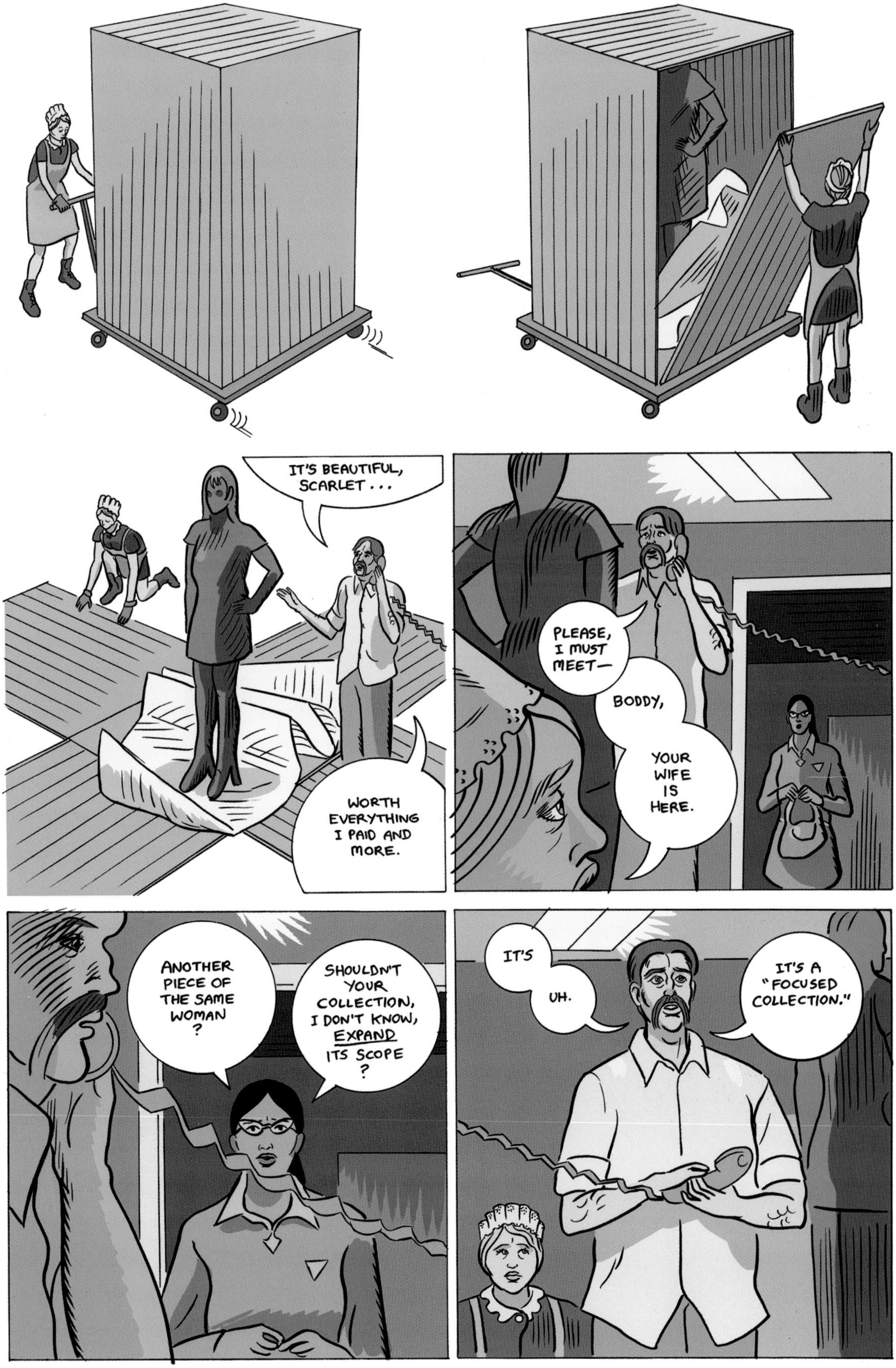
IT'S BEAUTIFUL, SCARLET . . .
WORTH EVERYTHING I PAID AND MORE.
PLEASE, I MUST MEET—
BODDY,
YOUR WIFE IS HERE.
ANOTHER PIECE OF THE SAME WOMAN ?
SHOULDN'T YOUR COLLECTION, I DON'T KNOW, EXPAND ITS SCOPE ?
IT'S
UH.
IT'S A "FOCUSED COLLECTION."

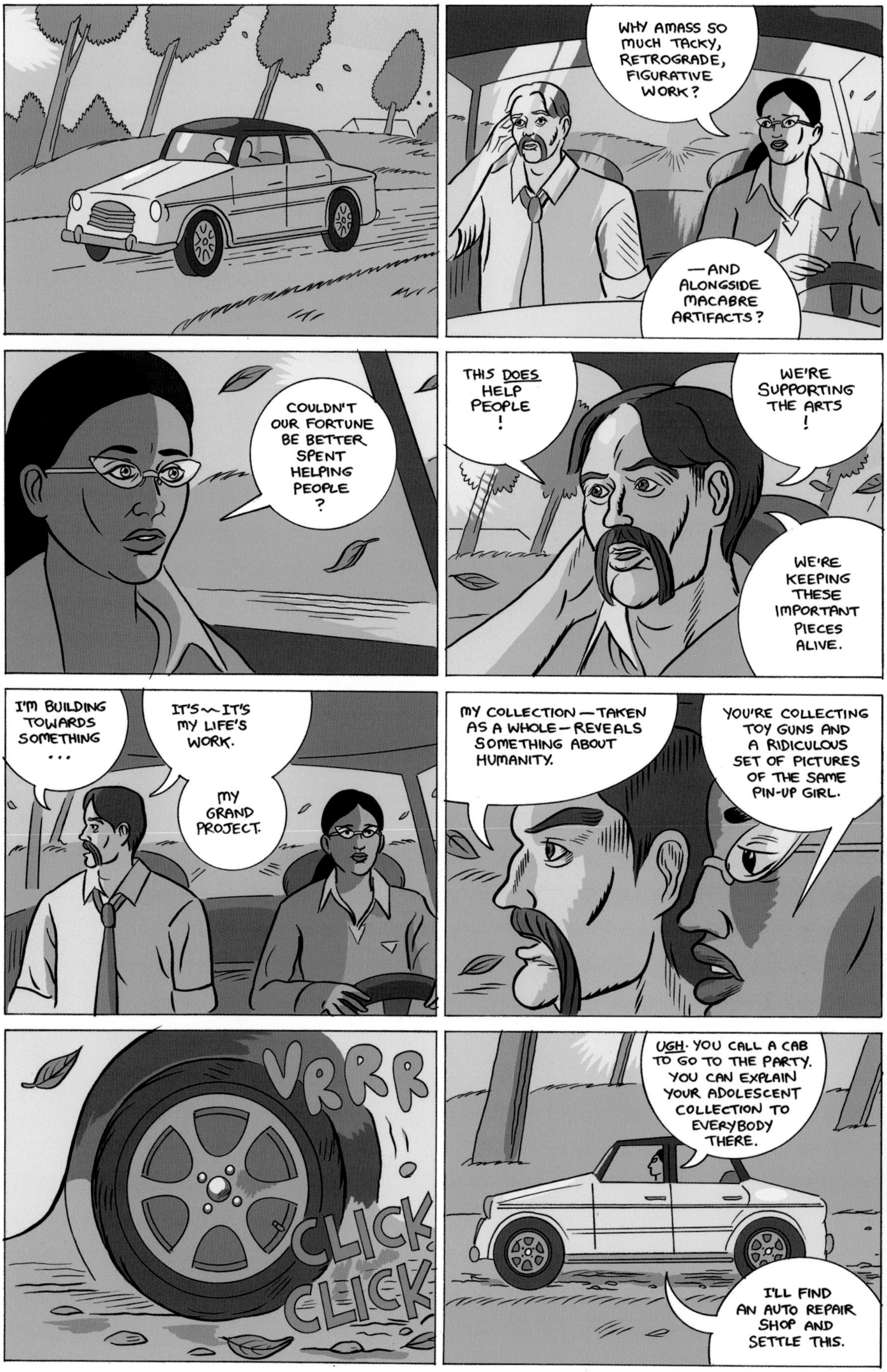
WHY AMASS SO MUCH TACKY, RETROGRADE, FIGURATIVE WORK?
—AND ALONGSIDE MACABRE ARTIFACTS?
COULDN'T OUR FORTUNE BE BETTER SPENT HELPING PEOPLE?
THIS DOES HELP PEOPLE!
WE'RE SUPPORTING THE ARTS!
WE'RE KEEPING THESE IMPORTANT PIECES ALIVE.
I'M BUILDING TOWARDS SOMETHING...
IT'S—IT'S MY LIFE'S WORK.
MY GRAND PROJECT.
MY COLLECTION—TAKEN AS A WHOLE—REVEALS SOMETHING ABOUT HUMANITY.
YOU'RE COLLECTING TOY GUNS AND A RIDICULOUS SET OF PICTURES OF THE SAME PIN-UP GIRL.
VRRR
CLICK
CLICK
UGH. YOU CALL A CAB TO GO TO THE PARTY. YOU CAN EXPLAIN YOUR ADOLESCENT COLLECTION TO EVERYBODY THERE.
I'LL FIND AN AUTO REPAIR SHOP AND SETTLE THIS.

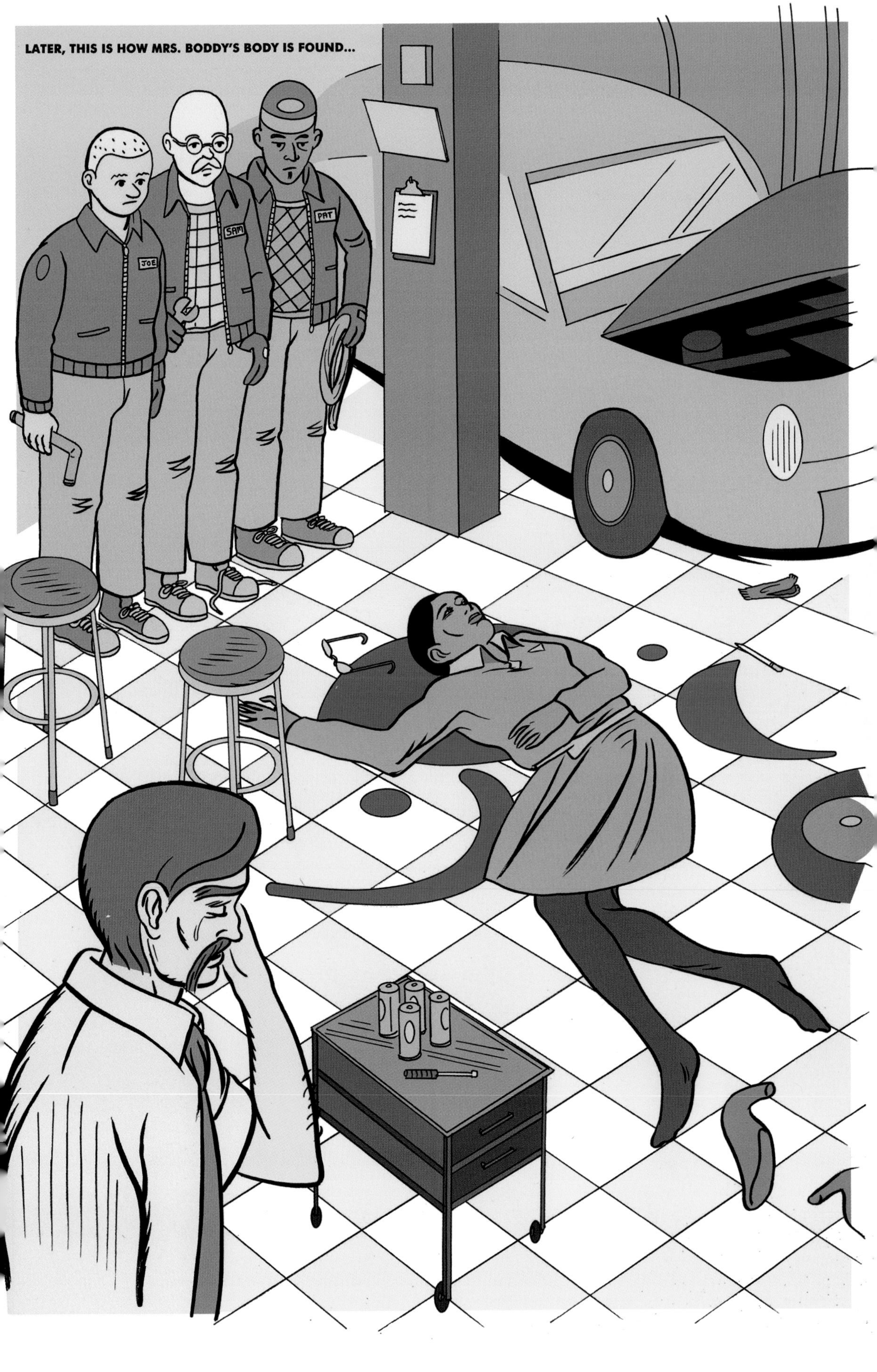
LATER, THIS IS HOW MRS. BODDY'S BODY IS FOUND...
JOE
SAM
PAT

WITHOUT TURNING BACK TO LOOK AT THE PREVIOUS PAGE, SEE IF YOU CAN IDENTIFY THE MURDERER...

THIS WILL TEST YOUR OBSERVATION SKILLS.
HE WAS THE MIDDLE OF THE THREE MEN IN THE AUTO SHOP.

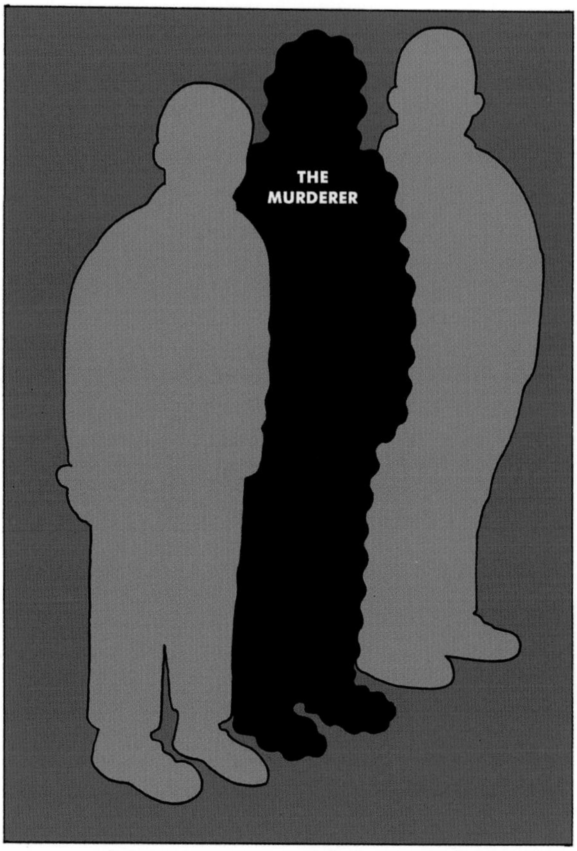
THE MURDERER

WHAT WAS HE HOLDING?

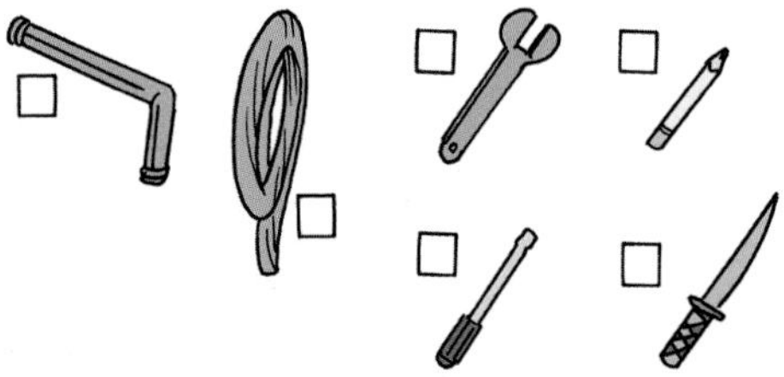

WHAT COLOR WERE HIS SHOES?

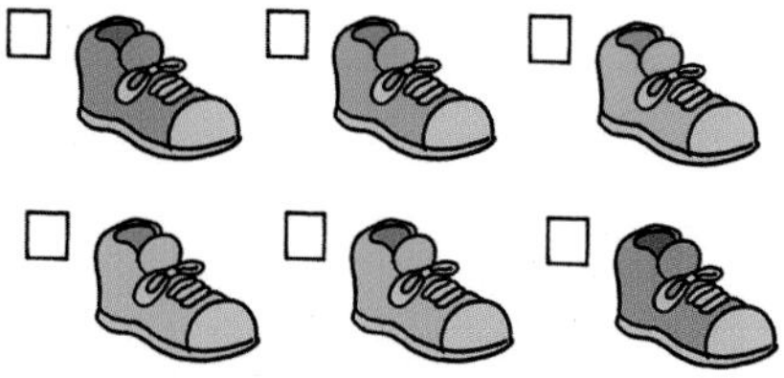

WAS ONE OF HIS SHOES UNTIED?

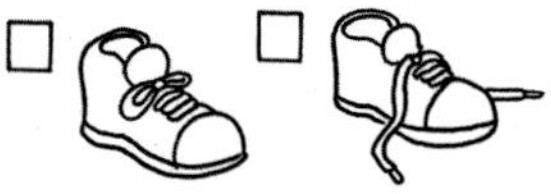

WHAT WAS THE PATTERN ON HIS SHIRT?

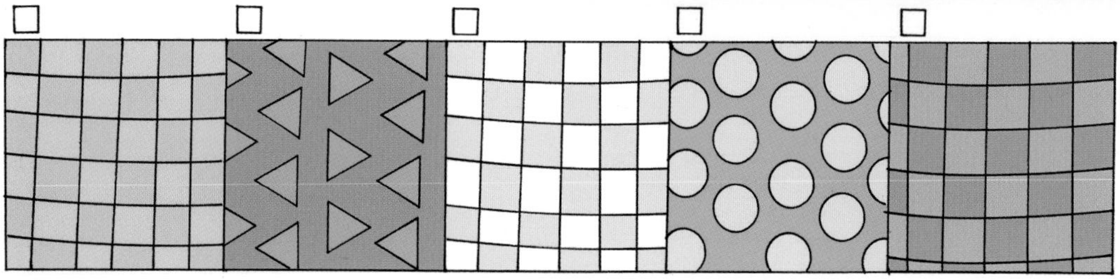

CAN YOU IDENTIFY HIS FACE HERE?

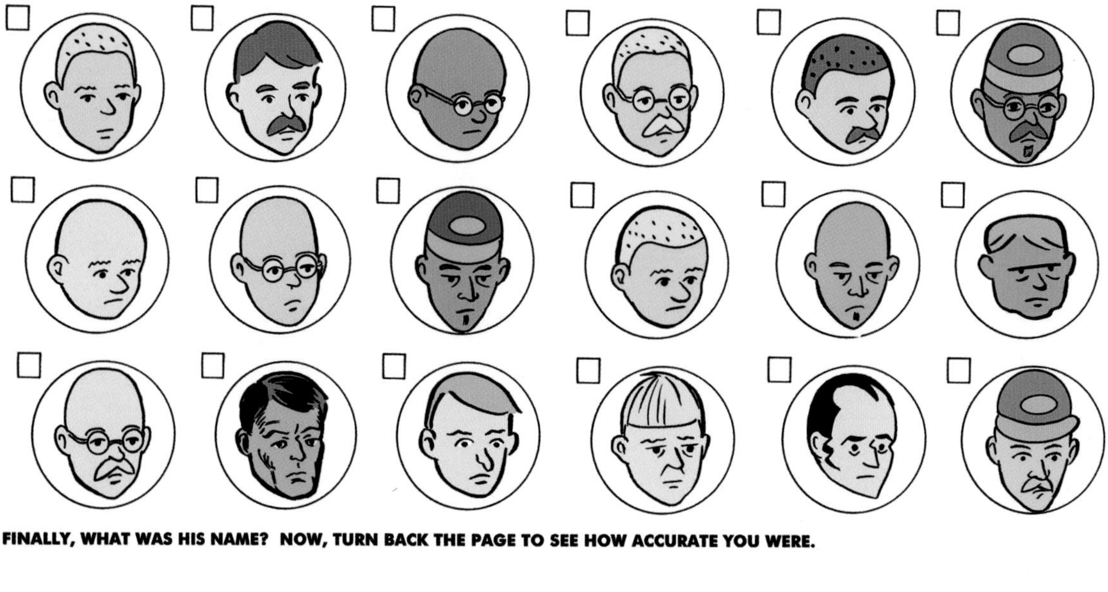

FINALLY, WHAT WAS HIS NAME? NOW, TURN BACK THE PAGE TO SEE HOW ACCURATE YOU WERE.

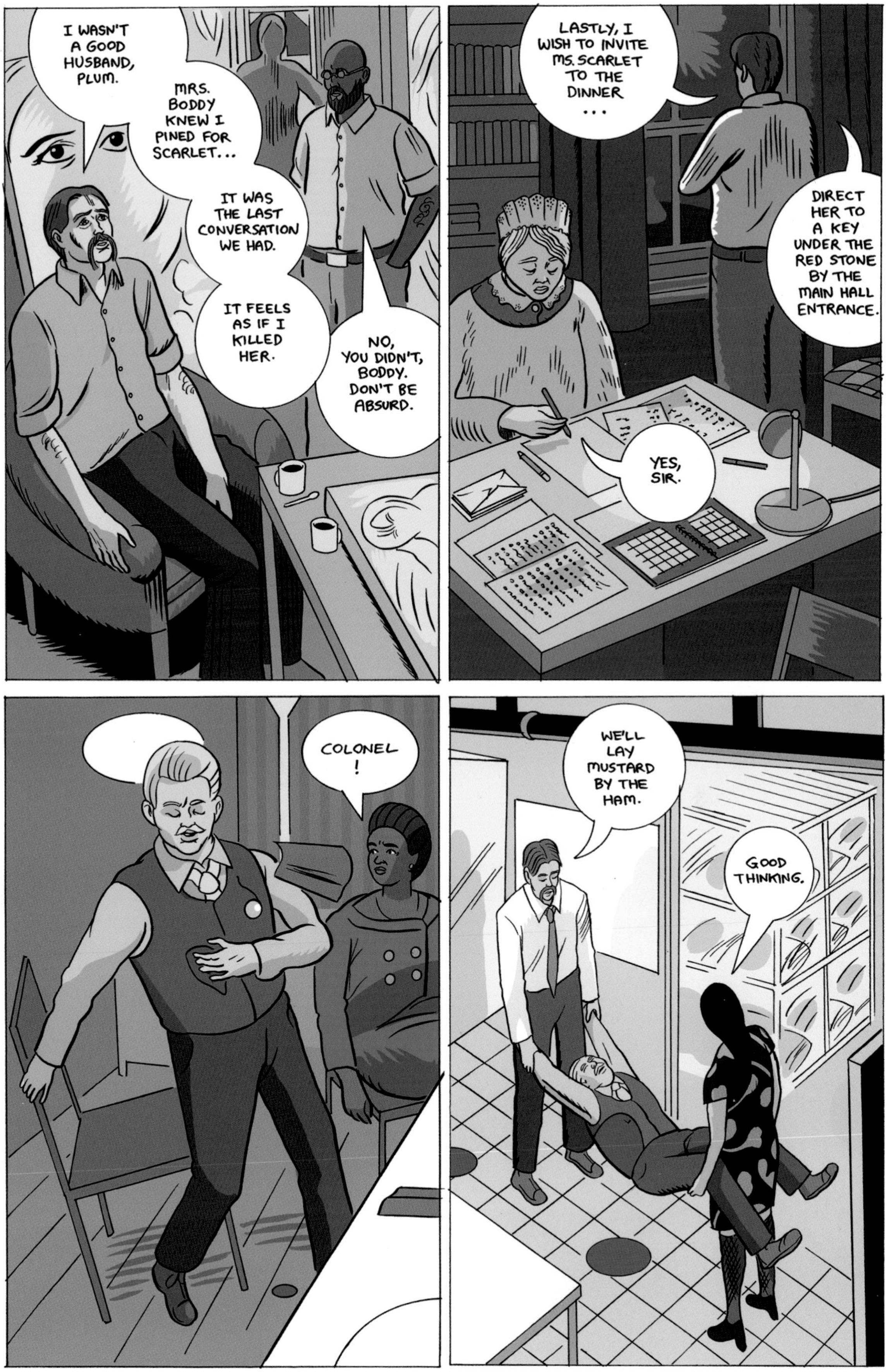
I WASN'T A GOOD HUSBAND, PLUM.
MRS. BODDY KNEW I PINED FOR SCARLET...
IT WAS THE LAST CONVERSATION WE HAD.
IT FEELS AS IF I KILLED HER.
NO, YOU DIDN'T, BODDY. DON'T BE ABSURD.
LASTLY, I WISH TO INVITE MS. SCARLET TO THE DINNER ...
DIRECT HER TO A KEY UNDER THE RED STONE BY THE MAIN HALL ENTRANCE.
YES, SIR.
COLONEL !
WE'LL LAY MUSTARD BY THE HAM.
GOOD THINKING.

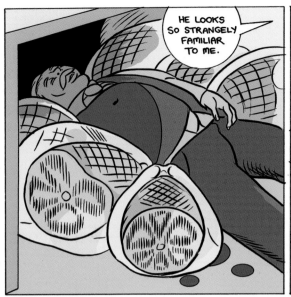

HE LOOKS SO STRANGELY FAMILIAR TO ME.

SCARLET...

I HAVEN'T BEEN HONEST WITH YOU . . .

IT SEEMS AS THOUGH NO ONE EVER IS . . .

I NEVER RECEIVED ANY DEATH THREATS.

HMM.

I HAD A SUSPICION THAT WAS THE CASE.

I~

I LOVE YOU, SCARLET.

I'VE LOVED YOU FOR A LONG TIME. BUT AFTER MY WIFE'S DEATH, I FELT GUILTY . . . HER GHOSTLY PRESENCE HANGS OVER THE MANOR.

I DON'T WANT HER HAUNTING ME— HAUNTING US— SO I FAKED THE DEATH THREATS TO MAKE A COVER. I WANT TO DISAPPEAR WITH YOU. I HAVE A FORTUNE STASHED ON AN ISLAND OFF WALES— NO ONE, ALIVE OR DEAD, WILL KNOW... WE CAN "DIE" TOGETHER.

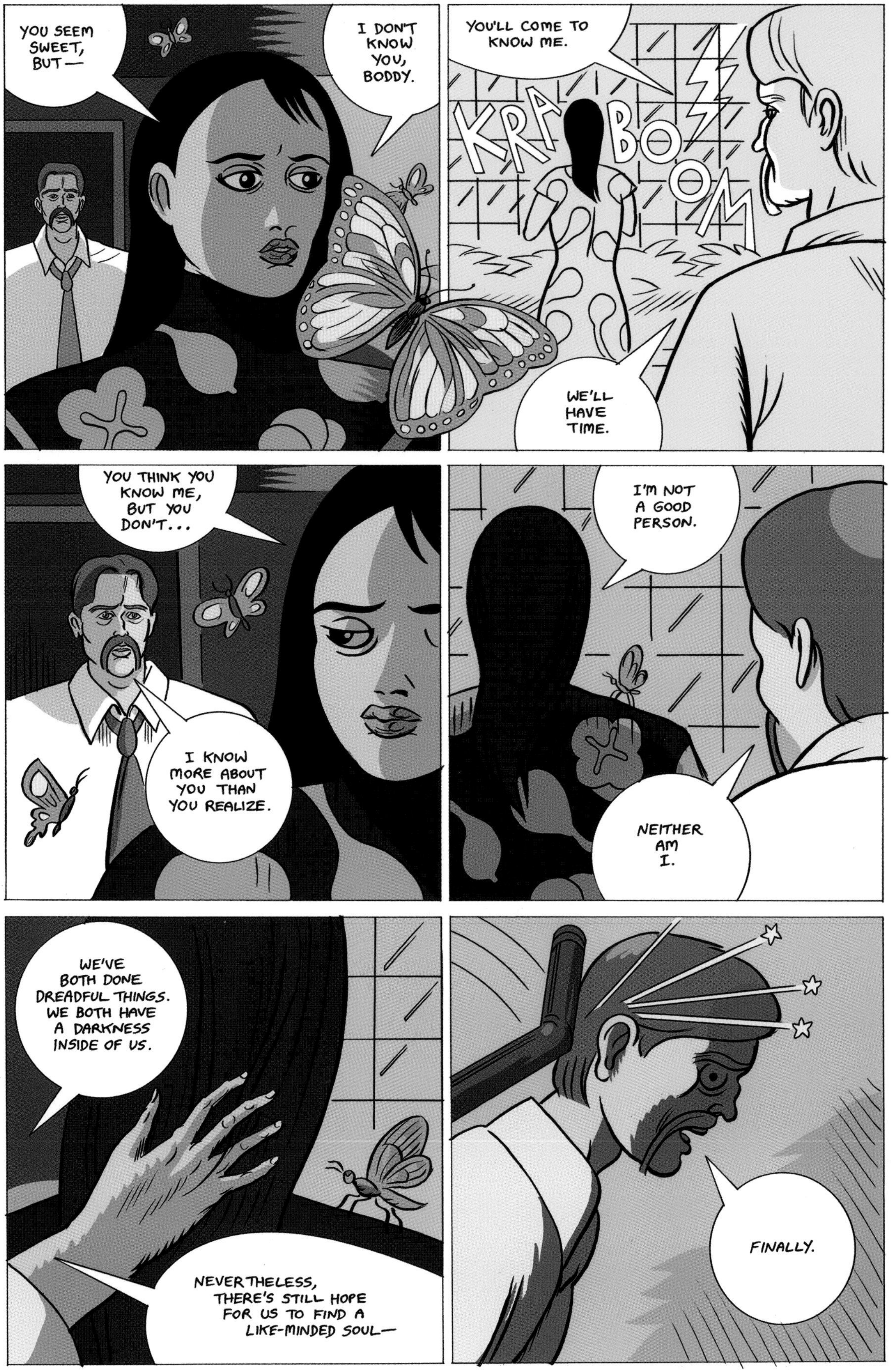
YOU SEEM SWEET, BUT—
I DON'T KNOW YOU, BODDY.
YOU'LL COME TO KNOW ME.
KRA BOOM
WE'LL HAVE TIME.
YOU THINK YOU KNOW ME, BUT YOU DON'T...
I KNOW MORE ABOUT YOU THAN YOU REALIZE.
I'M NOT A GOOD PERSON.
NEITHER AM I.
WE'VE BOTH DONE DREADFUL THINGS. WE BOTH HAVE A DARKNESS INSIDE OF US.
NEVERTHELESS, THERE'S STILL HOPE FOR US TO FIND A LIKE-MINDED SOUL—
FINALLY.

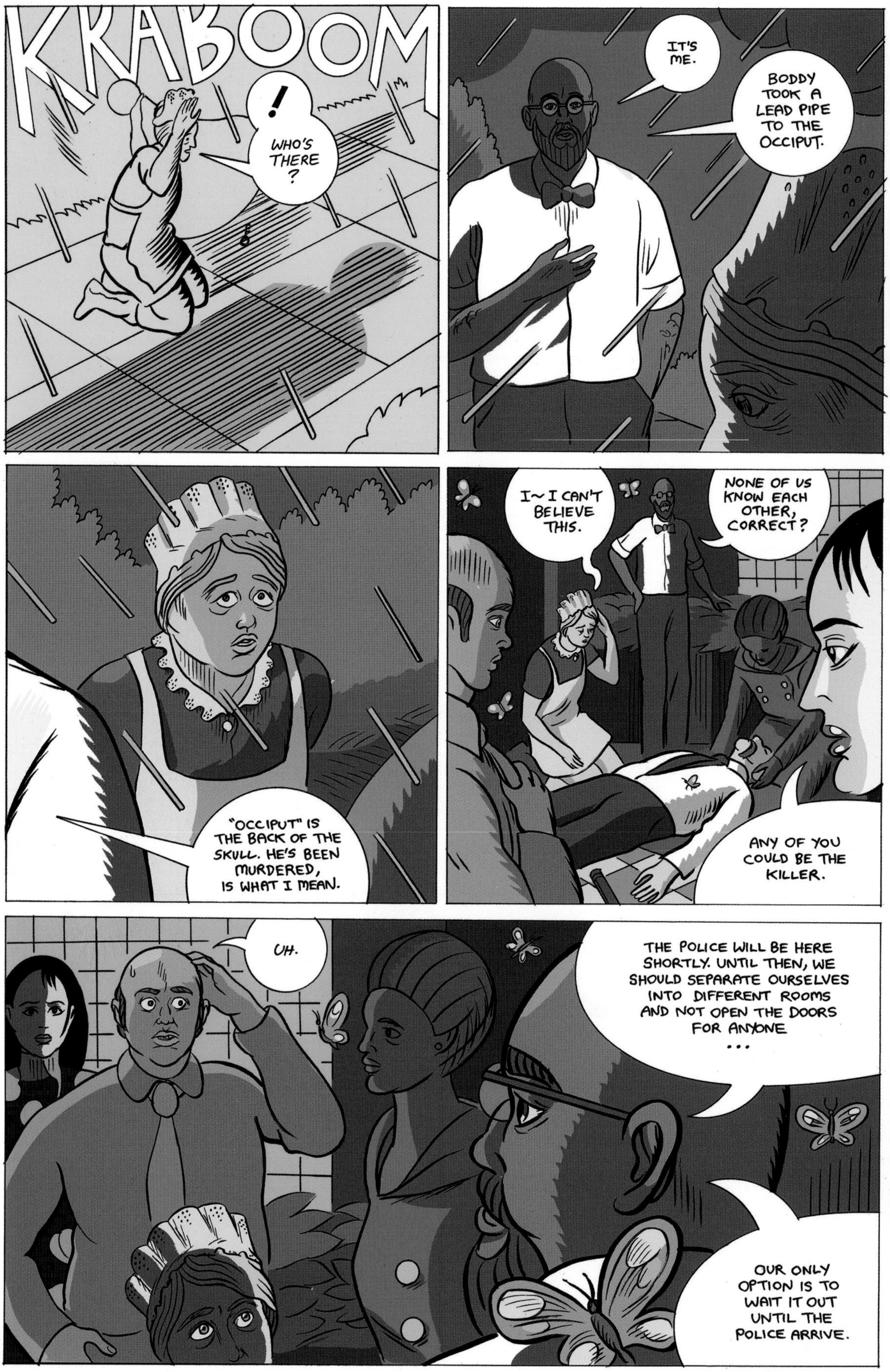
KRABOOM
!
WHO'S THERE ?
IT'S ME.
BODDY TOOK A LEAD PIPE TO THE OCCIPUT.
"OCCIPUT" IS THE BACK OF THE SKULL. HE'S BEEN MURDERED, IS WHAT I MEAN.
I~ I CAN'T BELIEVE THIS.
NONE OF US KNOW EACH OTHER, CORRECT?
ANY OF YOU COULD BE THE KILLER.
UH.
THE POLICE WILL BE HERE SHORTLY. UNTIL THEN, WE SHOULD SEPARATE OURSELVES INTO DIFFERENT ROOMS AND NOT OPEN THE DOORS FOR ANYONE ...
OUR ONLY OPTION IS TO WAIT IT OUT UNTIL THE POLICE ARRIVE.

SOLVE THIS PUZZLE TO DISCOVER WHERE EACH OF THE CHARACTERS HIDE...
DO THE NONOGRAM BY COLORING SQUARES IN GREEN (FOR MR. GREEN), BLUE (FOR MRS. PEACOCK), PURPLE (FOR PROF. PLUM), RED (FOR MS. SCARLET), OR BY LEAVING THEM BLANK (FOR MRS. WHITE).

2 2								O	
1 1 1		E		Y					
2 2								N	
1 1 1					U				
1 3 1				S					
1 2 1			H	D	T				
2 1 2		G				I		U	
1 3 1				H	T				
3				K		E			
5				L					
3						R			
1									
1			A						
1									
3				I					
3						A	L		
1									
1 1 1									
2 3 2	L		L	R					
1 7 1	C					Y		B	N
	5	3	1	1	3	1	1	3	5
	2	2	1	2	2	3	1	2	2
	1	1	1	2	11	2	1	1	1
		1		2		2		1	
				2		2			
				2					

IN A NONOGRAM, THE NUMBERS AT THE LEFT AND BOTTOM OF THE GRID MEASURE THE LENGTH OF UNBROKEN LINES OF COLOR IN THE CORRESPONDING ROW OR COLUMN. SO, A 5 WOULD REPRESENT FIVE CONSECUTIVE GREEN SQUARES, WHILE A 1 IS A SINGLE BLUE SQUARE WITH EITHER A BLANK SPACE OR ANOTHER COLOR ON EITHER SIDE.
THE ORDER IN WHICH THE SET IS LISTED IS THE SAME AS THE ORDER IN WHICH IT APPEARS IN THE PUZZLE...
SO, IF A CLUE IS 2 5, THE TWO BLUE SQUARES WILL BE LEFT OF THE FIVE PURPLE SQUARES.
THERE MAY BE ANY NUMBER OF BLANK SQUARES BETWEEN EACH SET!

FOR EXAMPLE, 3 1 1 2 MIGHT LOOK LIKE:

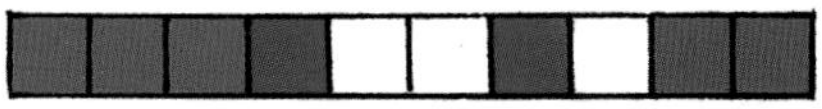

OR

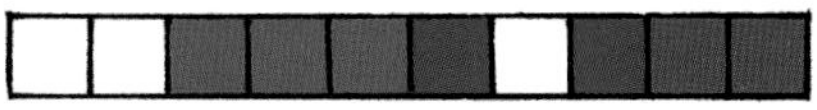

BUT NOT:

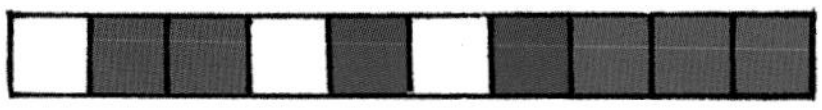

OR

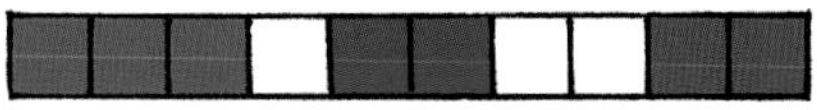

GETTING THE COLORS TO FOLLOW THE NUMBERS OF THE ROWS <u>AND</u> THE COLUMNS IS THE TRICKY PART!

ANOTHER THING: WHEN YOU COLOR OVER A LETTER, WRITE THE LETTER NEXT TO THE CHARACTER OF THE SAME COLOR...
WHEN YOU COMPLETE THE PUZZLE, THE LETTERS ON BLANK SQUARES BELONG TO MRS. WHITE.
WHEN YOU HAVE ALL THE LETTERS, YOU UNSCRAMBLE THEM TO DISCOVER WHICH ROOM EACH CHARACTER HIDES IN:

MR. GREEN ____________________

MRS. PEACOCK ____________________

PROF. PLUM ____________________

MS. SCARLET ____________________

MRS. WHITE ____________________

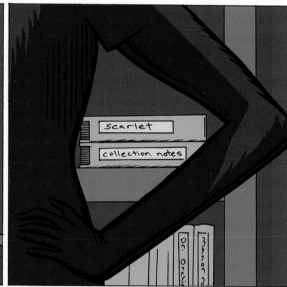

KRABOOM

scarlet

collection notes

lead white paint in wine

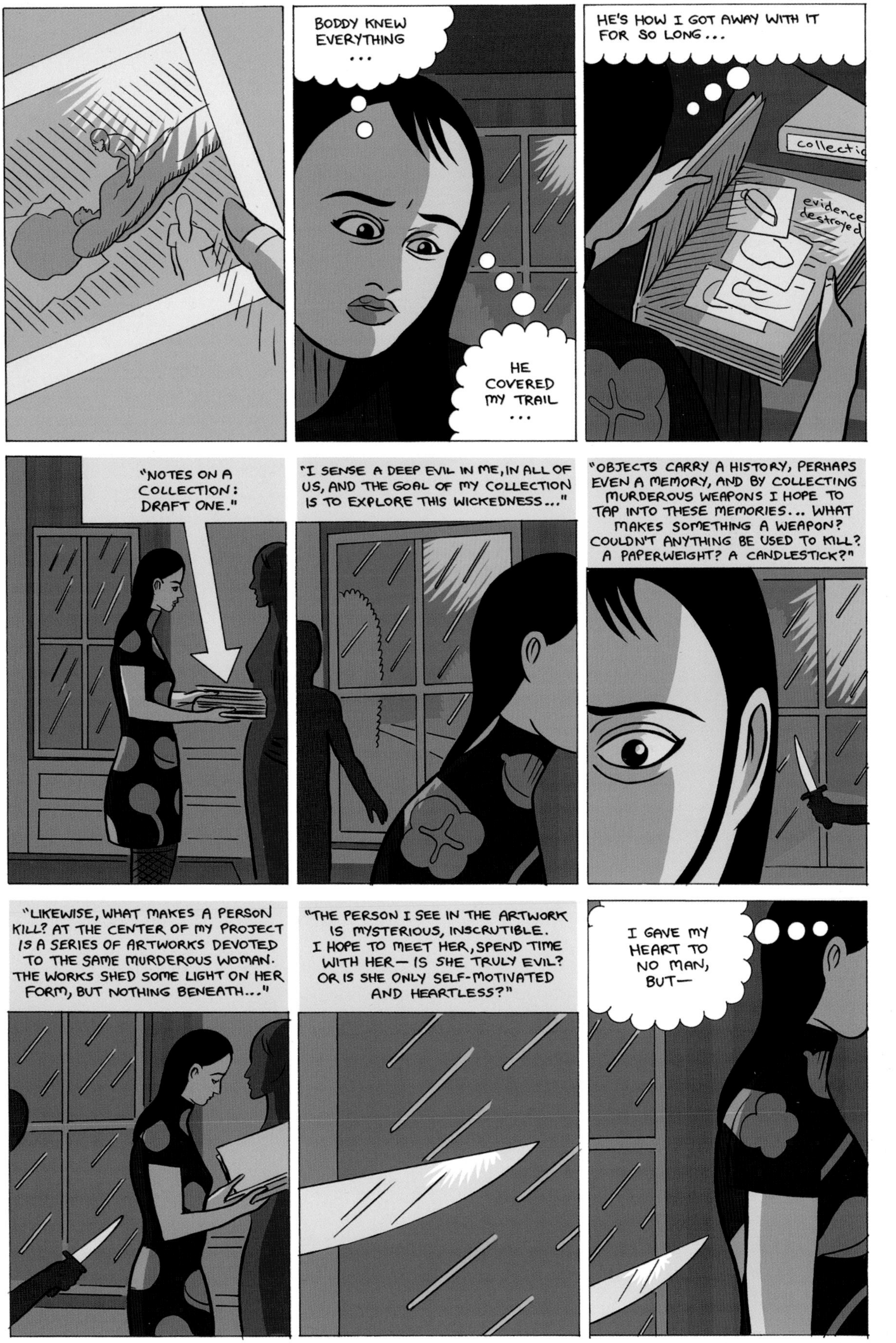
BODDY KNEW EVERYTHING ...
HE COVERED MY TRAIL ...
HE'S HOW I GOT AWAY WITH IT FOR SO LONG ...
collectio
evidence destroyed
"NOTES ON A COLLECTION: DRAFT ONE."
"I SENSE A DEEP EVIL IN ME, IN ALL OF US, AND THE GOAL OF MY COLLECTION IS TO EXPLORE THIS WICKEDNESS..."
"OBJECTS CARRY A HISTORY, PERHAPS EVEN A MEMORY, AND BY COLLECTING MURDEROUS WEAPONS I HOPE TO TAP INTO THESE MEMORIES... WHAT MAKES SOMETHING A WEAPON? COULDN'T ANYTHING BE USED TO KILL? A PAPERWEIGHT? A CANDLESTICK?"
"LIKEWISE, WHAT MAKES A PERSON KILL? AT THE CENTER OF MY PROJECT IS A SERIES OF ARTWORKS DEVOTED TO THE SAME MURDEROUS WOMAN. THE WORKS SHED SOME LIGHT ON HER FORM, BUT NOTHING BENEATH..."
"THE PERSON I SEE IN THE ARTWORK IS MYSTERIOUS, INSCRUTIBLE. I HOPE TO MEET HER, SPEND TIME WITH HER— IS SHE TRULY EVIL? OR IS SHE ONLY SELF-MOTIVATED AND HEARTLESS?"
I GAVE MY HEART TO NO MAN, BUT—

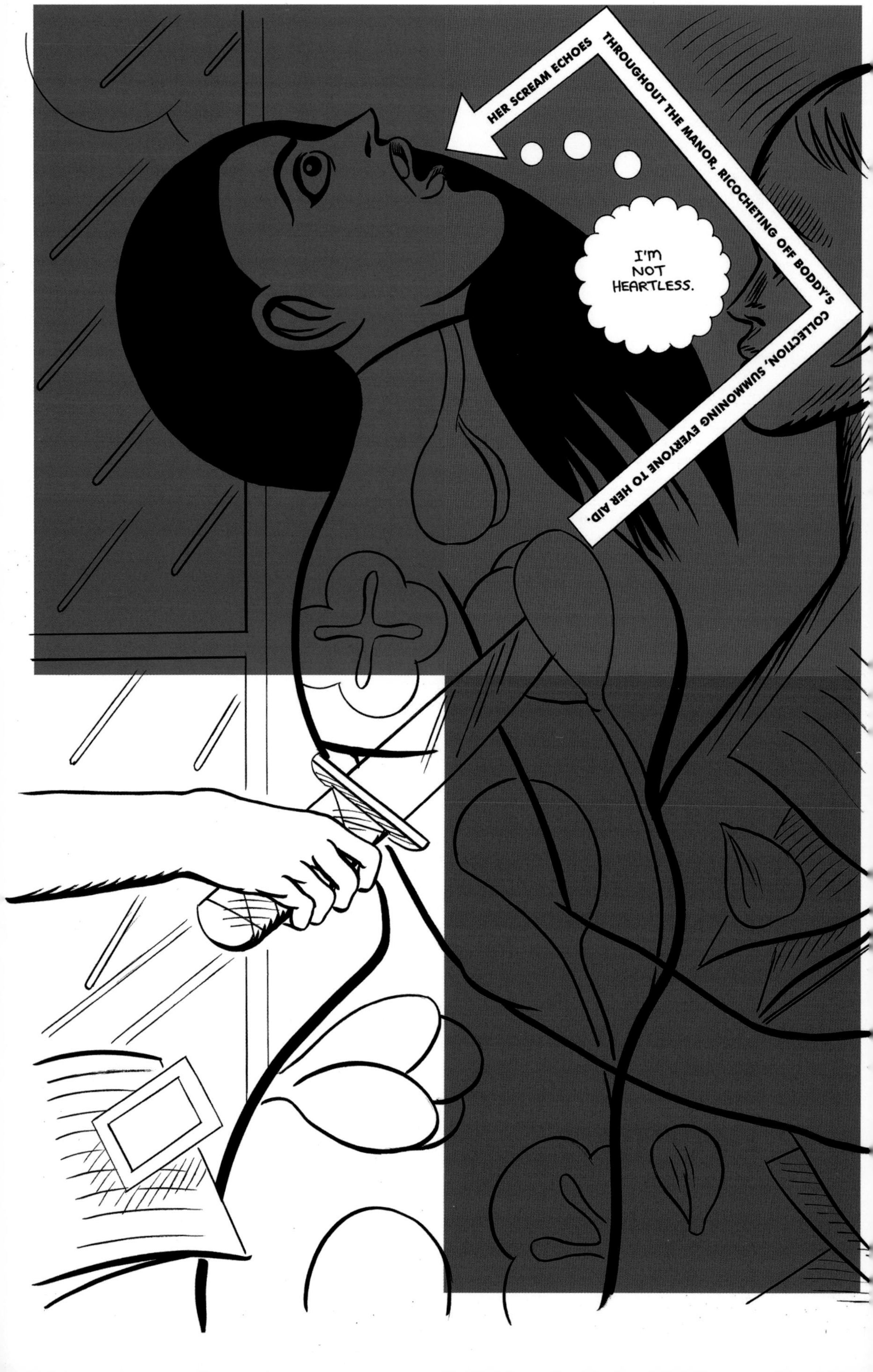
HER SCREAM ECHOES THROUGHOUT THE MANOR, RICOCHETING OFF BODDY'S COLLECTION, SUMMONING EVERYONE TO HER AID.
I'M NOT HEARTLESS.

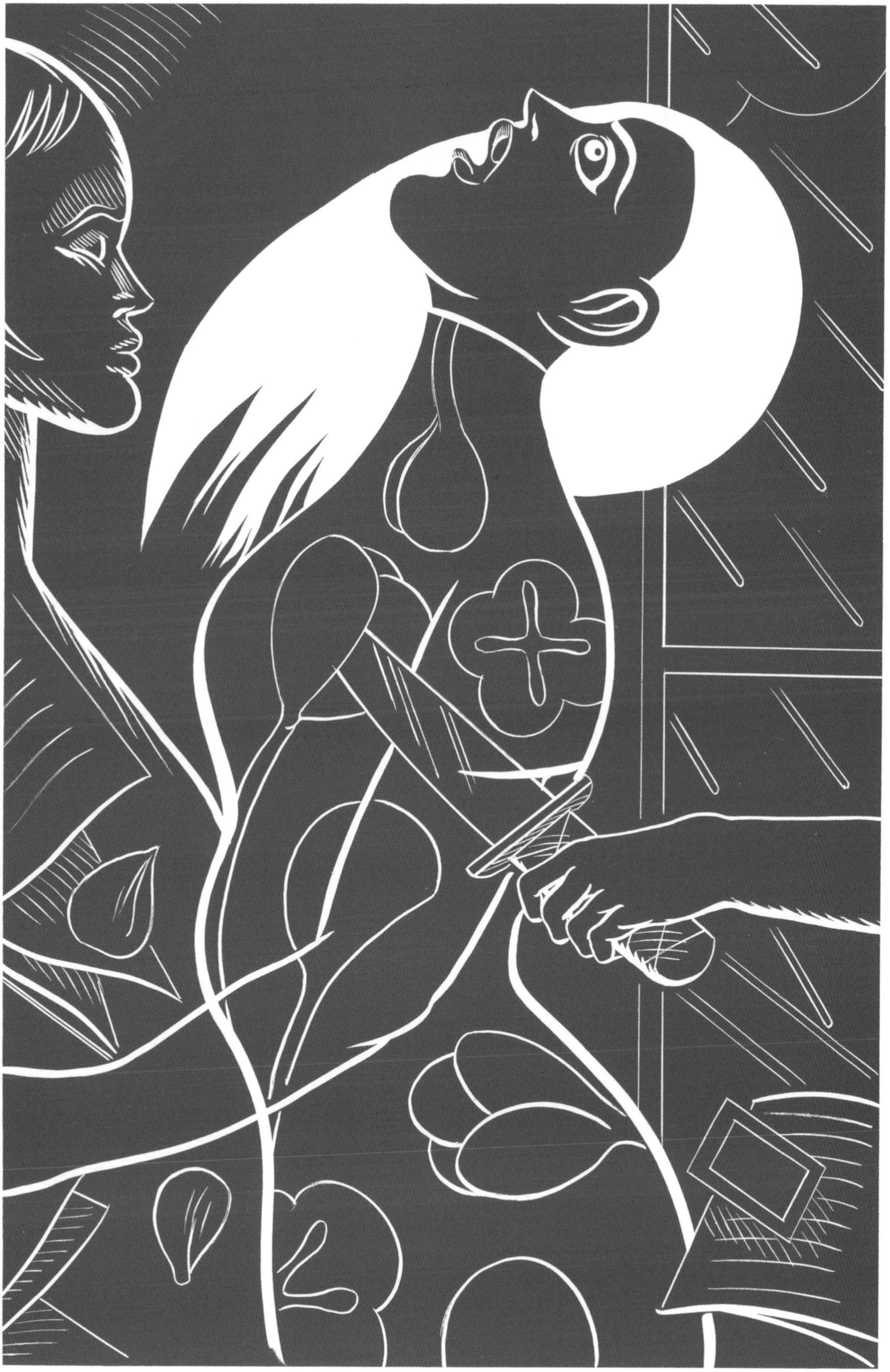

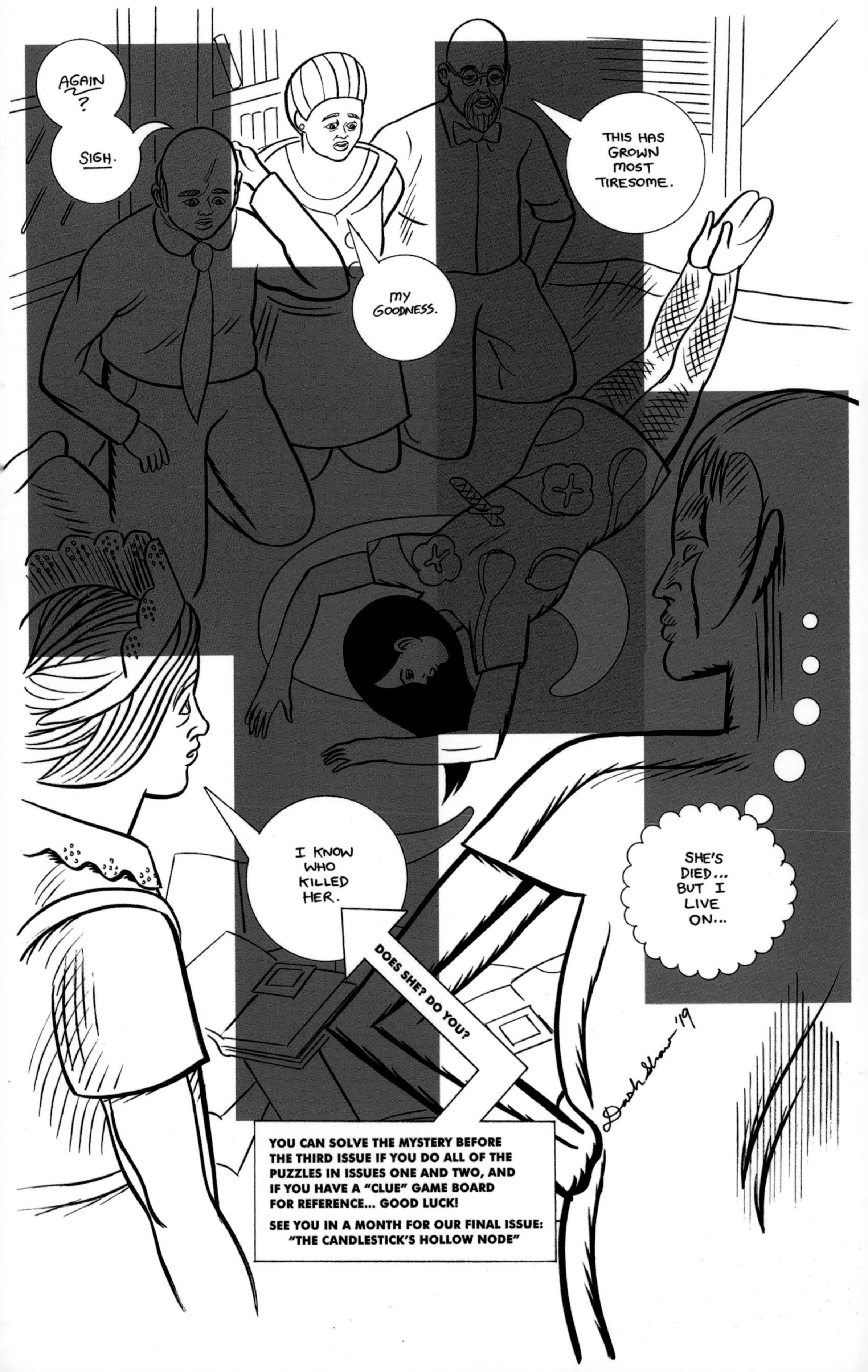
AGAIN?
SIGH.
MY GOODNESS.
THIS HAS GROWN MOST TIRESOME.
I KNOW WHO KILLED HER.
DOES SHE? DO YOU?
SHE'S DIED... BUT I LIVE ON...
YOU CAN SOLVE THE MYSTERY BEFORE THE THIRD ISSUE IF YOU DO ALL OF THE PUZZLES IN ISSUES ONE AND TWO, AND IF YOU HAVE A "CLUE" GAME BOARD FOR REFERENCE... GOOD LUCK!
SEE YOU IN A MONTH FOR OUR FINAL ISSUE: "THE CANDLESTICK'S HOLLOW NODE"
Dash Shaw '19

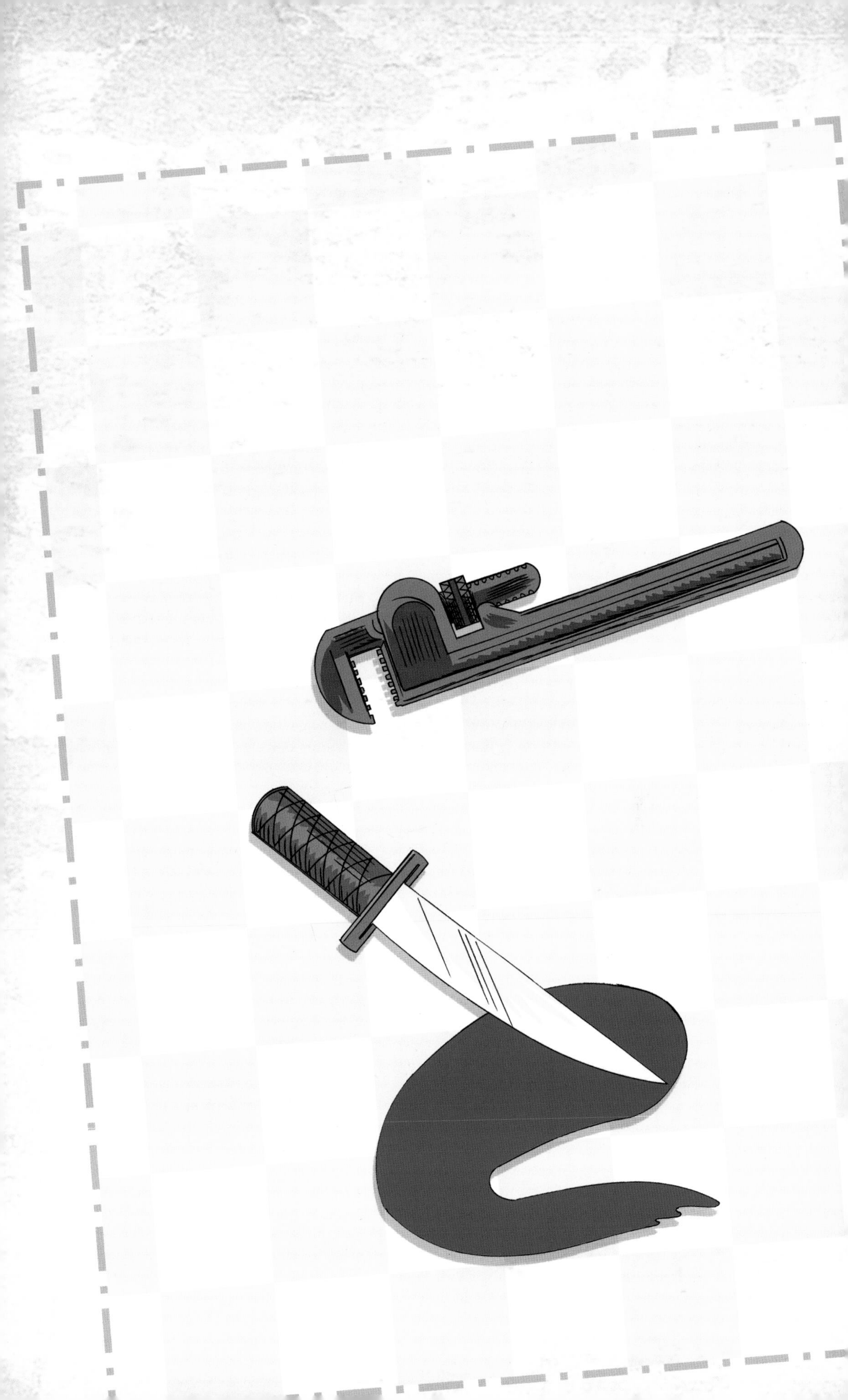

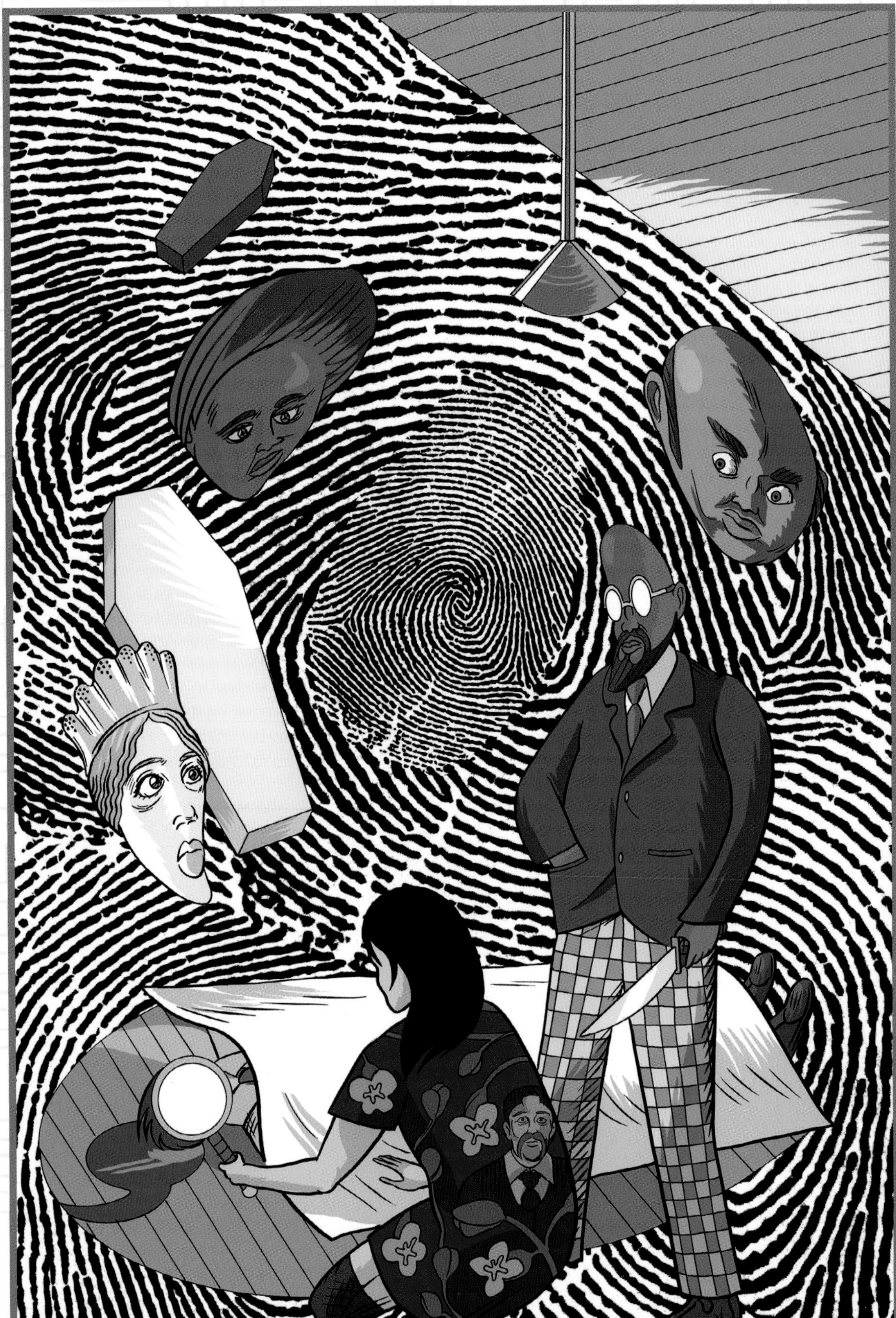

ART BY
DASH SHAW

I'D HIDE MY PARENTS' PULP MAGAZINES INSIDE MY SCHOOLBOOKS AND STAY UP LATE "STUDYING"...

IT'S BEDTIME, BIRDIE.

CLICK

HAUNTED

BUT...

I WANNA KEEP READING.

HERE— YOU CAN USE THIS FROM LAST NIGHT*. BE CAREFUL WITH IT.

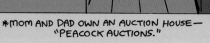

*MOM AND DAD OWN AN AUCTION HOUSE— "PEACOCK AUCTIONS."

COOL.

YOU HAVE ABOUT AN HOUR.

WHEN IT GOES OUT, YOU GO TO SLEEP.

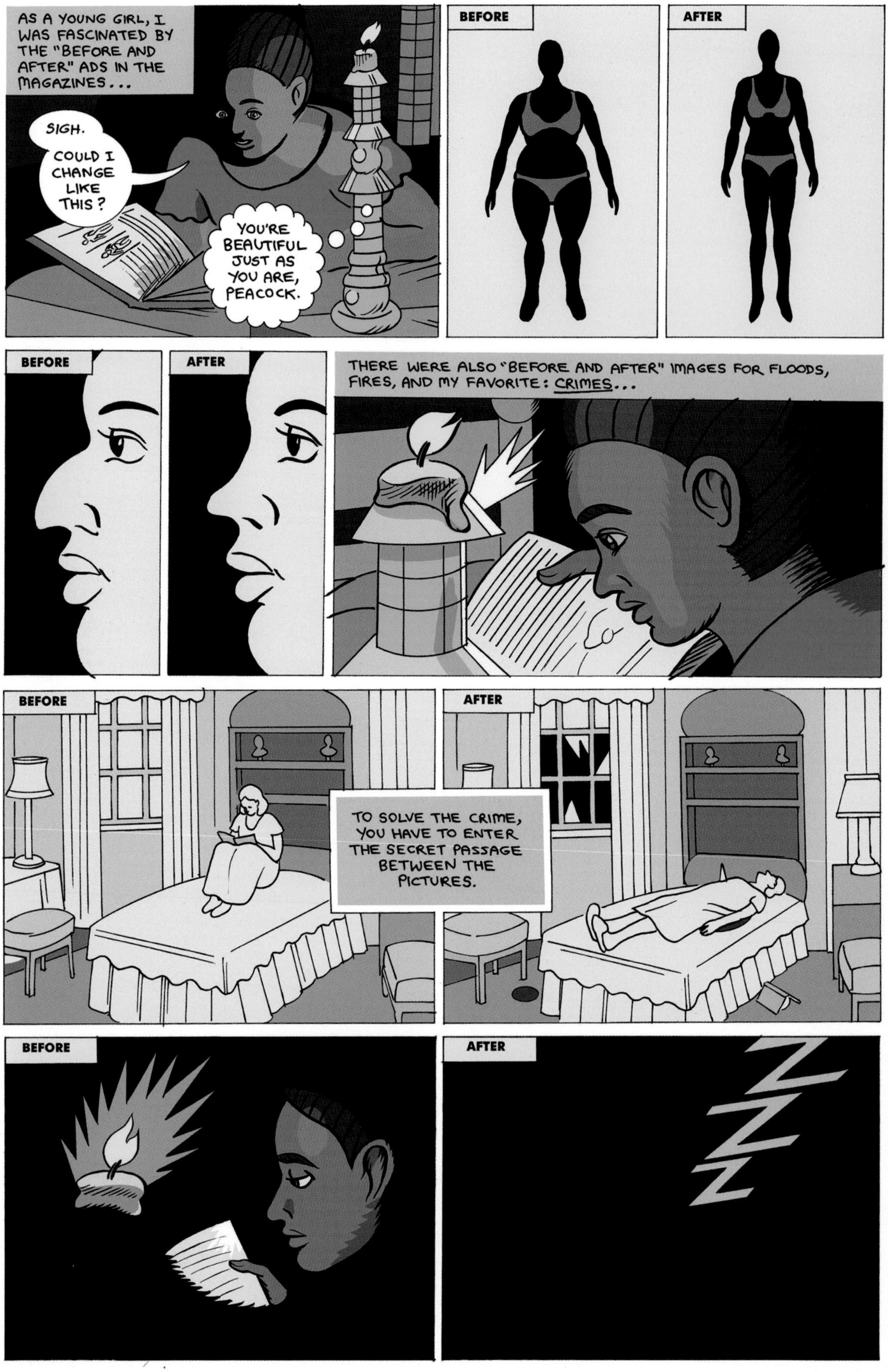
AS A YOUNG GIRL, I WAS FASCINATED BY THE "BEFORE AND AFTER" ADS IN THE MAGAZINES...
SIGH.
COULD I CHANGE LIKE THIS?
YOU'RE BEAUTIFUL JUST AS YOU ARE, PEACOCK.
BEFORE
AFTER
BEFORE
AFTER
THERE WERE ALSO "BEFORE AND AFTER" IMAGES FOR FLOODS, FIRES, AND MY FAVORITE: CRIMES...
BEFORE
TO SOLVE THE CRIME, YOU HAVE TO ENTER THE SECRET PASSAGE BETWEEN THE PICTURES.
AFTER
BEFORE
AFTER

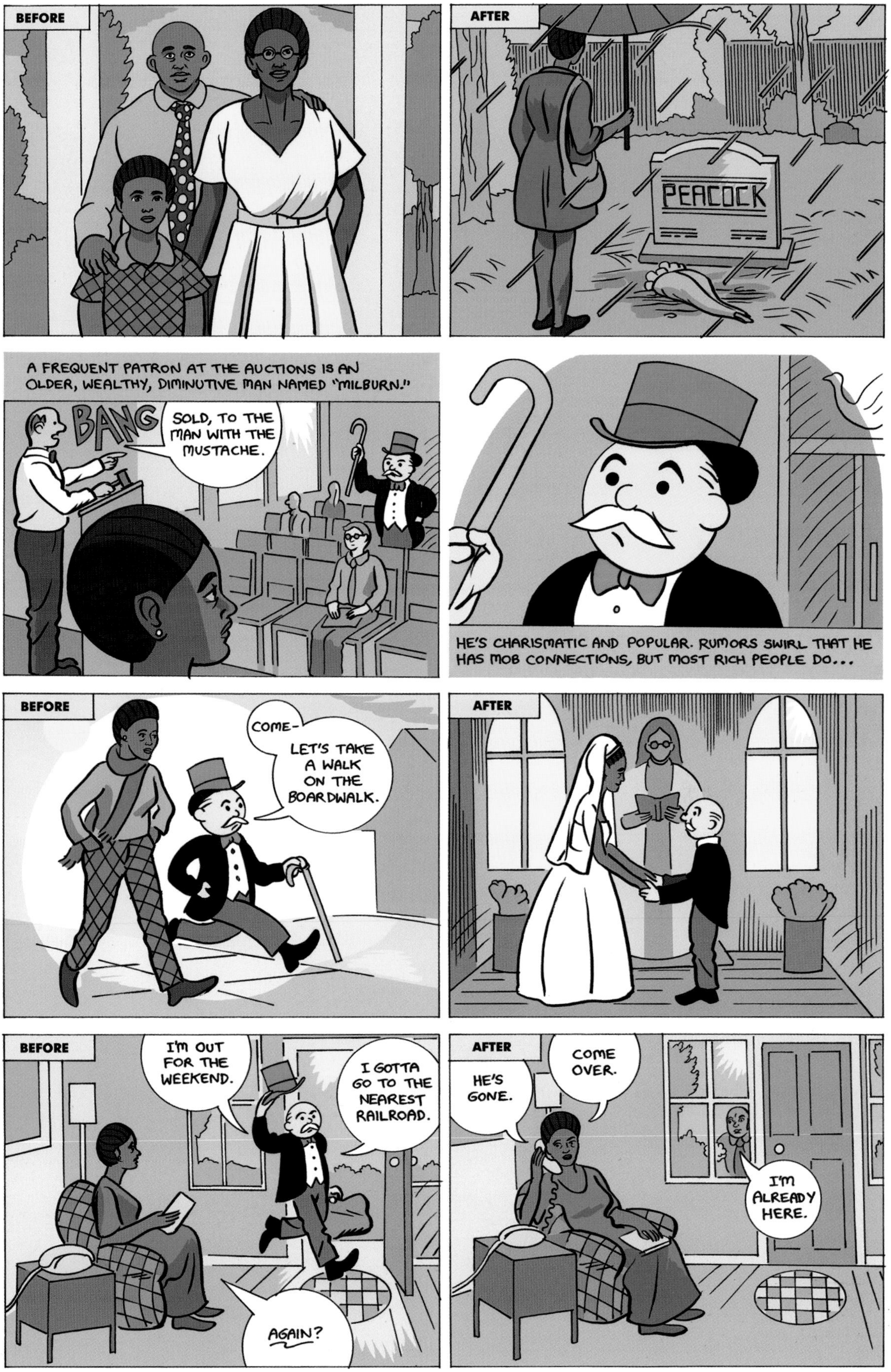
BEFORE
AFTER
PEACOCK
A FREQUENT PATRON AT THE AUCTIONS IS AN OLDER, WEALTHY, DIMINUTIVE MAN NAMED "MILBURN."
BANG
SOLD, TO THE MAN WITH THE MUSTACHE.
HE'S CHARISMATIC AND POPULAR. RUMORS SWIRL THAT HE HAS MOB CONNECTIONS, BUT MOST RICH PEOPLE DO...
BEFORE
COME-
LET'S TAKE A WALK ON THE BOARDWALK.
AFTER
BEFORE
I'M OUT FOR THE WEEKEND.
I GOTTA GO TO THE NEAREST RAILROAD.
AGAIN?
AFTER
HE'S GONE.
COME OVER.
I'M ALREADY HERE.

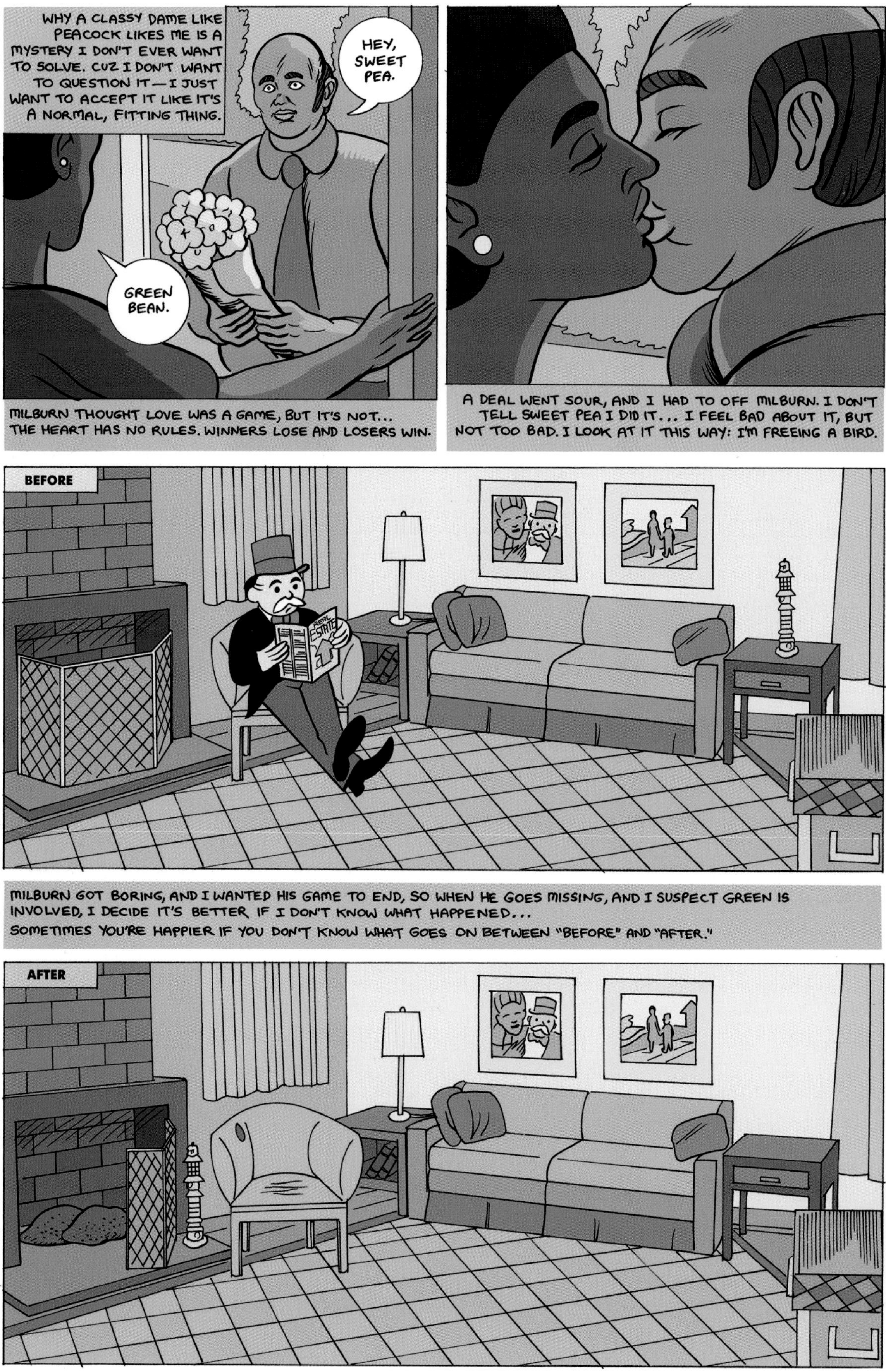
WHY A CLASSY DAME LIKE PEACOCK LIKES ME IS A MYSTERY I DON'T EVER WANT TO SOLVE. CUZ I DON'T WANT TO QUESTION IT—I JUST WANT TO ACCEPT IT LIKE IT'S A NORMAL, FITTING THING.
HEY, SWEET PEA.
GREEN BEAN.
MILBURN THOUGHT LOVE WAS A GAME, BUT IT'S NOT... THE HEART HAS NO RULES. WINNERS LOSE AND LOSERS WIN.
A DEAL WENT SOUR, AND I HAD TO OFF MILBURN. I DON'T TELL SWEET PEA I DID IT... I FEEL BAD ABOUT IT, BUT NOT TOO BAD. I LOOK AT IT THIS WAY: I'M FREEING A BIRD.
BEFORE
REAL ESTATE
MILBURN GOT BORING, AND I WANTED HIS GAME TO END, SO WHEN HE GOES MISSING, AND I SUSPECT GREEN IS INVOLVED, I DECIDE IT'S BETTER IF I DON'T KNOW WHAT HAPPENED...
SOMETIMES YOU'RE HAPPIER IF YOU DON'T KNOW WHAT GOES ON BETWEEN "BEFORE" AND "AFTER."
AFTER

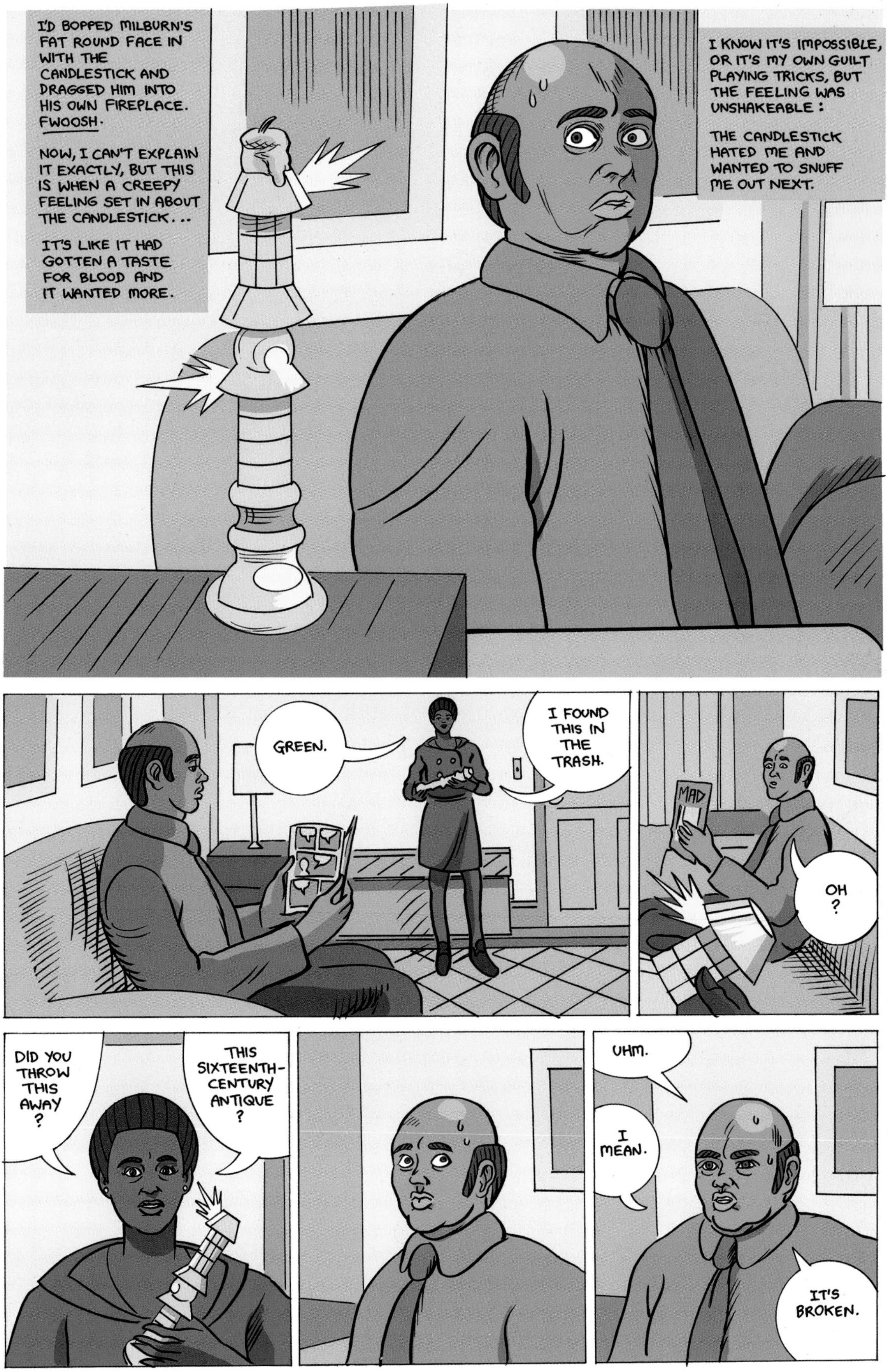
I'D BOPPED MILBURN'S FAT ROUND FACE IN WITH THE CANDLESTICK AND DRAGGED HIM INTO HIS OWN FIREPLACE. FWOOSH.
NOW, I CAN'T EXPLAIN IT EXACTLY, BUT THIS IS WHEN A CREEPY FEELING SET IN ABOUT THE CANDLESTICK...
IT'S LIKE IT HAD GOTTEN A TASTE FOR BLOOD AND IT WANTED MORE.
I KNOW IT'S IMPOSSIBLE, OR IT'S MY OWN GUILT PLAYING TRICKS, BUT THE FEELING WAS UNSHAKEABLE:
THE CANDLESTICK HATED ME AND WANTED TO SNUFF ME OUT NEXT.
GREEN.
I FOUND THIS IN THE TRASH.
MAD
OH?
DID YOU THROW THIS AWAY?
THIS SIXTEENTH-CENTURY ANTIQUE?
UHM.
I MEAN.
IT'S BROKEN.

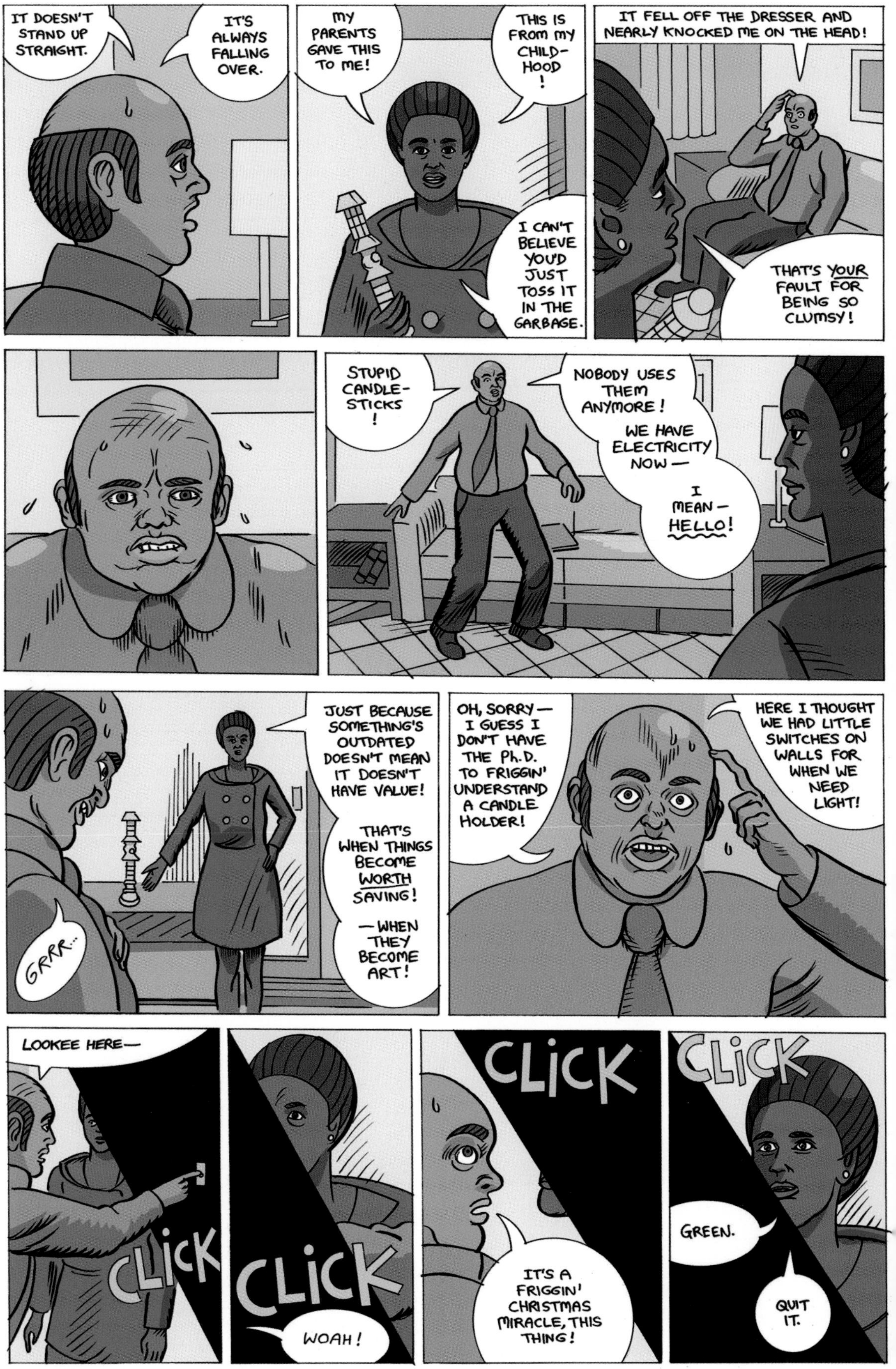
IT DOESN'T STAND UP STRAIGHT.
IT'S ALWAYS FALLING OVER.
MY PARENTS GAVE THIS TO ME!
THIS IS FROM MY CHILDHOOD!
I CAN'T BELIEVE YOU'D JUST TOSS IT IN THE GARBAGE.
IT FELL OFF THE DRESSER AND NEARLY KNOCKED ME ON THE HEAD!
THAT'S YOUR FAULT FOR BEING SO CLUMSY!
STUPID CANDLE-STICKS!
NOBODY USES THEM ANYMORE!
WE HAVE ELECTRICITY NOW—
I MEAN—HELLO!
JUST BECAUSE SOMETHING'S OUTDATED DOESN'T MEAN IT DOESN'T HAVE VALUE!
THAT'S WHEN THINGS BECOME WORTH SAVING!
—WHEN THEY BECOME ART!
GRRR...
OH, SORRY— I GUESS I DON'T HAVE THE Ph.D. TO FRIGGIN' UNDERSTAND A CANDLE HOLDER!
HERE I THOUGHT WE HAD LITTLE SWITCHES ON WALLS FOR WHEN WE NEED LIGHT!
LOOKEE HERE—
CLICK
CLICK
WOAH!
CLICK
IT'S A FRIGGIN' CHRISTMAS MIRACLE, THIS THING!
CLICK
GREEN.
QUIT IT.

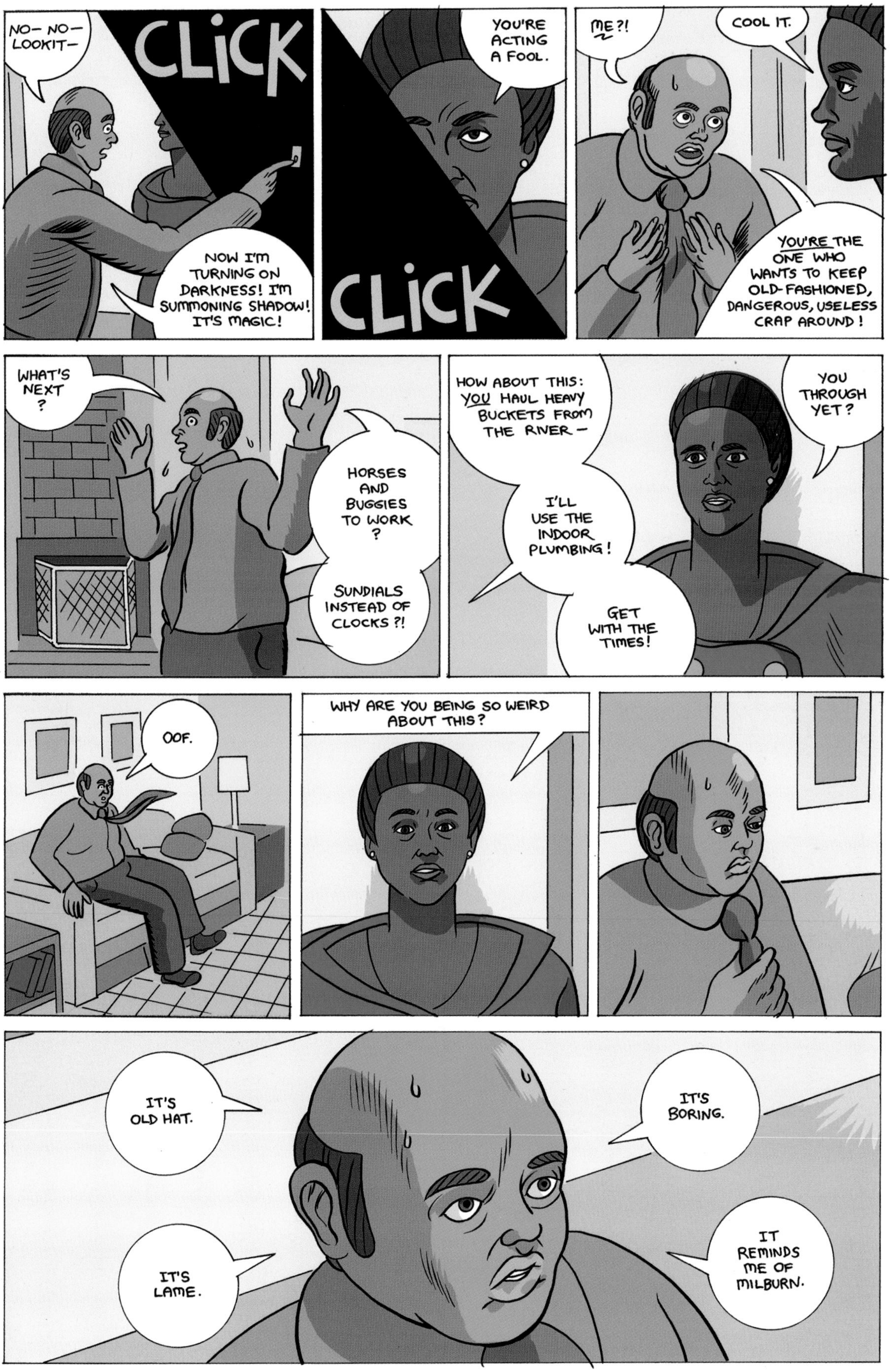
NO— NO— LOOKIT—
CLICK
NOW I'M TURNING ON DARKNESS! I'M SUMMONING SHADOW! IT'S MAGIC!
YOU'RE ACTING A FOOL.
CLICK
ME?!
COOL IT.
YOU'RE THE ONE WHO WANTS TO KEEP OLD-FASHIONED, DANGEROUS, USELESS CRAP AROUND!
WHAT'S NEXT?
HORSES AND BUGGIES TO WORK?
SUNDIALS INSTEAD OF CLOCKS?!
HOW ABOUT THIS: YOU HAUL HEAVY BUCKETS FROM THE RIVER—
I'LL USE THE INDOOR PLUMBING!
YOU THROUGH YET?
GET WITH THE TIMES!
OOF.
WHY ARE YOU BEING SO WEIRD ABOUT THIS?
IT'S OLD HAT.
IT'S BORING.
IT'S LAME.
IT REMINDS ME OF MILBURN.

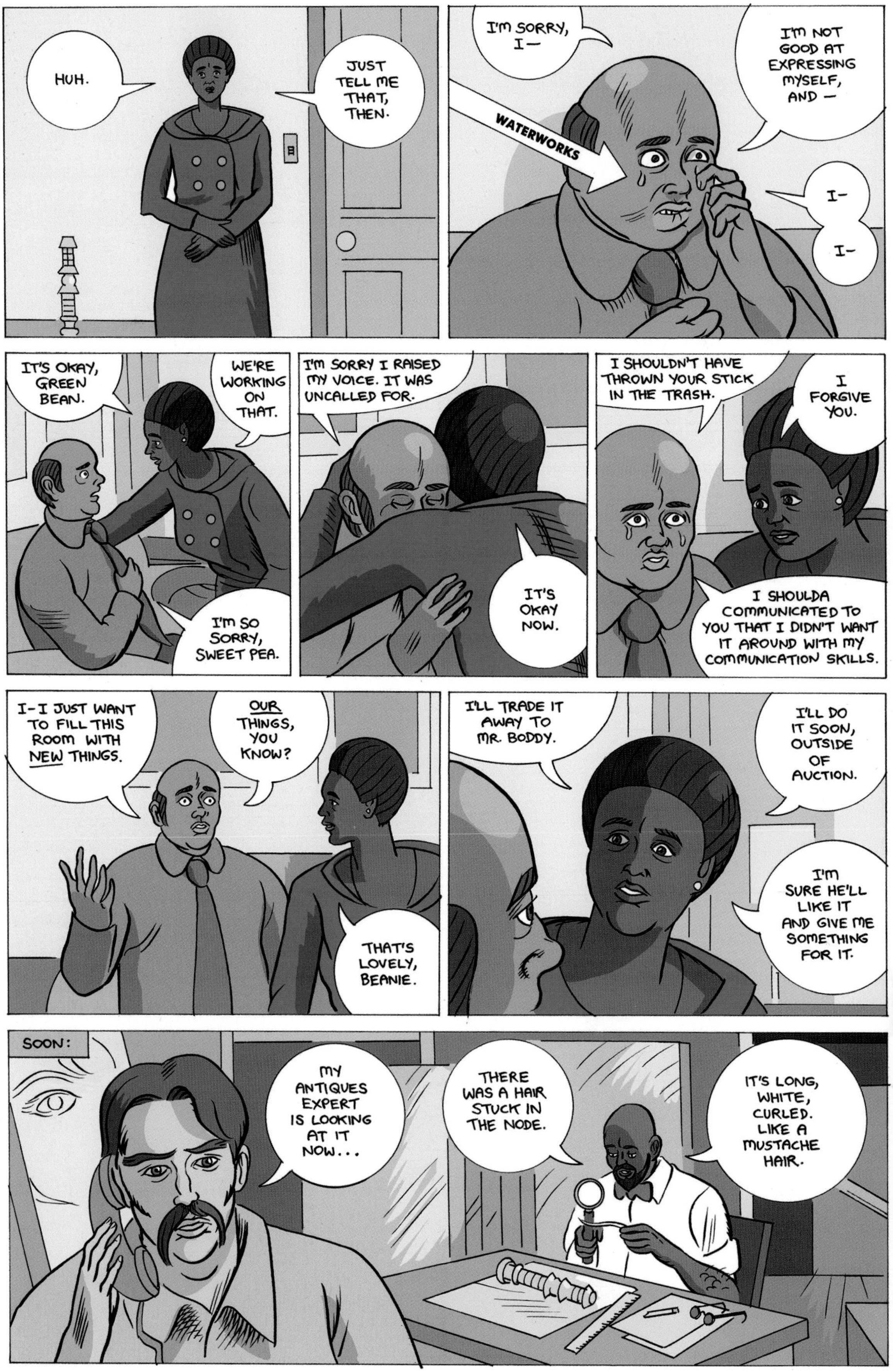
HUH.
JUST TELL ME THAT, THEN.
I'M SORRY, I—
I'M NOT GOOD AT EXPRESSING MYSELF, AND —
WATERWORKS
I-
I-
IT'S OKAY, GREEN BEAN.
WE'RE WORKING ON THAT.
I'M SO SORRY, SWEET PEA.
I'M SORRY I RAISED MY VOICE. IT WAS UNCALLED FOR.
IT'S OKAY NOW.
I SHOULDN'T HAVE THROWN YOUR STICK IN THE TRASH.
I FORGIVE YOU.
I SHOULDA COMMUNICATED TO YOU THAT I DIDN'T WANT IT AROUND WITH MY COMMUNICATION SKILLS.
I- I JUST WANT TO FILL THIS ROOM WITH NEW THINGS.
OUR THINGS, YOU KNOW?
THAT'S LOVELY, BEANIE.
I'LL TRADE IT AWAY TO MR. BODDY.
I'LL DO IT SOON, OUTSIDE OF AUCTION.
I'M SURE HE'LL LIKE IT AND GIVE ME SOMETHING FOR IT.
SOON:
MY ANTIQUES EXPERT IS LOOKING AT IT NOW...
THERE WAS A HAIR STUCK IN THE NODE.
IT'S LONG, WHITE, CURLED. LIKE A MUSTACHE HAIR.

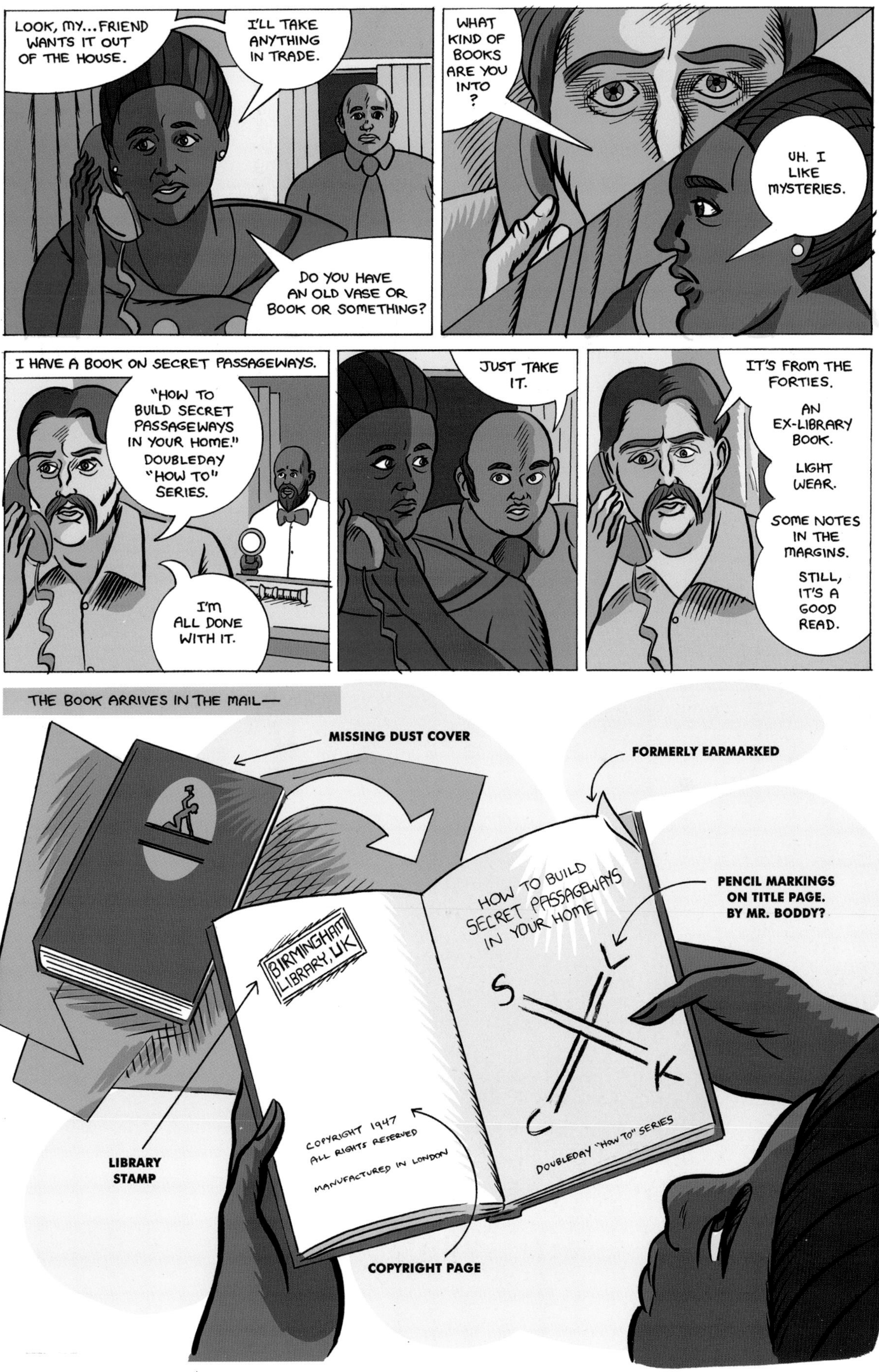
LOOK, MY...FRIEND WANTS IT OUT OF THE HOUSE.
I'LL TAKE ANYTHING IN TRADE.
DO YOU HAVE AN OLD VASE OR BOOK OR SOMETHING?
WHAT KIND OF BOOKS ARE YOU INTO?
UH. I LIKE MYSTERIES.
I HAVE A BOOK ON SECRET PASSAGEWAYS.
"HOW TO BUILD SECRET PASSAGEWAYS IN YOUR HOME." DOUBLEDAY "HOW TO" SERIES.
I'M ALL DONE WITH IT.
JUST TAKE IT.
IT'S FROM THE FORTIES.
AN EX-LIBRARY BOOK.
LIGHT WEAR.
SOME NOTES IN THE MARGINS.
STILL, IT'S A GOOD READ.
THE BOOK ARRIVES IN THE MAIL—
MISSING DUST COVER
FORMERLY EARMARKED
BIRMINGHAM LIBRARY, UK
HOW TO BUILD SECRET PASSAGEWAYS IN YOUR HOME
PENCIL MARKINGS ON TITLE PAGE. BY MR. BODDY?
S L C K
COPYRIGHT 1947
ALL RIGHTS RESERVED
MANUFACTURED IN LONDON
DOUBLEDAY "HOW TO" SERIES
LIBRARY STAMP
COPYRIGHT PAGE

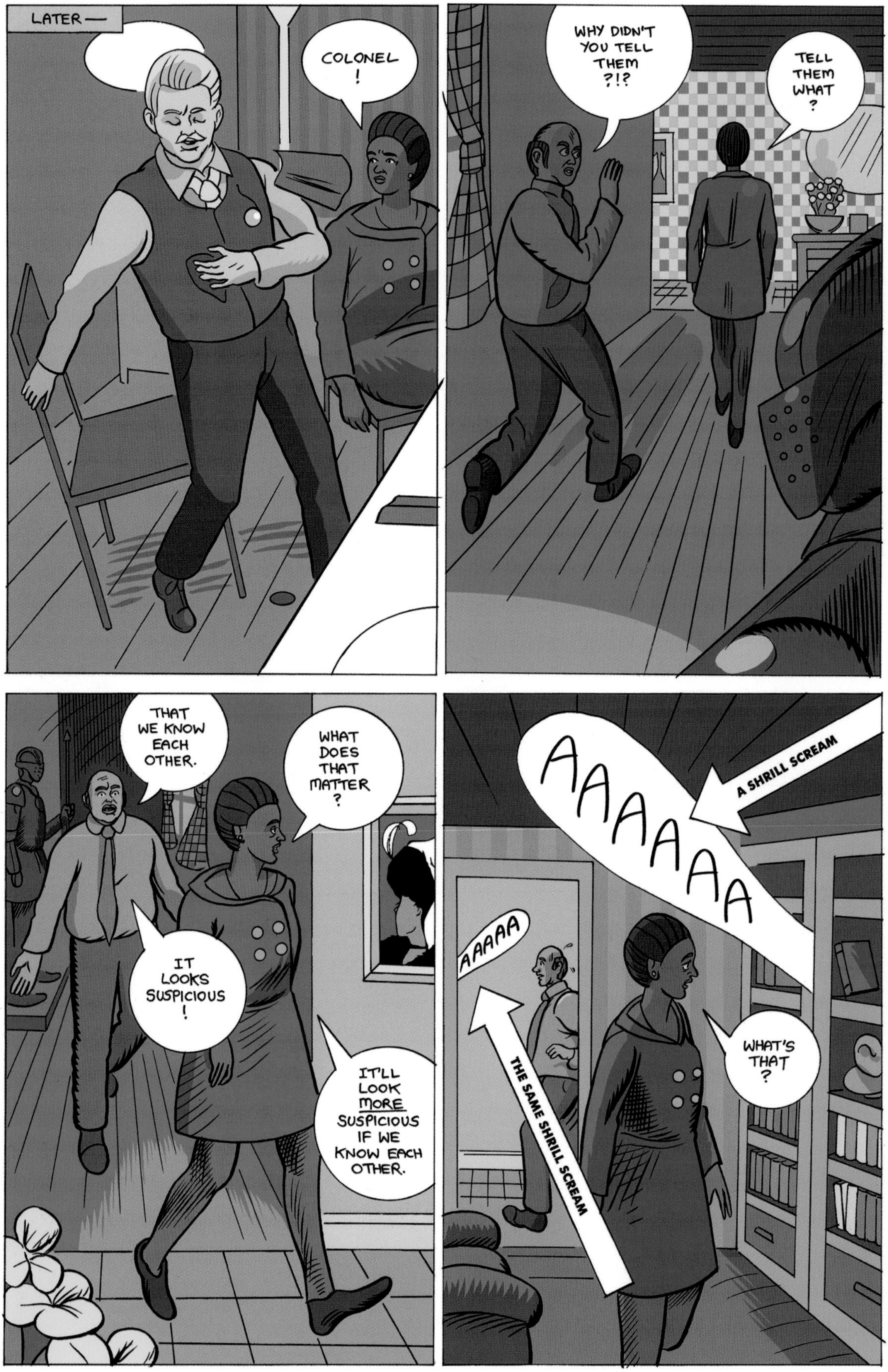
LATER —
COLONEL !
WHY DIDN'T YOU TELL THEM ?!?
TELL THEM WHAT ?
THAT WE KNOW EACH OTHER.
WHAT DOES THAT MATTER ?
IT LOOKS SUSPICIOUS !
IT'LL LOOK MORE SUSPICIOUS IF WE KNOW EACH OTHER.
AAAAAA
A SHRILL SCREAM
AAAAA
THE SAME SHRILL SCREAM
WHAT'S THAT ?

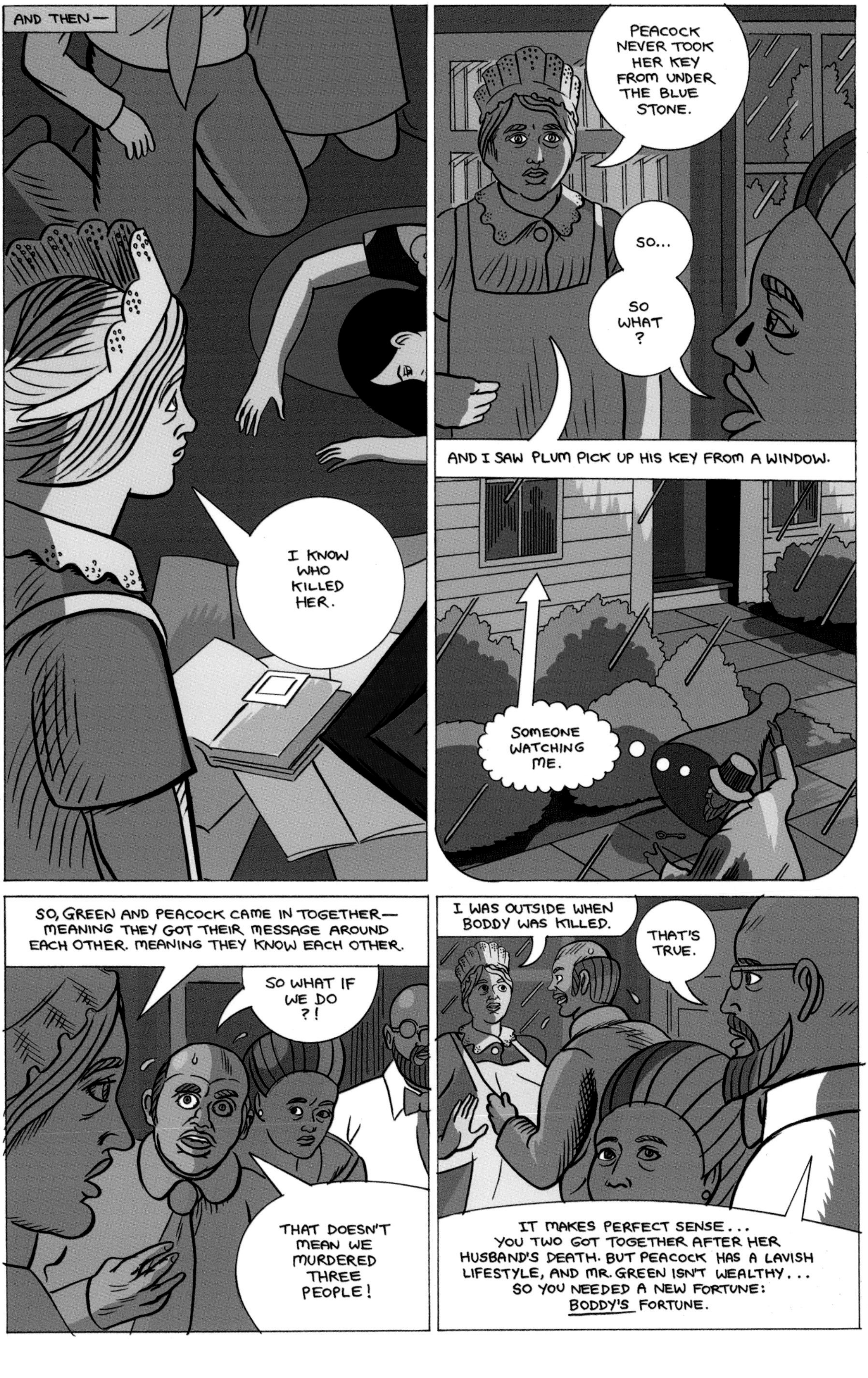
AND THEN—
I KNOW WHO KILLED HER.
PEACOCK NEVER TOOK HER KEY FROM UNDER THE BLUE STONE.
SO...
SO WHAT ?
AND I SAW PLUM PICK UP HIS KEY FROM A WINDOW.
SOMEONE WATCHING ME.
SO, GREEN AND PEACOCK CAME IN TOGETHER— MEANING THEY GOT THEIR MESSAGE AROUND EACH OTHER. MEANING THEY KNOW EACH OTHER.
SO WHAT IF WE DO ?!
THAT DOESN'T MEAN WE MURDERED THREE PEOPLE!
I WAS OUTSIDE WHEN BODDY WAS KILLED.
THAT'S TRUE.
IT MAKES PERFECT SENSE... YOU TWO GOT TOGETHER AFTER HER HUSBAND'S DEATH. BUT PEACOCK HAS A LAVISH LIFESTYLE, AND MR. GREEN ISN'T WEALTHY... SO YOU NEEDED A NEW FORTUNE: BODDY'S FORTUNE.

IF THE REST OF US DIED, THE COLLECTION WOULD GO TO PEACOCK'S AUCTION. PEACOCK WOULD CONTROL IT— SHE COULD MANIPULATE IT TO HER AND GREEN'S FAVOR.

DING DONG ♪ ♪

YOU'RE MAKING AN AWFUL LOT OF PRESUMPTIONS, MISS WHITE!

YOU WERE BOTH SITTING BESIDE MUSTARD AT THE DINNER TABLE.

KRA-BOOM

YOU COULD HAVE EASILY SHOT HIM FROM BELOW THE TABLE WITHOUT ANYONE ELSE SEEING.

POLICE!

KNOCK KNOCK

DON'T BE ABSURD!

THEN, YOU FOUGHT BEING PAIRED WITH ME TO SEARCH THE MANOR. YOU WANTED TO BE WITH YOUR LOVEBIRD, PEACOCK, SO YOU TWO COULD GO TOGETHER AND, HAND IN HAND, BLUDGEON RICH MR. BODDY.

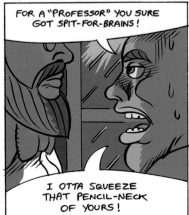

FOR A "PROFESSOR" YOU SURE GOT SPIT-FOR-BRAINS!

I OTTA SQUEEZE THAT PENCIL-NECK OF YOURS!

WE'RE COMMIN' IN!

KRACK

AND BEING A "FORMER" MOB MAN, MR. GREEN WOULD KNOW HOW TO PICK A LOCK TO GET INTO THE STUDY TO SLAY SCARLET.

GRRR.

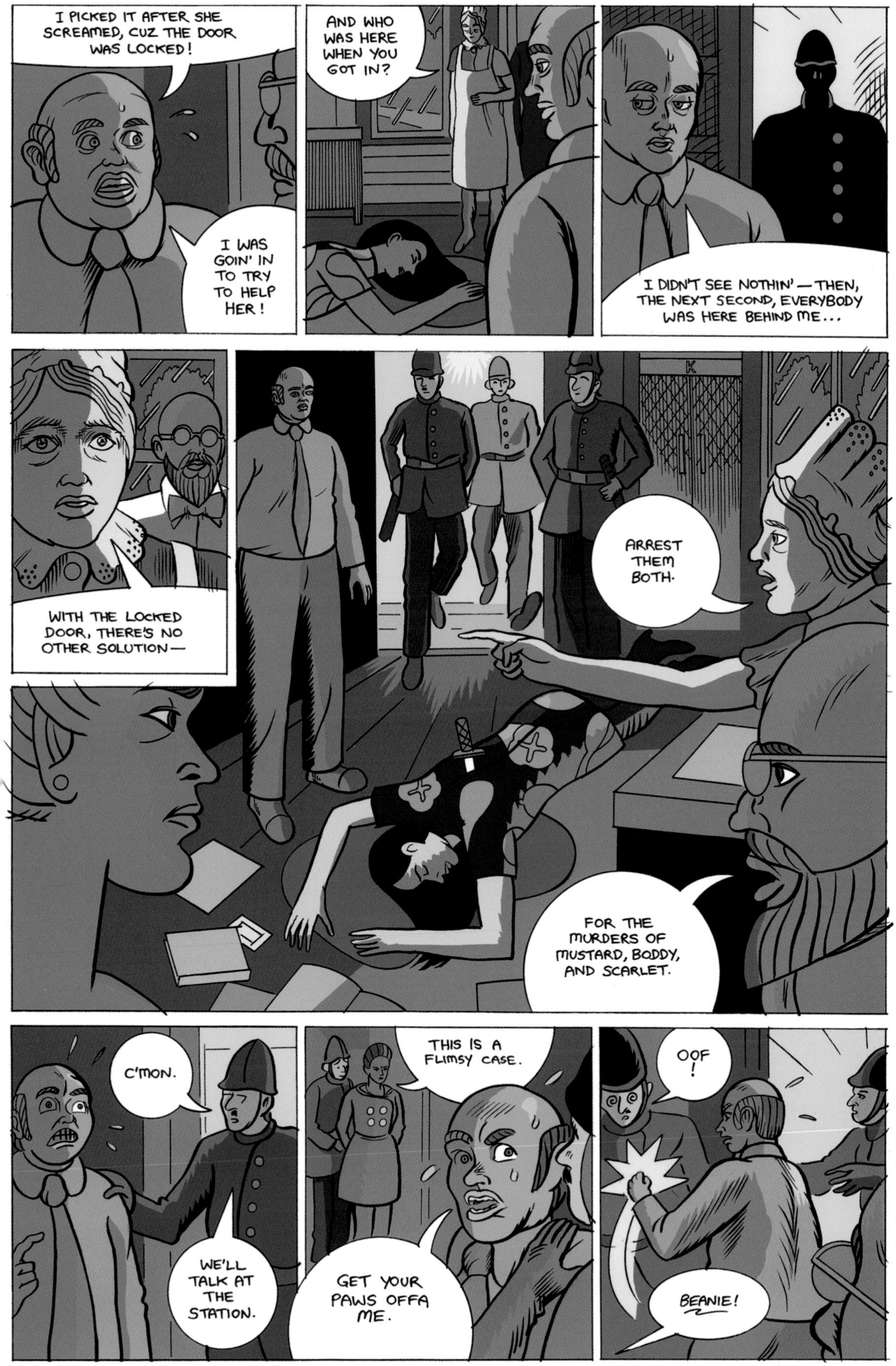
I PICKED IT AFTER SHE SCREAMED, CUZ THE DOOR WAS LOCKED!
I WAS GOIN' IN TO TRY TO HELP HER!
AND WHO WAS HERE WHEN YOU GOT IN?
I DIDN'T SEE NOTHIN' — THEN, THE NEXT SECOND, EVERYBODY WAS HERE BEHIND ME...
WITH THE LOCKED DOOR, THERE'S NO OTHER SOLUTION—
K
ARREST THEM BOTH.
FOR THE MURDERS OF MUSTARD, BODDY, AND SCARLET.
C'MON.
WE'LL TALK AT THE STATION.
THIS IS A FLIMSY CASE.
GET YOUR PAWS OFFA ME.
OOF!
BEANIE!

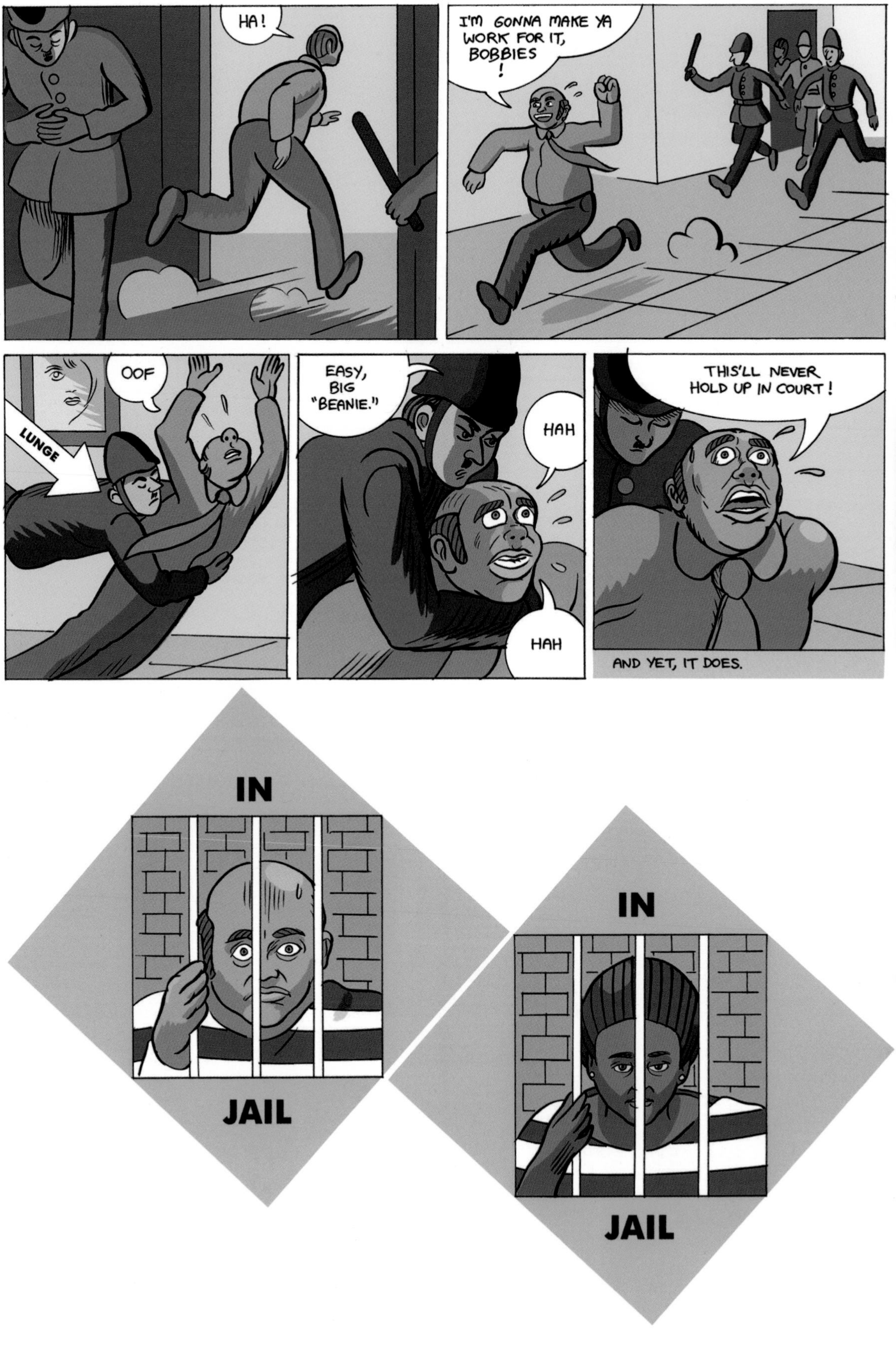
HA!
I'M GONNA MAKE YA WORK FOR IT, BOBBIES!
OOF
LUNGE
EASY, BIG "BEANIE."
HAH
HAH
THIS'LL NEVER HOLD UP IN COURT!
AND YET, IT DOES.
IN
JAIL
IN
JAIL

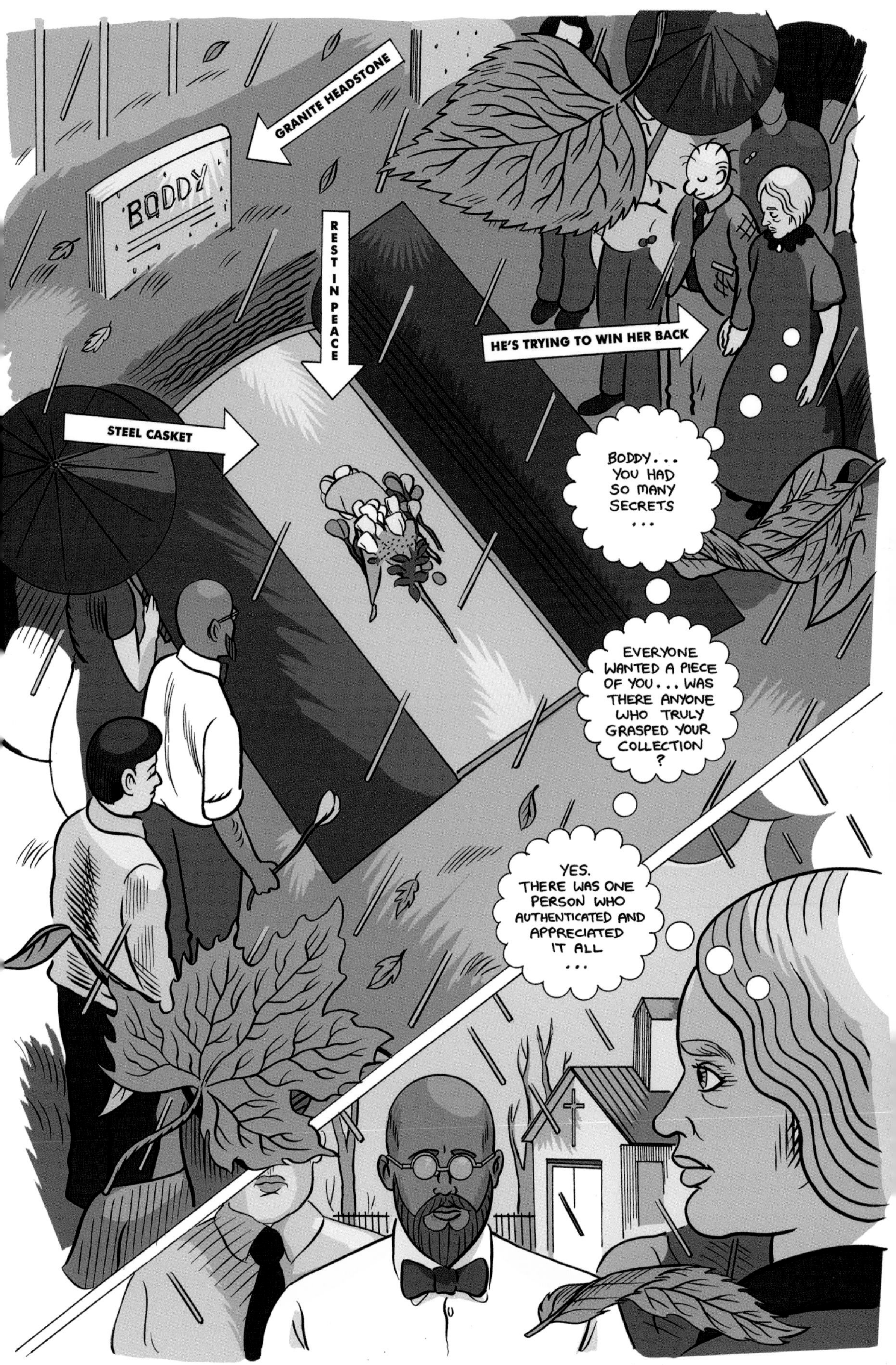
GRANITE HEADSTONE
BODDY
REST IN PEACE
HE'S TRYING TO WIN HER BACK
STEEL CASKET
BODDY... YOU HAD SO MANY SECRETS...
EVERYONE WANTED A PIECE OF YOU... WAS THERE ANYONE WHO TRULY GRASPED YOUR COLLECTION?
YES. THERE WAS ONE PERSON WHO AUTHENTICATED AND APPRECIATED IT ALL...

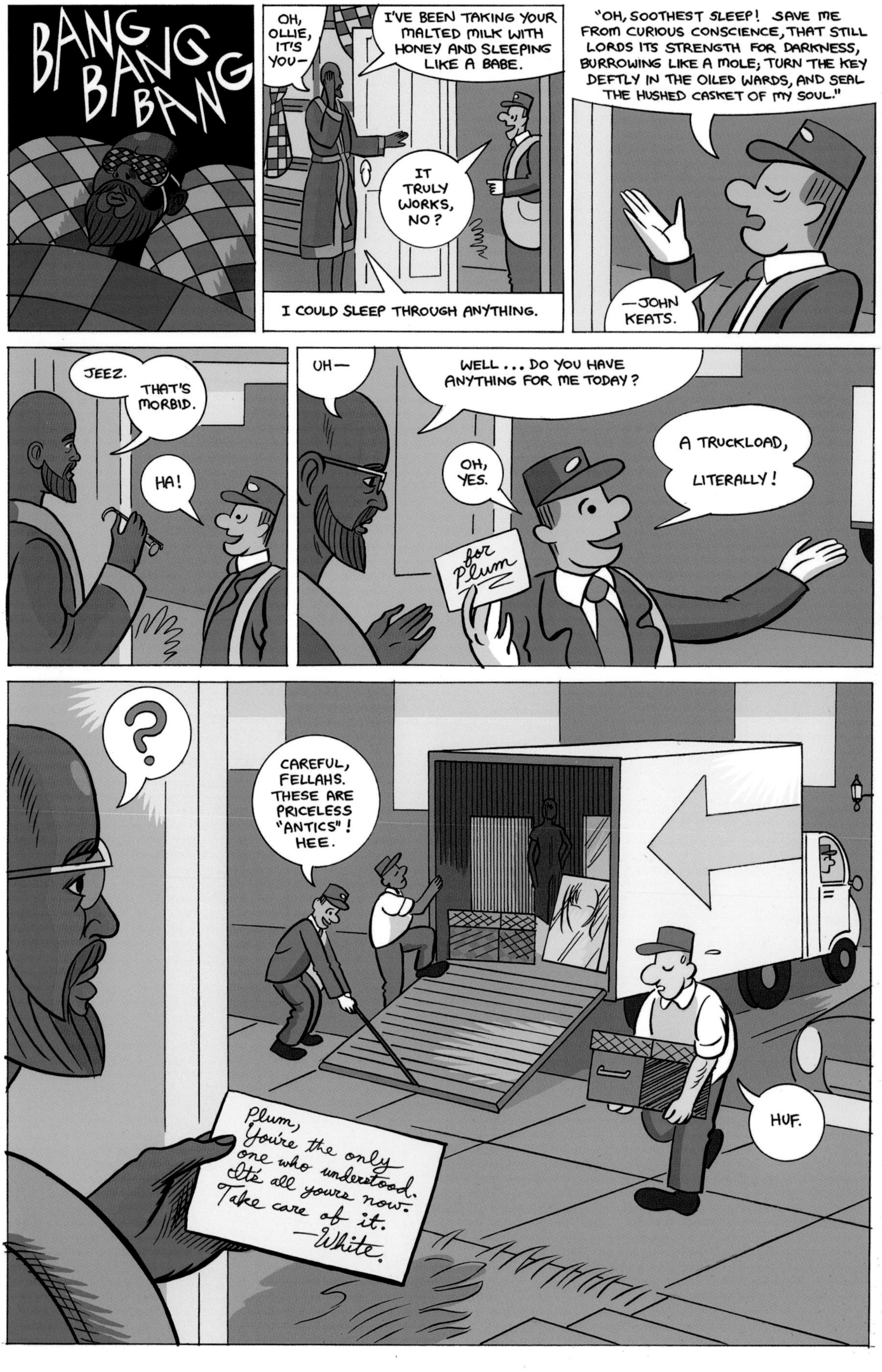
BANG BANG BANG
OH, OLLIE, IT'S YOU—
I'VE BEEN TAKING YOUR MALTED MILK WITH HONEY AND SLEEPING LIKE A BABE.
IT TRULY WORKS, NO?
I COULD SLEEP THROUGH ANYTHING.
"OH, SOOTHEST SLEEP! SAVE ME FROM CURIOUS CONSCIENCE, THAT STILL LORDS ITS STRENGTH FOR DARKNESS, BURROWING LIKE A MOLE; TURN THE KEY DEFTLY IN THE OILED WARDS, AND SEAL THE HUSHED CASKET OF MY SOUL."
—JOHN KEATS.
JEEZ.
THAT'S MORBID.
HA!
UH—
WELL ... DO YOU HAVE ANYTHING FOR ME TODAY?
OH, YES.
A TRUCKLOAD,
LITERALLY!
for Plum
?
CAREFUL, FELLAHS. THESE ARE PRICELESS "ANTICS"! HEE.
HUF.
Plum,
You're the only one who understood.
It's all yours now.
Take care of it.
—White.

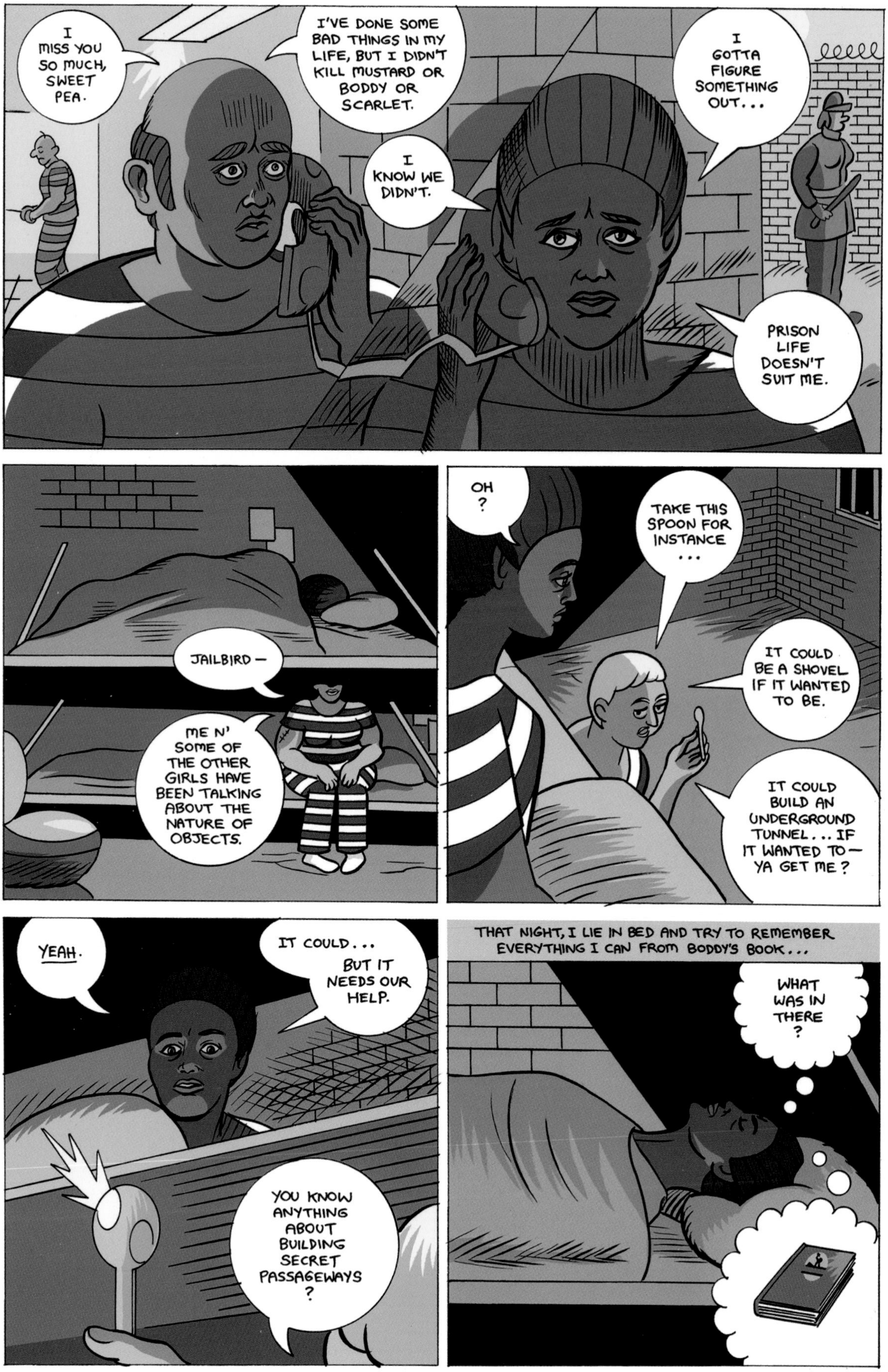
I MISS YOU SO MUCH, SWEET PEA.
I'VE DONE SOME BAD THINGS IN MY LIFE, BUT I DIDN'T KILL MUSTARD OR BODDY OR SCARLET.
I KNOW WE DIDN'T.
I GOTTA FIGURE SOMETHING OUT...
PRISON LIFE DOESN'T SUIT ME.
JAILBIRD—
ME N' SOME OF THE OTHER GIRLS HAVE BEEN TALKING ABOUT THE NATURE OF OBJECTS.
OH?
TAKE THIS SPOON FOR INSTANCE...
IT COULD BE A SHOVEL IF IT WANTED TO BE.
IT COULD BUILD AN UNDERGROUND TUNNEL... IF IT WANTED TO— YA GET ME?
YEAH.
IT COULD... BUT IT NEEDS OUR HELP.
YOU KNOW ANYTHING ABOUT BUILDING SECRET PASSAGEWAYS?
THAT NIGHT, I LIE IN BED AND TRY TO REMEMBER EVERYTHING I CAN FROM BODDY'S BOOK...
WHAT WAS IN THERE?

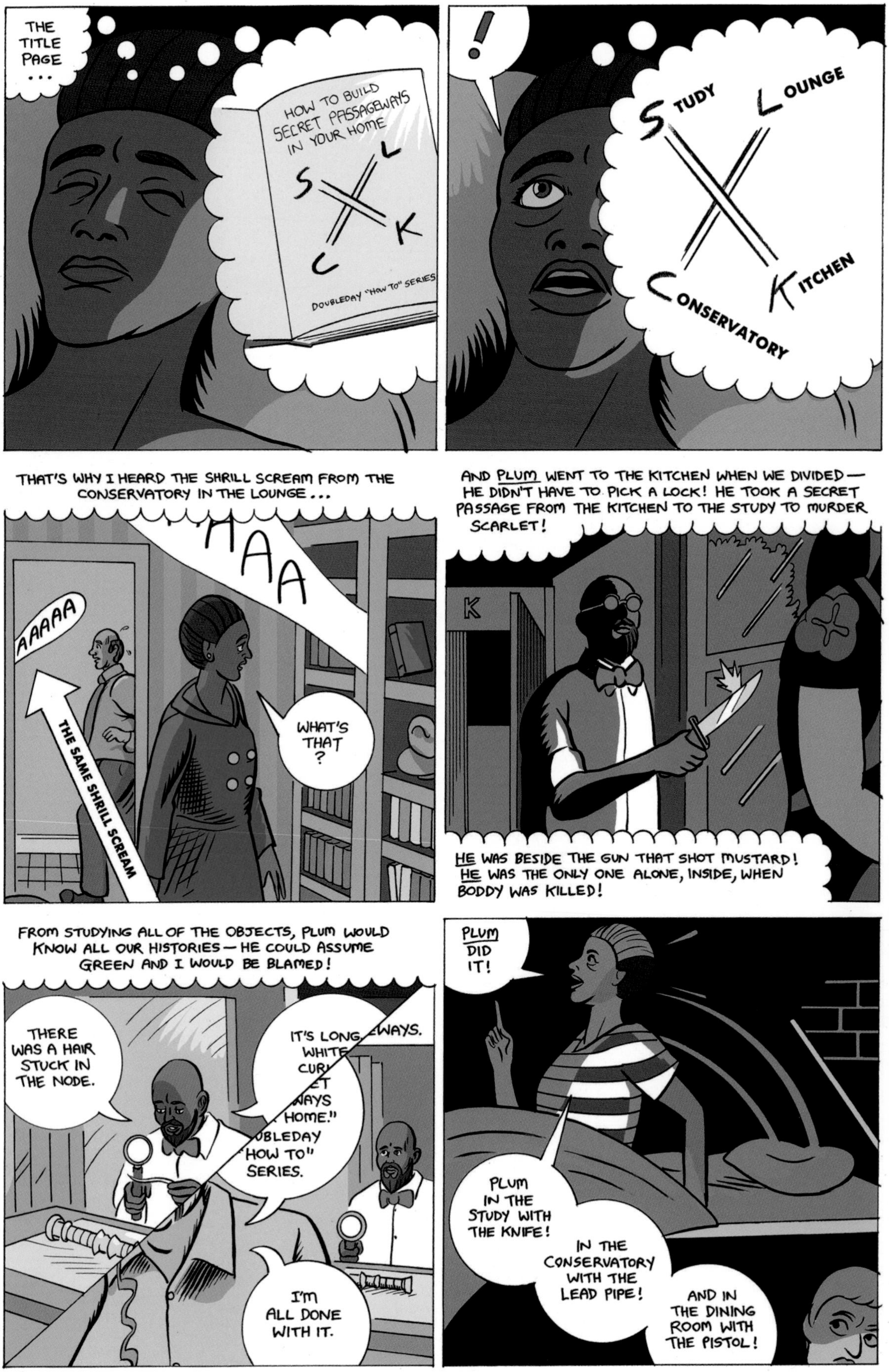
THE TITLE PAGE . . .
HOW TO BUILD SECRET PASSAGEWAYS IN YOUR HOME
S L C K
DOUBLEDAY "HOW TO" SERIES
!
STUDY LOUNGE
CONSERVATORY KITCHEN
THAT'S WHY I HEARD THE SHRILL SCREAM FROM THE CONSERVATORY IN THE LOUNGE . . .
HAA
AAAAA
THE SAME SHRILL SCREAM
WHAT'S THAT ?
AND PLUM WENT TO THE KITCHEN WHEN WE DIVIDED— HE DIDN'T HAVE TO PICK A LOCK! HE TOOK A SECRET PASSAGE FROM THE KITCHEN TO THE STUDY TO MURDER SCARLET!
K
HE WAS BESIDE THE GUN THAT SHOT MUSTARD! HE WAS THE ONLY ONE ALONE, INSIDE, WHEN BODDY WAS KILLED!
FROM STUDYING ALL OF THE OBJECTS, PLUM WOULD KNOW ALL OUR HISTORIES— HE COULD ASSUME GREEN AND I WOULD BE BLAMED!
THERE WAS A HAIR STUCK IN THE NODE.
IT'S LONG, WHITE CURL
WAYS.
ET
WAYS
HOME."
OUBLEDAY "HOW TO" SERIES.
I'M ALL DONE WITH IT.
PLUM DID IT!
PLUM IN THE STUDY WITH THE KNIFE!
IN THE CONSERVATORY WITH THE LEAD PIPE!
AND IN THE DINING ROOM WITH THE PISTOL!

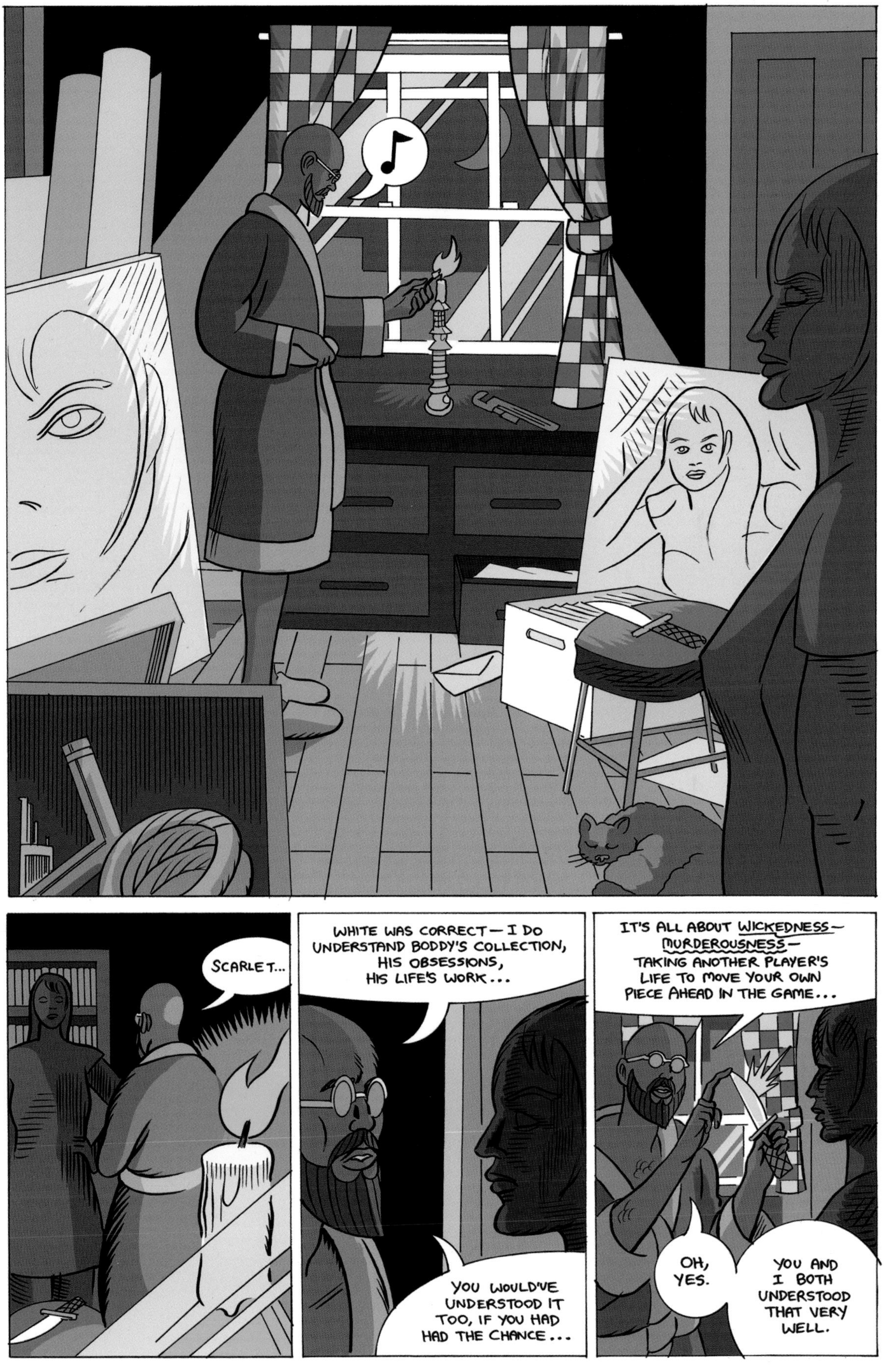
SCARLET...
WHITE WAS CORRECT— I DO UNDERSTAND BODDY'S COLLECTION, HIS OBSESSIONS, HIS LIFE'S WORK...
YOU WOULD'VE UNDERSTOOD IT TOO, IF YOU HAD HAD THE CHANCE...
IT'S ALL ABOUT WICKEDNESS— MURDEROUSNESS— TAKING ANOTHER PLAYER'S LIFE TO MOVE YOUR OWN PIECE AHEAD IN THE GAME...
OH, YES.
YOU AND I BOTH UNDERSTOOD THAT VERY WELL.

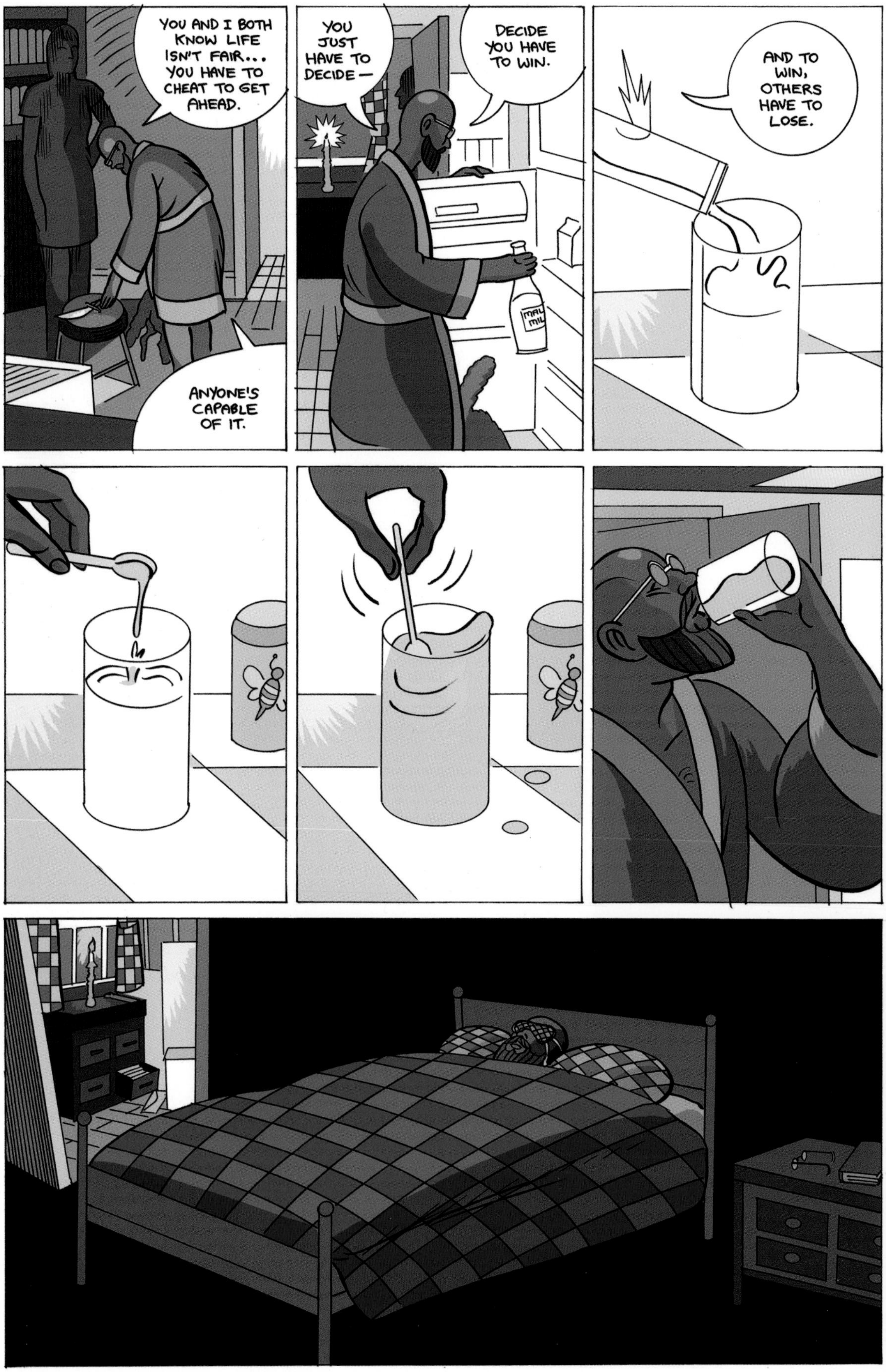
YOU AND I BOTH KNOW LIFE ISN'T FAIR... YOU HAVE TO CHEAT TO GET AHEAD.
ANYONE'S CAPABLE OF IT.
YOU JUST HAVE TO DECIDE—
DECIDE YOU HAVE TO WIN.
AND TO WIN, OTHERS HAVE TO LOSE.

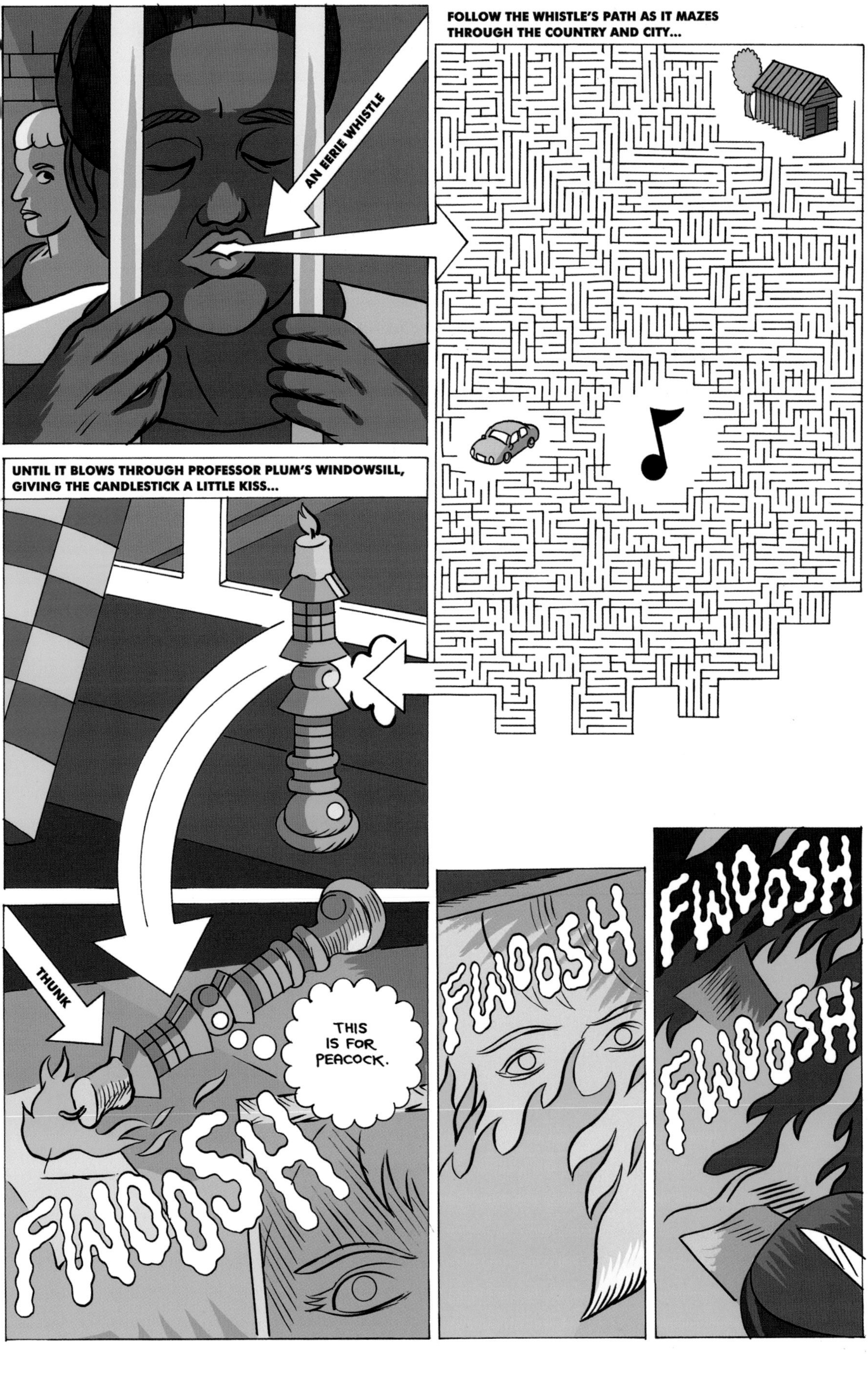
AN EERIE WHISTLE
FOLLOW THE WHISTLE'S PATH AS IT MAZES THROUGH THE COUNTRY AND CITY...
UNTIL IT BLOWS THROUGH PROFESSOR PLUM'S WINDOWSILL, GIVING THE CANDLESTICK A LITTLE KISS...
THUNK
THIS IS FOR PEACOCK.
FWOOSH
FWOOSH
FWOOSH
FWOOSH

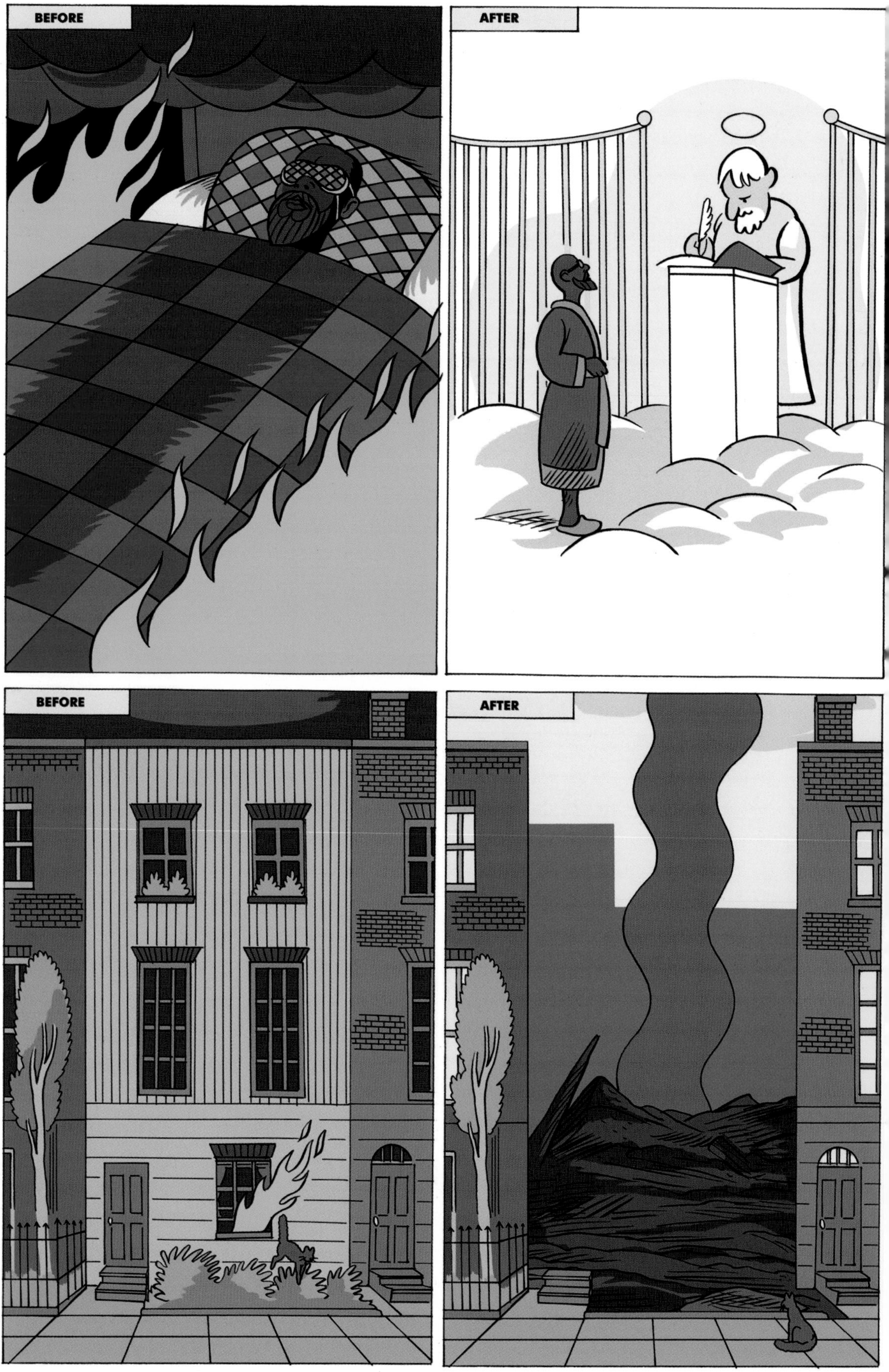
BEFORE
AFTER
BEFORE
AFTER

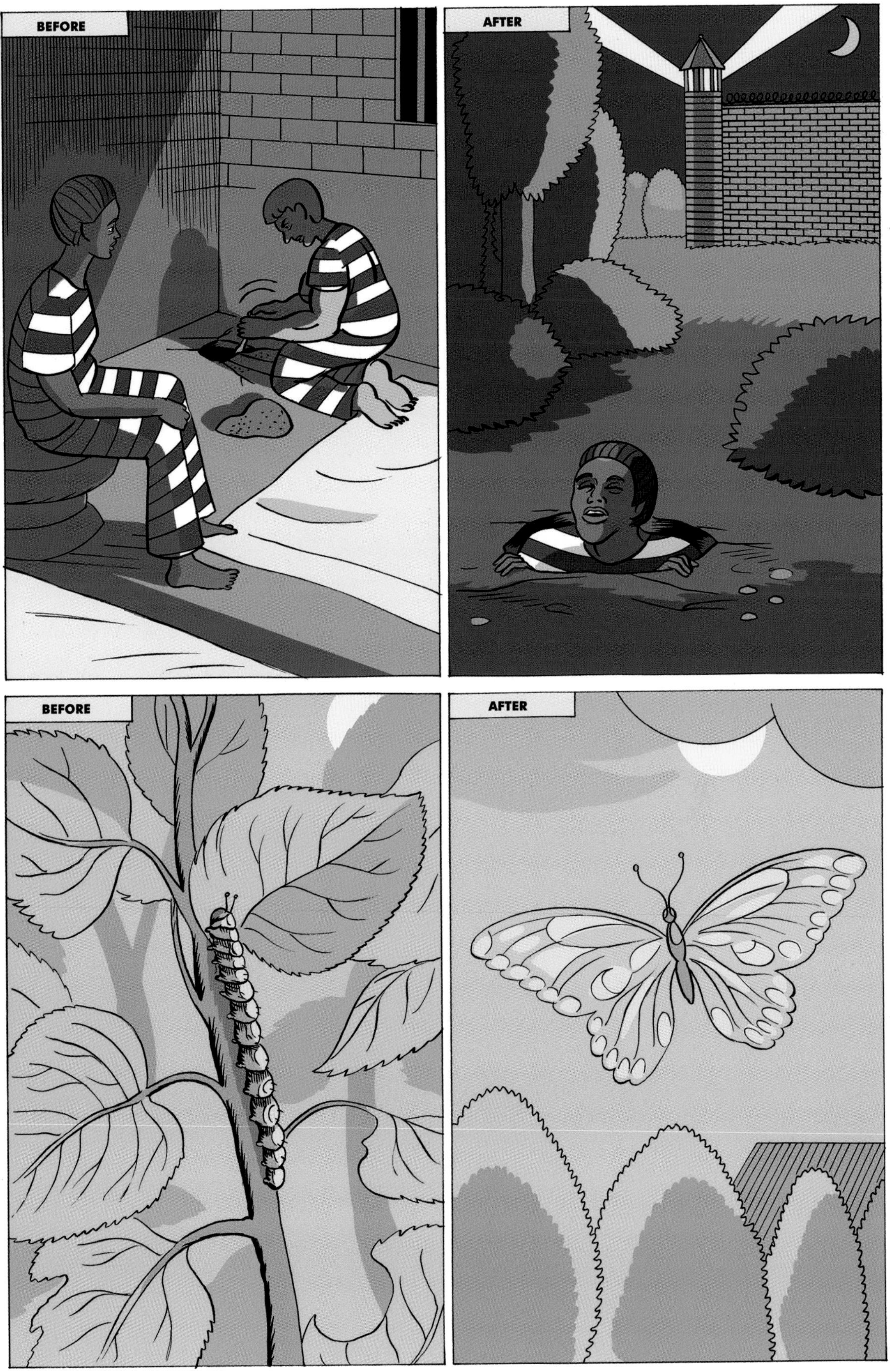
BEFORE
AFTER
BEFORE
AFTER

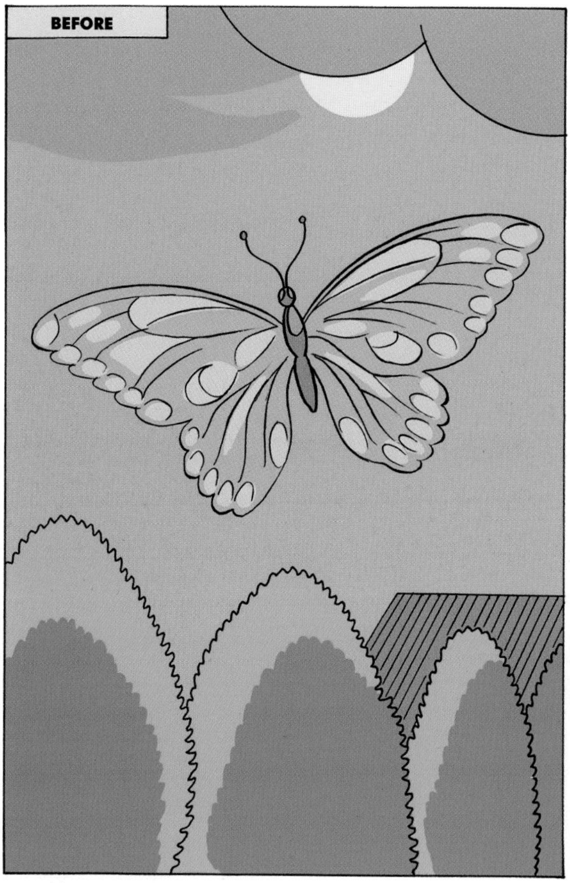
BEFORE

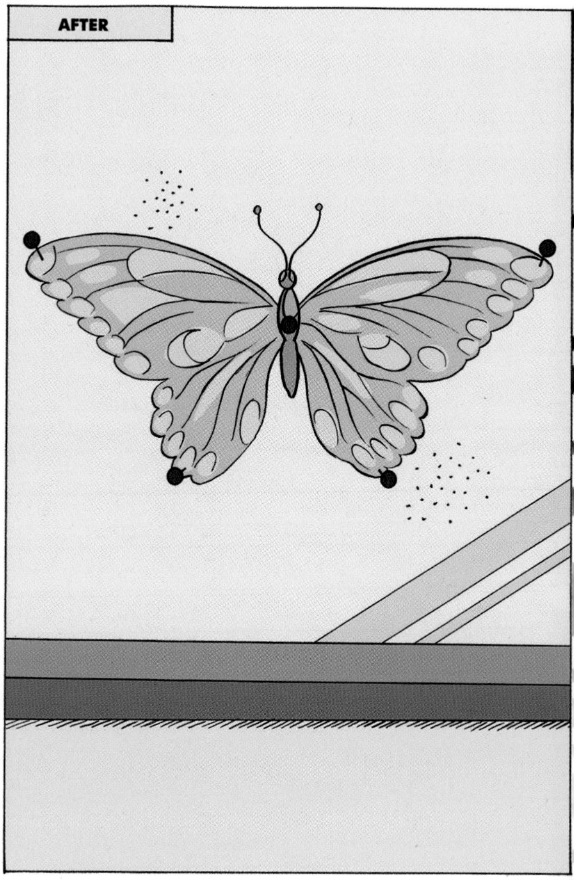
AFTER

BEFORE

Once upon

AFTER

ever after.

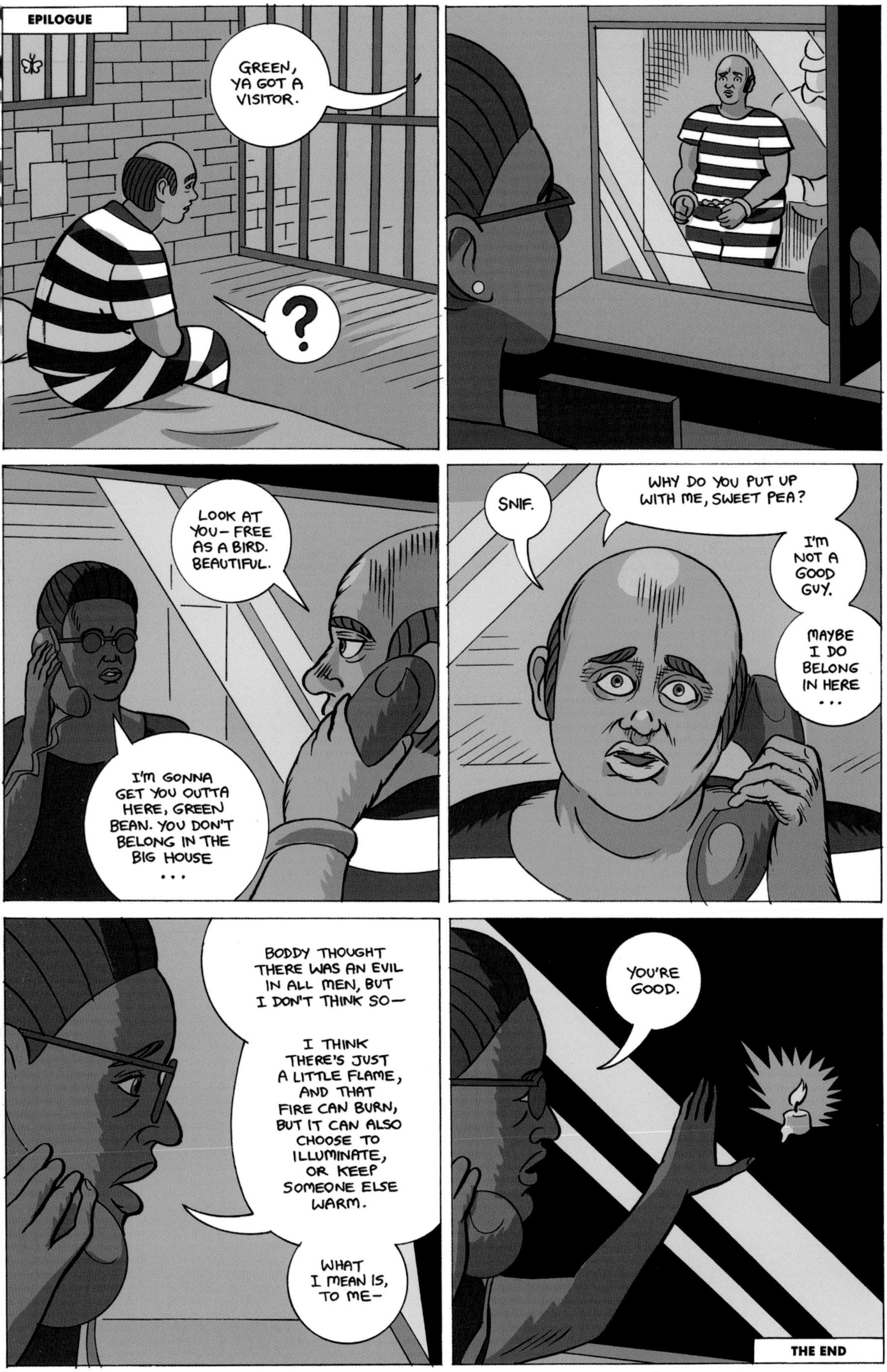
EPILOGUE
GREEN, YA GOT A VISITOR.
?
LOOK AT YOU— FREE AS A BIRD. BEAUTIFUL.
I'M GONNA GET YOU OUTTA HERE, GREEN BEAN. YOU DON'T BELONG IN THE BIG HOUSE . . .
SNIF.
WHY DO YOU PUT UP WITH ME, SWEET PEA?
I'M NOT A GOOD GUY.
MAYBE I DO BELONG IN HERE . . .
BODDY THOUGHT THERE WAS AN EVIL IN ALL MEN, BUT I DON'T THINK SO—
I THINK THERE'S JUST A LITTLE FLAME, AND THAT FIRE CAN BURN, BUT IT CAN ALSO CHOOSE TO ILLUMINATE, OR KEEP SOMEONE ELSE WARM.
WHAT I MEAN IS, TO ME—
YOU'RE GOOD.
THE END

Dash Shaw '19

ON MURDER CONSIDERED AS A RECREATIONAL ACTIVITY

By Tim Hodler

The first version of *Clue* I can remember playing came in a battered old box. My brothers and I had to climb a small stepladder to pry it out from where it was stored, crammed between sets of backgammon, *Trivial Pursuit*, and the *Raiders of the Lost Ark* tie-in board game on the top shelf of a closet at my grandparents' house in Arkansas. It was the 1972 edition, a fact I only know because that was the edition that, for the first time in the game's history, used photographs of real models for its illustrations.

I don't think it's just nostalgia that makes me prefer those photographs to the Art Deco-esque line drawings and Virgil Partsch-style space-age cartoons of earlier editions. The images are all online on countless fan sites now, but even without those visual aids I can still see them in my mind's eye: the mustachioed and mutton-chopped Colonel Mustard, wearing a monocle and safari jacket; the bald, frowning, choleric Mr. Green in an ill-fitting suit, looking like the ultimate child-hating vice principal, one tirade away from cardiac arrest; mousy, middle-aged Mrs. White in a traditional maid's outfit, holding a candlestick (which seemed like a cheat—why would she use any other weapon?); the aristocratic Mrs. Peacock, a prim spinster who clearly disapproved of any and all human frailties; and of course, Miss Scarlet, a stereotypical Mata Hari-style femme fatale, wearing a tight wrap dress and smoking out of an outdated and quite Freudian cigarette holder. My favorite character to play was Professor Plum, because he wore glasses (as I did) and was the only relatively young and heroic-looking man available (I would never have dared play as a girl, unless it was absolutely necessary—if I had been able to get over my sexism, I would have realized that Miss Scarlet, who always goes first, is obviously the optimal choice). Looking at Plum's photograph now, it's fairly obvious that, with his steepled fingers and self-satisfied smirk, he was meant to register as just as ridiculous a figure as the others.

I don't believe the 1972 *Clue* contained any biographical information about the characters other than what you could glean from the images (if it did, we lost or overlooked it). Still, it seems clear to me today that the game's characters, as minimal as their development was, provided one of the key attractions of *Clue*—unlike other games with abstract pegs, counters, wheels, and toy cars, in this one you played as an actual person. And not just any person, but an unpleasant, probably immoral one. There was little worthy of aspiration here. No child could be expected to want to grow up to be like Mr. Green or Mrs. Peacock; only an adult could be so undiscerning. Why that was appealing may take some explaining.

Obviously, *Clue* does not require *Dungeons & Dragons*-level engagement with character; it is very rudimentary role-play. And it is not the only game that asks the players to pretend to be dull adults. In *Life*, for example, you find yourself outfitted with a spouse, children, and even a job. That seemed like the kind of imagining that adults thought was good for you: you should start planning how you'll eventually pay the bills as soon as possible. *Clue*, on the other hand, seemed to reveal the kind of fantasy that adults themselves engaged in; this was not the "life lessons" they wanted to impart to younger generations, but the escapism they used to avoid those lessons themselves. That *Clue* offered such bizarre and frankly unattractive imaginary roles only made it seem more adult, giving it an air of mysterious sophistication that no other board game possessed. If grown-ups wanted to be like *this*, then... well, there was a lot to take in.

Incidentally, the 2015 edition of *Clue* that I purchased for my own daughter a couple years ago has left those old photographs long behind. The characters are all illustrated now, in bright, computer-rendered colors. They are decades younger than the 1972 versions, too: Mr. Green now has a full head of hair and a noir hero's trench coat (his bio calls him a "suave con man" who has previously impersonated a prince, a pilot, and a priest, among other things); Mrs. Peacock wears a strapless dress and her hair down; Miss Scarlet's a blue-eyed blonde with no tobacco products in sight; Colonel Mustard has more contemporary grooming, with only a large mustache and an ascot reminding us of his colonialist past; and Mrs. White has transformed from a hapless English maidservant to the young Asian orphan known as Dr. Orchid, expert in plant toxicology and adopted daughter of the permanent victim Mr. Boddy. Only Professor Plum is almost exactly his old, insufferable self. The new images are not nearly as evocative as their photographic predecessors, but the background textual material included is far more involved, so perhaps when put together they achieve a similar effect. (I have not annoyed my daughter by comparing it to the game of my childhood and finding out for certain.)

The game's emphasis on character types, spanning a fairly wide range of class and gender (or at least wide for a board game), stems directly from the classic detective mystery literature that inspired it. As many have noted before, one of the key pleasures of detective stories is the way they allow the reader access to an entire society, including people and places normally cordoned off from the average middle class literary consumer; the detective interacts with everyone from the wealthiest 1% living in palatial mansions to street-level criminals selling illicit substances out of front businesses, exploring all the various ways these hidden worlds intertwine with and inform everyday "civil" society. Obviously, *Clue* strips almost all of that substantive critique away, except for the veneer hinted at by the characters' costumes and evident backgrounds. But even that tiny remnant, which we find in the imperialist exploiter Colonel Mustard, Victorian prude Mrs. Peacock, and the ineffectual academic Professor Plum, evokes a flavor of adult social commentary difficult to find in any of the other classic early 20th century board games—with the exception of *Monopoly* (which even in its toned-down modern incarnation still contains faint echoes of the anti-capitalist politics of its origins in Lizzie Magie's "Landlord's Game").

Am I claiming too much? Perhaps.

One other key attraction of *Clue* can't possibly be denied, however: the game inescapably hinges on a horrific topic, murder. As a brief glance at network television listings or a bestseller list will attest, there appears to be no more popular artistic object of contemplation than crime, and the undisputed king of crime is homicide. To my knowledge, *Clue* was one of the first games to take full advantage of this fact.

Killings of one form or another are implied in many other keystone games, from *Battleship* (1931) and *Stratego* (1947) all the way back to the knights and pawns of chess (6th century), but those "deaths" are so theoretical as to hardly register. In *Clue*, the entire game revolves around the intentional killing of a human being—and not just abstract killing, but murder incorporating easily available household objects: rope, candlesticks, lead pipes, wrenches, knives. It is hard to play *Clue* and not imagine a lead pipe swinging down on a man's head, crushing his skull. The game's designers simplified things by not including motive along with means and opportunity among the factors the players must discover, and so avoid a too-close examination of the many possible reasons why a person may want to end the life of another. But by doing so, they kept the emphasis even more firmly on the brute physical facts of murder.

Explaining why so many people enjoy thinking about intentionally caused violent death is a subject for another essay, and so I won't belabor this point too much further. (Homicide's appeal is hardly that mysterious anyway, and if you don't agree, why did you buy this comic?) But it is perhaps noteworthy that *Clue* was first dreamed up in 1944, a year before the end of World War II, the most destructive era in human history, during which up to 50 million human lives were taken. The man who thought the game up was a middle-aged former musician from England named Anthony Pratt, who was spending his days working a drilling machine in a factory devoted to manufacturing parts for armored tanks, which themselves were to be used in battle for the purpose of snuffing out life.

As the story goes, while working that drilling machine, Pratt had a lot of time to think, and started reminiscing about one of his musical gigs. Before the war, Pratt had often performed at "murder parties," a fad of that pre-television time, in which guests would gather in a country hotel and band together to solve the mysterious "death" of one of the other guests. It was a sort of early, high-class version of LARPing, inspired by the works of writers like Agatha Christie and Dorothy Sayers rather than the fantasies of J.R.R. Tolkien and Jack Vance. (This last odd link to *Dungeons & Dragons* makes me wonder: what if *Clue* had inspired breathless news stories about children being unable to separate imagination from reality, doing serious damage with a dagger in the billiards room or the conservatory? The idea seems ridiculous, but why? Comic books and video games have also proved to be popular scapegoats for juvenile delinquency; why not board games? Perhaps our society is more afraid of sorcery and gore than traditional in-home murder.)

Pratt decided to recreate those mystery party experiences in a board game, recruited his wife Elva to design the imagery, and sold it to a UK games manufacturer called Waddingtons. The first edition came out a few years later in 1948, and the following seventy-one years saw dozens of new editions, spin-off games, VCR adaptations, licensed tie-in games (including Alfred Hitchcock, *Scooby-Doo*, and *Seinfeld* editions, and, yes, even a *Dungeons & Dragons Clue*). There's also the almost-good 1985 film starring Tim Curry and Madeline Kahn, of which many people seem to have fond memories, so perhaps the less said here about it the better. (One note too good to resist sharing: according to *Clue* fansite *The Art of Murder,* Tom Stoppard spent several months working on an early version of the screenplay before quitting in frustration at the idea of turning the game into a workable story, noting that it was the first time he had ever been unable to complete a commission.)

The so-called "Golden Age" mysteries that provided Pratt with his literary inspiration are essentially games themselves. They were supposed to be written according to well-known "rules of fair play," in which the reader competed with the detective (and ultimately, the author) to see who could solve the mysteries first using the same set of clues. Anyone who has read an early Ellery Queen novel will remember the "Challenge to the Reader" which would appear near the story's end, informing the reader that everything needed to determine the culprit had by that point been revealed. It seems only natural that such a genre would evolve into real out-and-out games, and *Clue* is only the first of many that would take their lead from the detective story.

But it was the first, and it was the first I learned to win at, which is perhaps the biggest reason I loved *Clue* as a child. All games determine their winners based on a combination of luck, strategy, and skill. Some games, such as *Candyland,* almost entirely come down to luck (though as any adult who has played against a child knows, there are ways to lose even *Candyland* on purpose). Others, such as Tic-Tac-Toe, revolve largely around strategy, but that strategy is so easy to learn (and so hard to improve upon) that when you play against anyone with even the most moderate experience, it is almost impossible not to end the game in a draw. *Clue,* on the other hand, is balanced just right, at least for an intelligent child. If that child pays close enough attention, she can learn more sophisticated strategies for taking notes and interpreting her opponents' moves, and then she can *win,* more often than not—at least until the other players eventually catch up. The only object of contemplation more rewarding than murder may be one's own Sherlock Holmes-like brilliance.

Perhaps the most profound aspect of all in *Clue* is the way it handles guilt. Every time you play the game, there is a one-in-six chance that, at the end of your quest for the truth, you will find, just like the first great literary detective Oedipus, that you yourself are in fact the very murderer whom you have vowed to expose. Is there any more satisfying feeling than this: intellectually outdoing your opponents (let's leave aside the role of luck involved in game-piece placement here—it's psychologically irrelevant), turning over the final cards, and revealing that you were the culprit who put everything in motion in the first place? There is nothing more truly adult than this: doubling as both hero and villain, thrilling at triumph over your opponents while also reveling in the guilty knowledge that you were the one who really did wrong.

And you would have gotten away with it, too, if it wasn't for you meddling kids.

About the Author: Tim Hodler is the co-editor of the Comics Journal *website.*

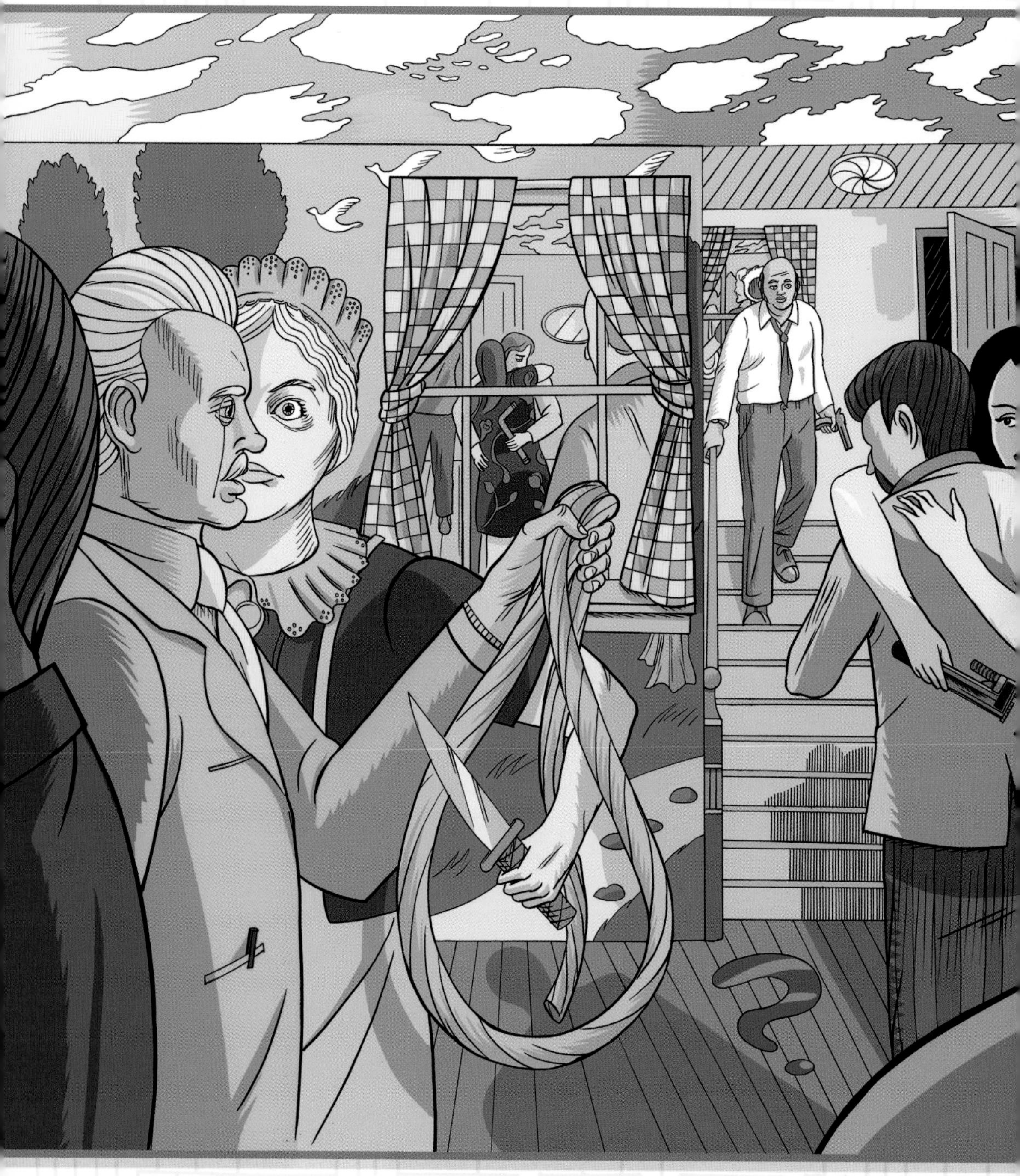

ART BY
DASH SHAW

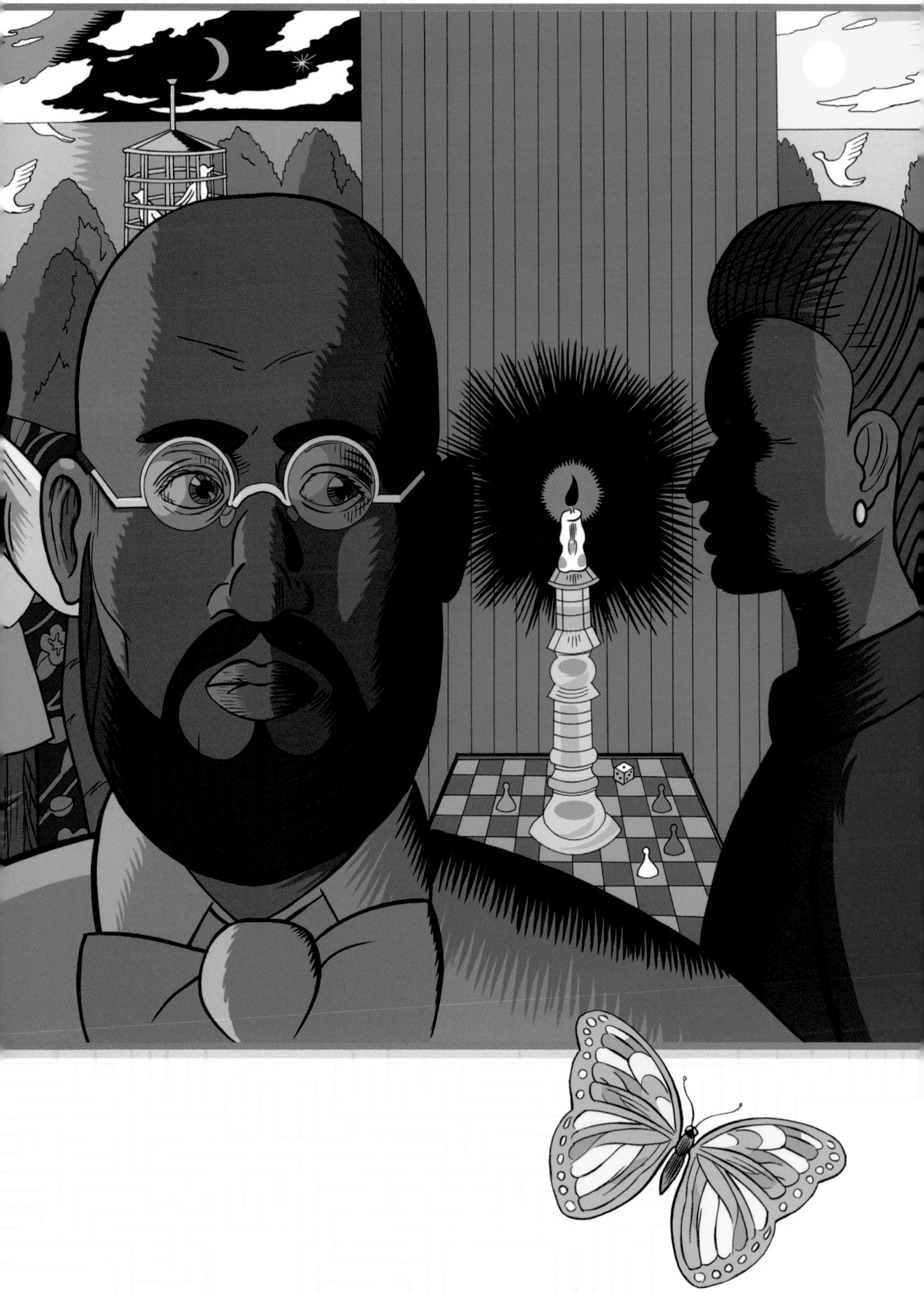

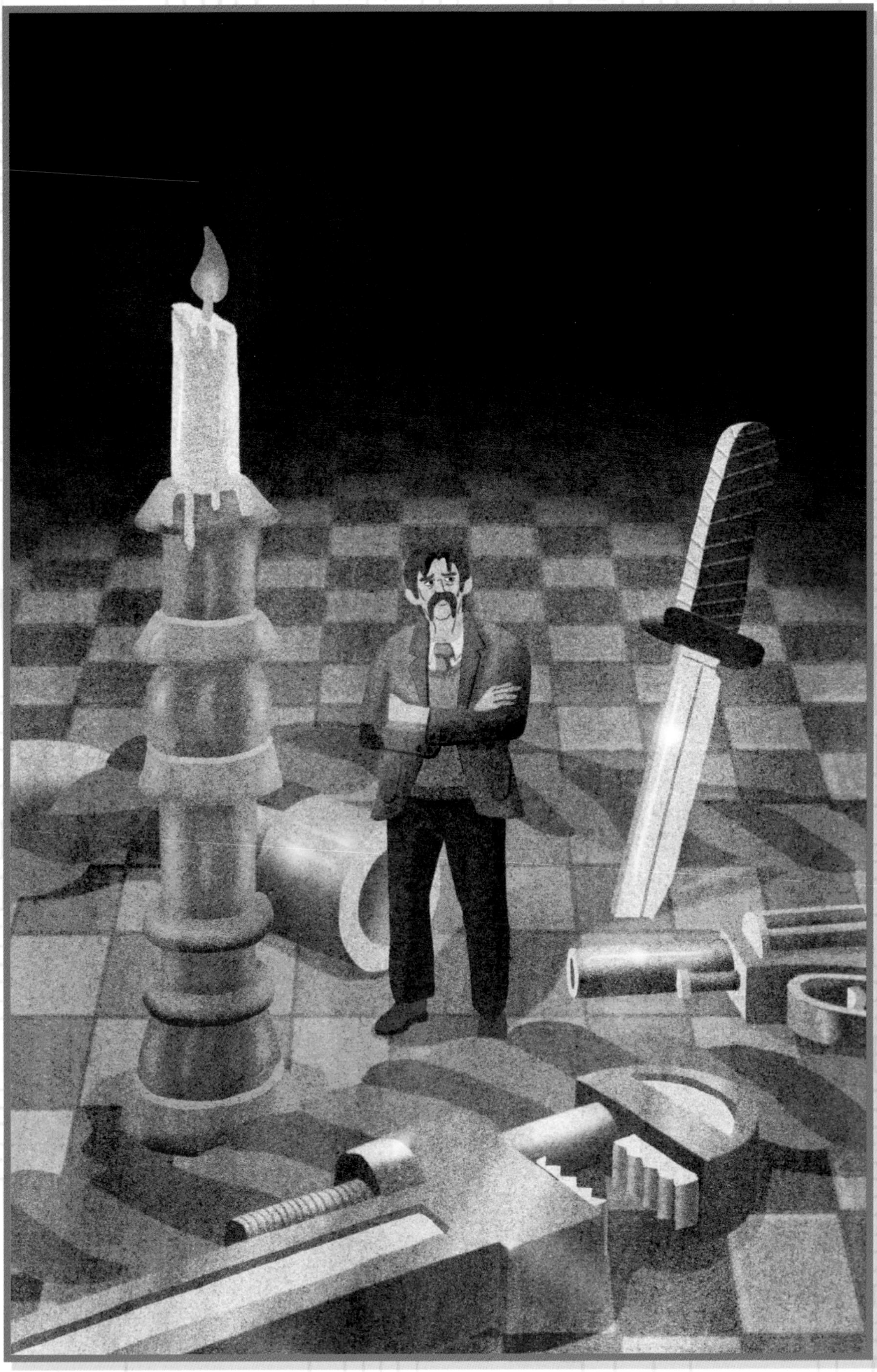

ART BY
JED McGOWAN

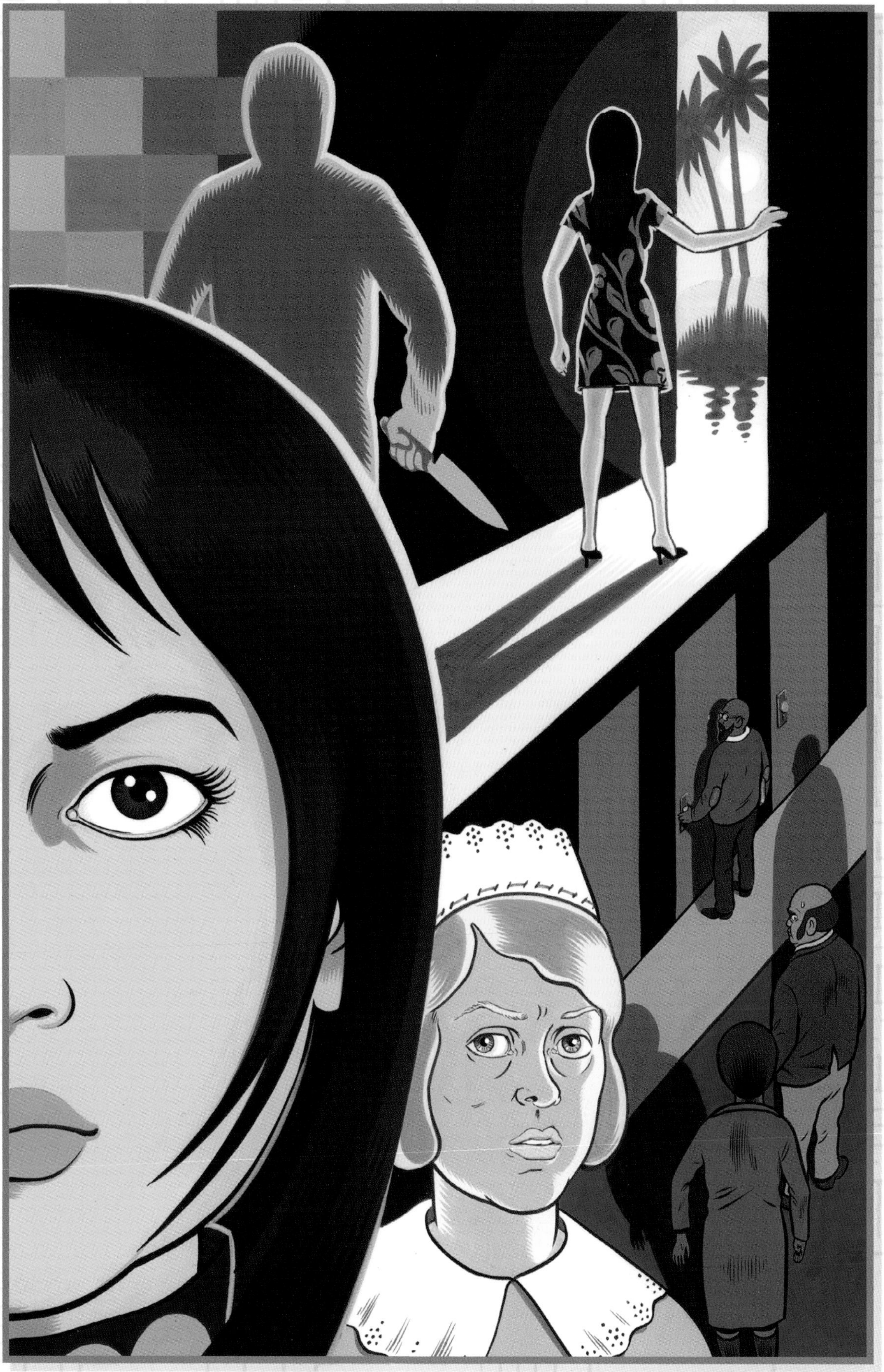

ART BY
SOPHIE FRANZ

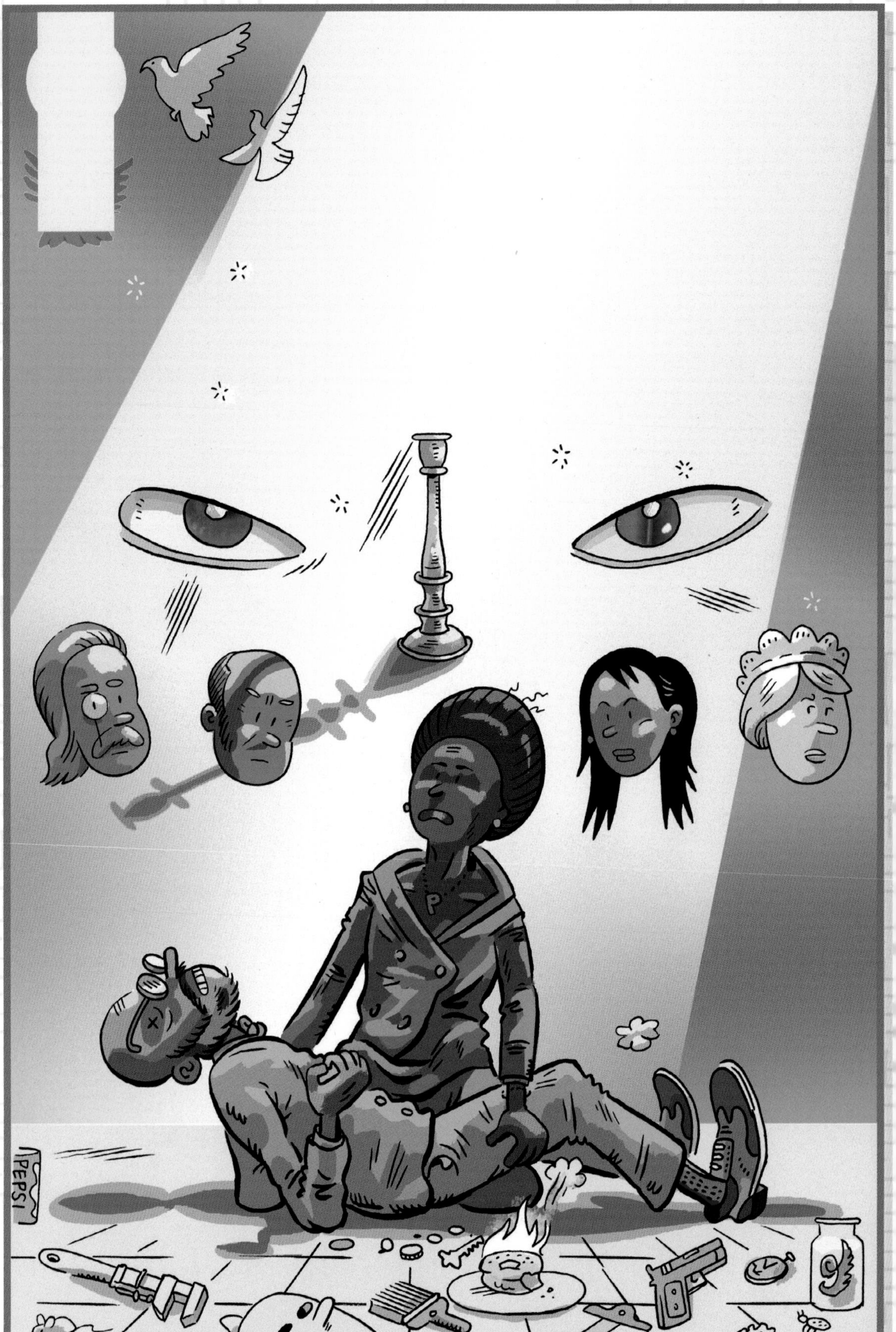
PEPSI

ART BY
KEVIN HUIZENGA

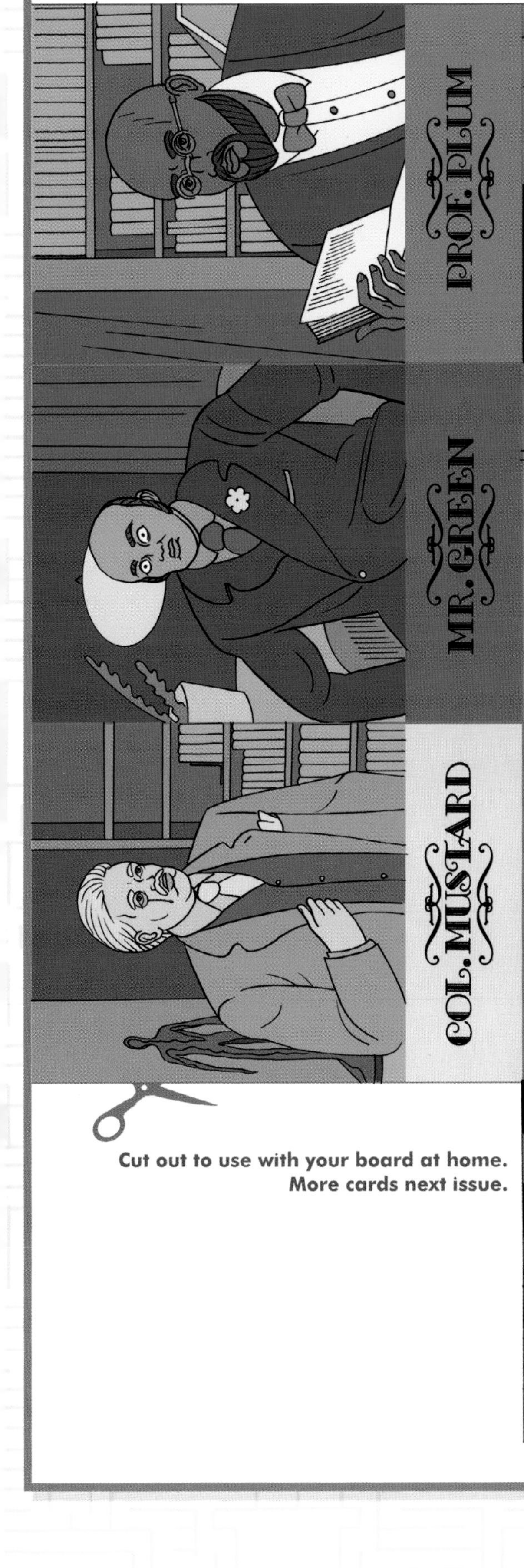
COL. MUSTARD
MR. GREEN
PROF. PLUM

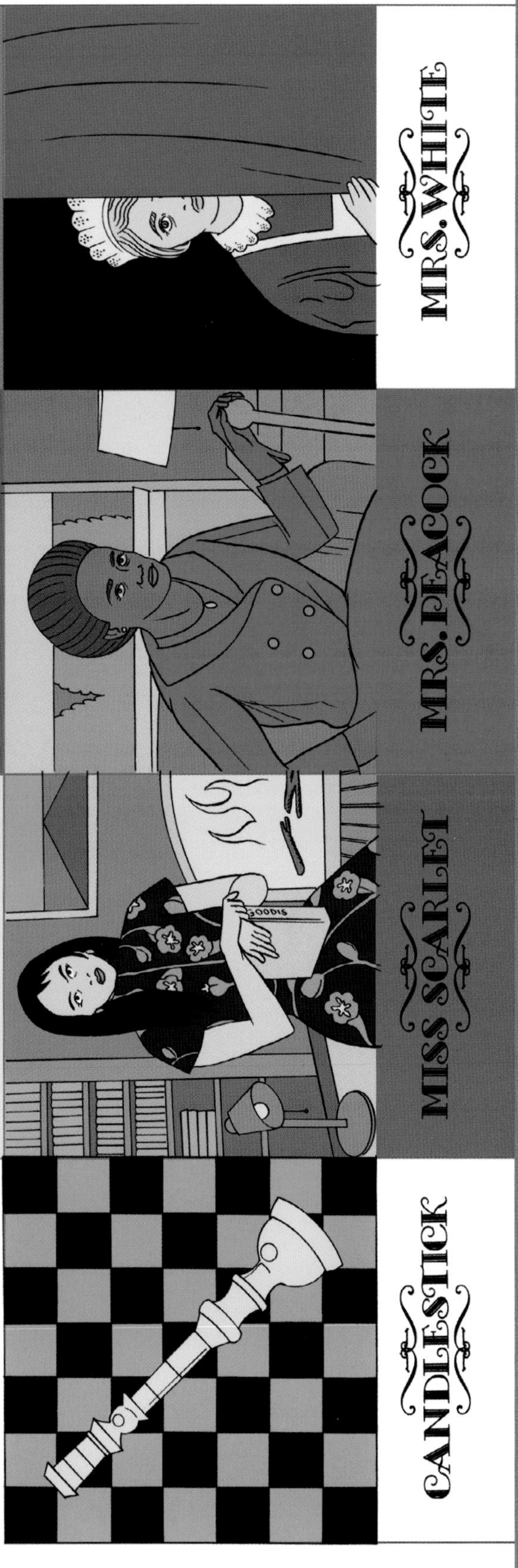
CANDLESTICK
MISS SCARLET
MRS. PEACOCK
MRS. WHITE

Cut out to use with your board at home.
More cards next issue.

ART BY
DASH SHAW

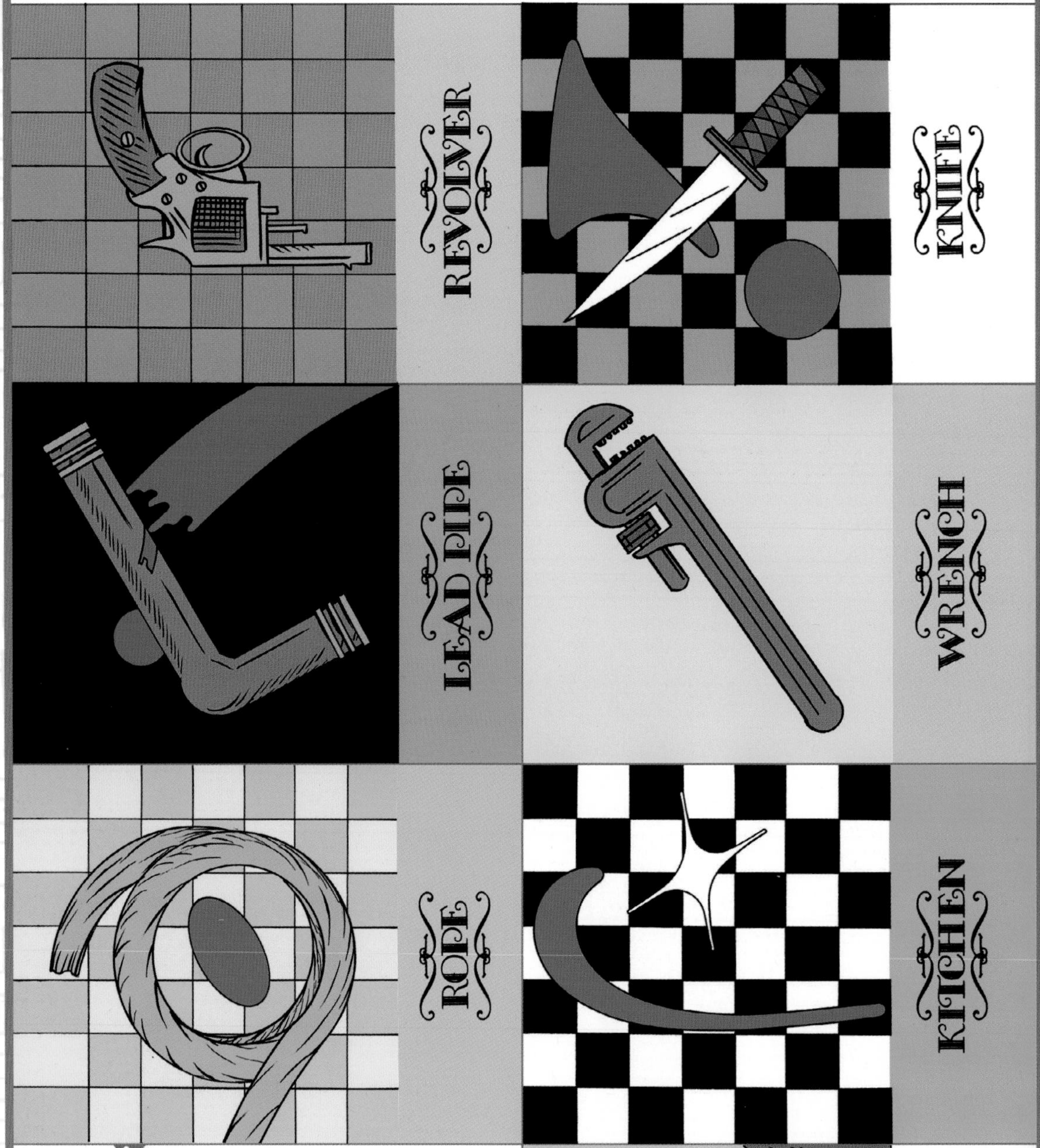
REVOLVER
KNIFE
LEAD PIPE
WRENCH
ROPE
KITCHEN

Cut out to use with your board at home.
More cards next issue.

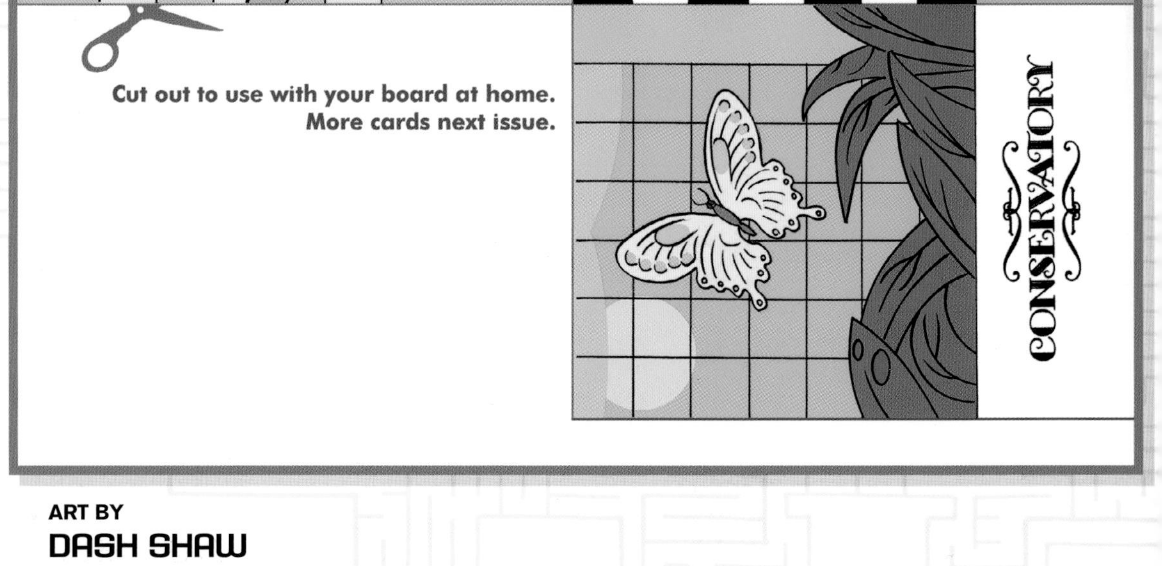
CONSERVATORY

ART BY
DASH SHAW

Cut out to use with your board at home.

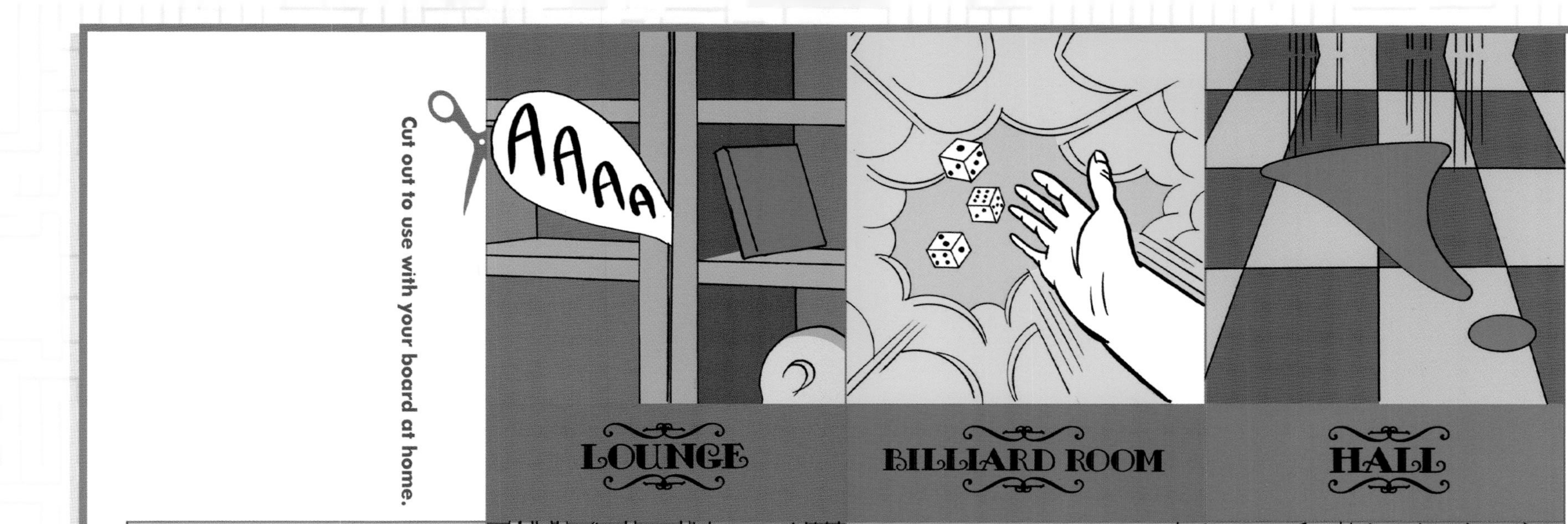
AAAA
LOUNGE
BILLIARD ROOM
HALL

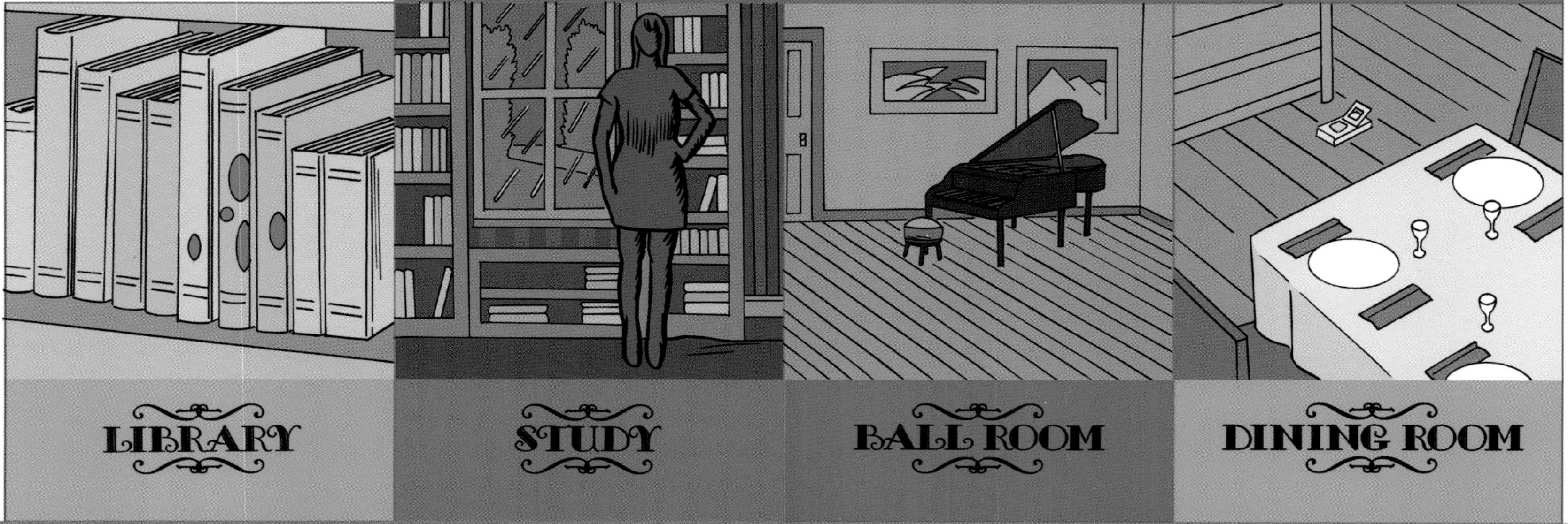
LIBRARY
STUDY
BALL ROOM
DINING ROOM

ART BY
DASH SHAW

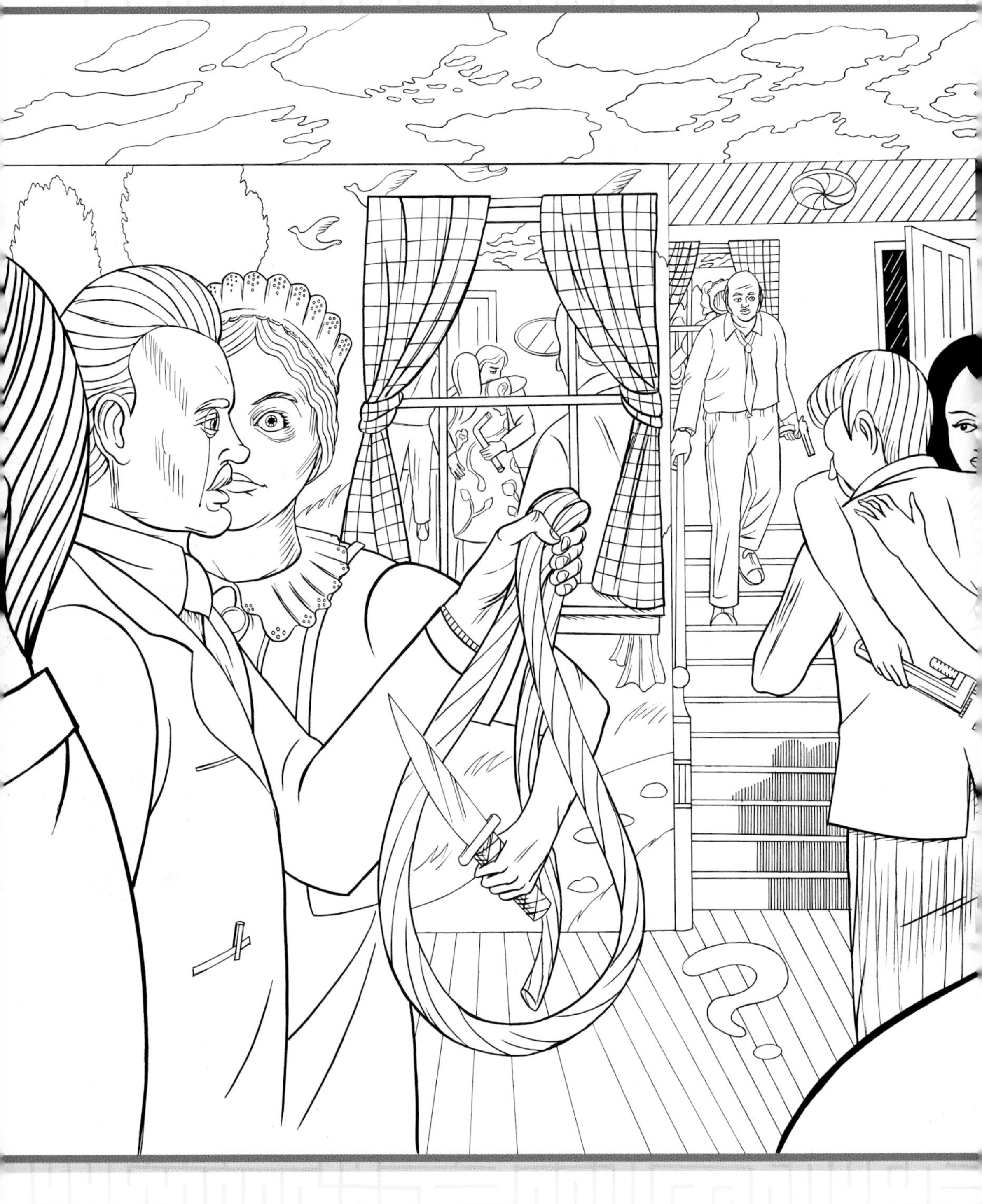

ART BY
DASH SHAW

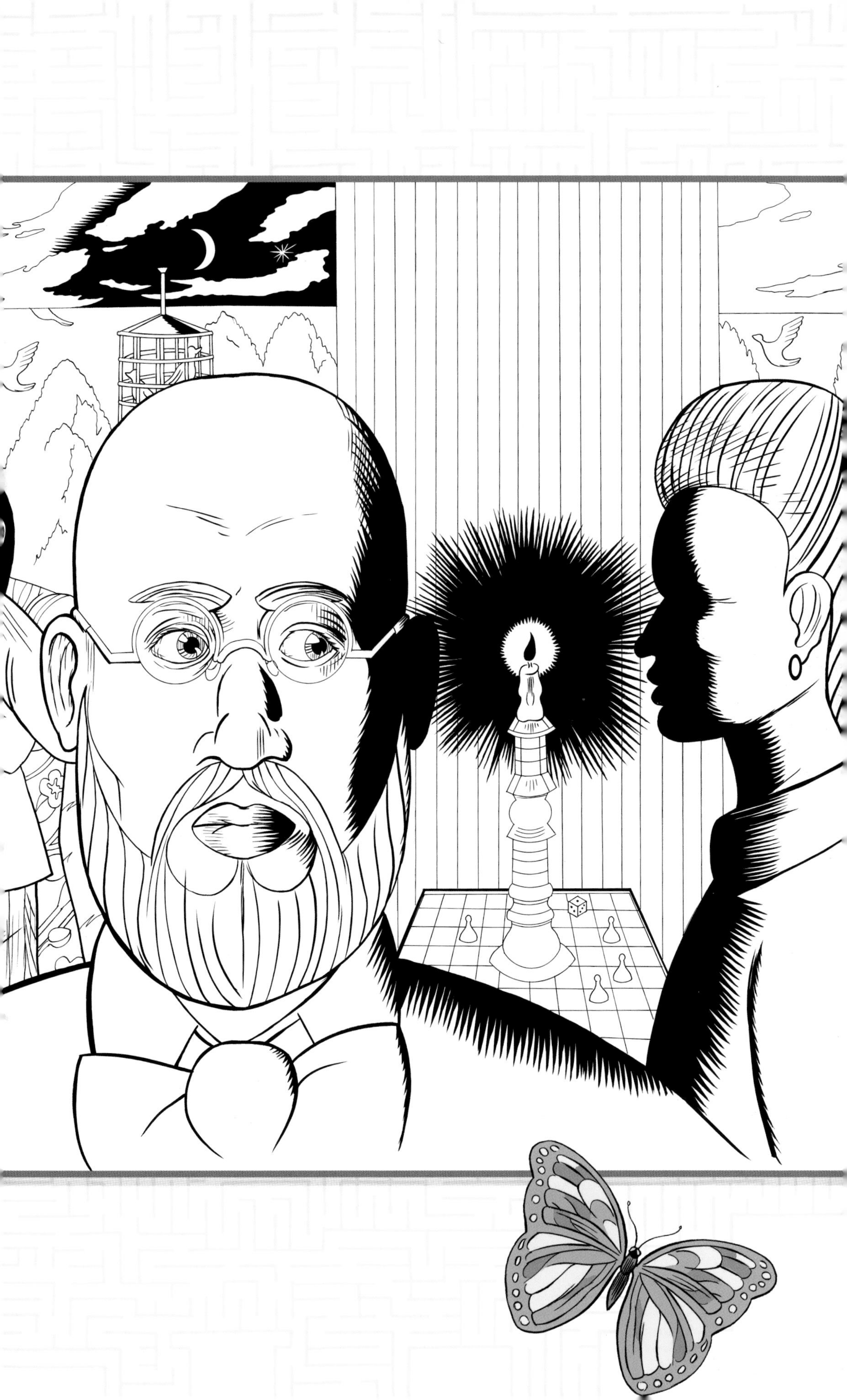

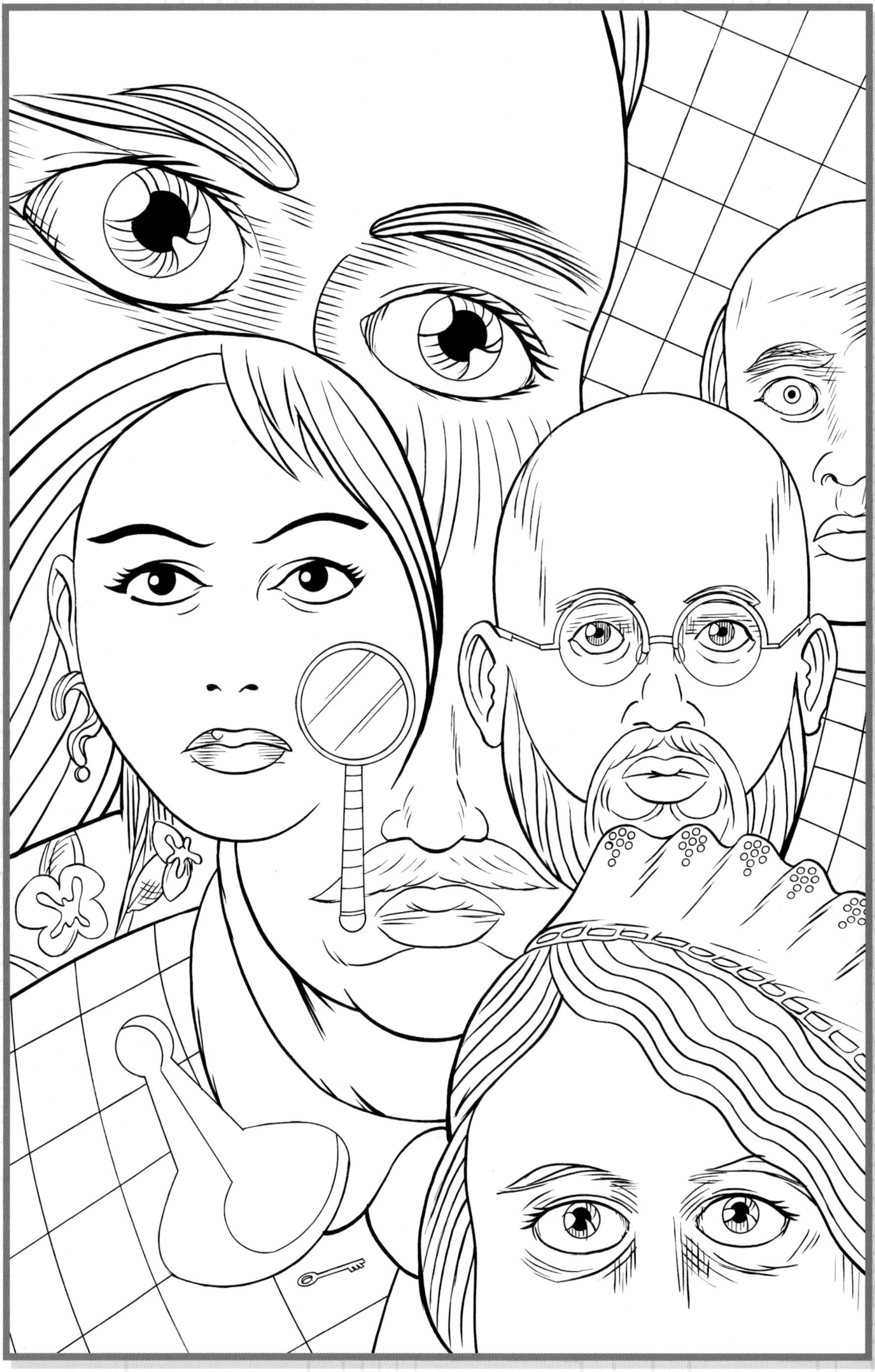

ART BY
DASH SHAW

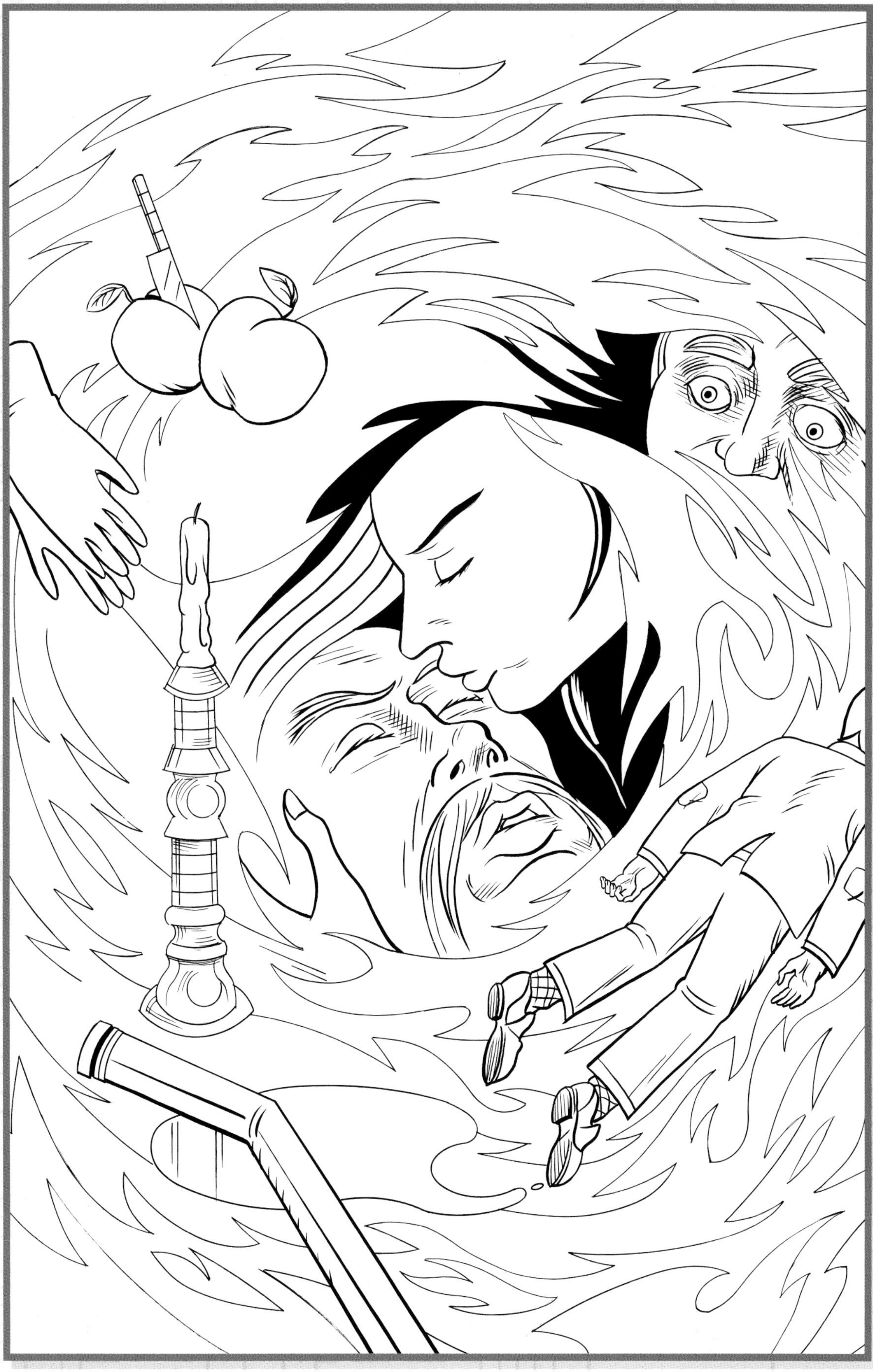

ART BY
DASH SHAW

SHAW IN THE STUDIO WITH THE CANDLESTICK

By Suzette Smith

What's your background with *Clue*? Did you play the game much when you were young?

I always liked it. I don't have a great memory, but the characters and the location stuck around in my mind. I did a short comic story in college that used *Clue* characters. I liked that they were kind of these quirky, colorful characters.

When I was a kid I loved the *Clue* Scholastic books series. They follow a similar format to *Encyclopedia Brown*, where each chapter has a mystery. I found some online and ordered them when I was doing research for this project.

Is the Scholastic series from a single perspective?

It's a third person narrator with a mystery in every chapter. And they aren't all murder. It's like, "Who stole Miss Scarlet's cat?"

What other research did you do into the *Clue* game?

I started with online histories. It was born out of the Great Depression. Sherlock Holmes was super popular at the time. It was also a board game version of murder mystery games people played at parties. I ordered a bunch of the old game boards—the '60s and the '70s versions. I grew up with the '80s game.

When I was telling other people I was working on this, Dan Nadel got very excited about it. One of his favorite artists—George Hardie, who drew the Pink Floyd *Dark Side of the Moon* cover—did a *Clue* book. It was written by Lawrence Treat. Treat did a number of other picture-mystery books and some were illustrated by the cartoonist Paul Karasik. I had never seen those before, so I immediately ordered them. They were inspirational because they included lots of coded pictures and puzzles and I thought it would be really fun to have some of that in my *Clue* comics.

Like the code Professor Plum is translating in issue one, that's a real solvable code, right?

Yeah.

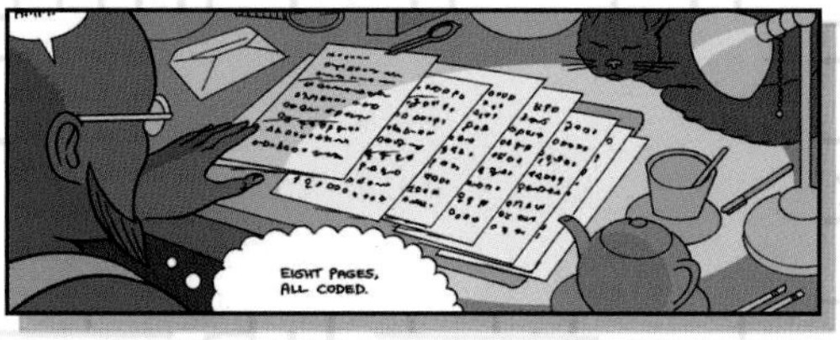
EIGHT PAGES,
ALL CODED.

So now you have a stack of *Clue* memorabilia?

It's a stack, yeah.

Did you watch the *Clue* movie?

I watched it again, but it didn't influence me much. When I told people I was doing a *Clue* thing, they immediately thought of the movie because it was very popular, especially among people my age. It wasn't popular when it came out, but it had a kind of second life on Comedy Central syndication.

There was definitely a summer where it was always on.

It became a cult classic because of that. *Clue* automatically has a dry humor aspect. The movie has it, but I think it's also

STUDY
HALL
LOUNGE
LIBRARY
WHERE WE ARE NOW (THE DINING ROOM)*
BILLIARD ROOM
CONSERVATORY
BALLROOM
KITCHEN

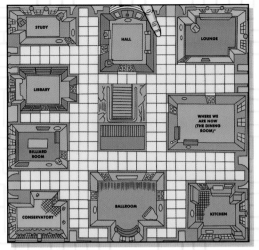

intrinsically in the names of the characters, in the board game, and the fact that all these murderous, suspicious people have gathered in this one mansion.

It definitely feels like a Dash Shaw comic poured into a *Clue* mystery or vice versa.

Dry humor is gonna be in anything that I do. With this project, I just wanted to make another comic book and the fact that it's also a *Clue* book is fun, or a bonus. Ideally it stands on its own. But I think it will also satisfy anyone who doesn't know who I am and just wants to read a *Clue* comic.

How did you end up working on a *Clue* comic?

While I was touring *My Entire High School Sinking Into the Sea* through Pittsburgh, I saw Tom Scioli and got to tell him how much I liked *Transformers vs G.I. Joe*, which he'd done for IDW Publishing.

Y'know, I still go to the comics shop once a week and I always want to buy a new comic. But a lot of it isn't interesting to me, or the alternative comics don't come out in pamphlet comic form. Scioli's work gave me something to buy there, and, because his work on *Transformers* and *Super Powers* was always so great, I would just get them as they came out.

I think that he was surprised that I was following it so closely. When he did *Go-Bots*, he asked me to do a bunch of covers for it. Then the editor David Hedgecock said, "Would you like to draw a comic for us?"

He told me some of the Hasbro properties I could make a comic about, and *Clue* immediately jumped out to me because I'd already drawn a comic with the characters—which was kind of a nice sign—and, also, I liked that it was a mystery. I like a serialized format for a mystery, as opposed to a graphic novel where it can be solved in one read. I hope people will be reading it as it comes out and, maybe like *Twin Peaks*, it can milk some suspense or the mysterious aspects of new clues.

And I liked that it didn't have a big history already established. For so many properties, you have to read a bunch of *Spider-Man* comics to even figure out if you have something to contribute to it.

I'm interested in its symbols. The murder weapons stand out immediately. Were you trying to create myths for the Clue weapons?

JACK THE RIPPER'S MOST BELOVED KNIFE.
THIS ARRIVED TO ME THROUGH MY MAID, OF ALL PEOPLE. I'VE NEVER VENTURED TO ASK HOW... WE ARE ALL ALLOWED OUR SECRETS, AREN'T WE?
ON A LESS MORBID NOTE, A SIXTEENTH-CENTURY CANDLESTICK, GIVEN TO ME BY A WEALTHY COLLECTOR AFTER HER HUSBAND'S PREMATURE DEMISE.
I PERSONALLY FIND CANDLESTICKS RATHER STODGY, AND I PREFER THE EIGHTEENTH CENTURY IN ALL THINGS, BUT THIS PIECE HAS A UNIQUE PRESENCE THAT CAN'T BE PUT INTO WORDS...
IT SHOULD REALLY BE HELD FOR ITS FULL EFFECT.

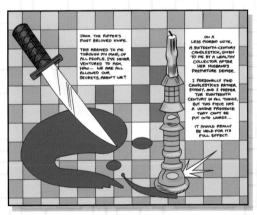

In issue one of *Clue*, I'm making histories for the objects, which takes some of the symbolic nature out of them. I'm making the knife a *specific* knife instead of just a knife. But it was the first idea I had because, growing up, one of the things I remember about *Clue* [was that there were] candlesticks as a murder weapon. As a kid born in 1983, I didn't know what a candlestick was. Candlesticks weren't around me. I guess just because it's a blunt object it means that it could kill someone. You'd think they would have picked poison.

Yeah, three of the murder weapons are just bludgeoning tools.

I thought all that was funny, but about those objects as symbols—in *Clue*, you have this deck like a tarot deck: a deck of symbols. You shuffle these characters, locations, and weapons into different arrangements to make a story. And I'm just giving the reader my version of the story.

Each comic is like a cool object in itself.

When I started working on this, I told a friend about it and he said, "It's so cool that you get to do this as a job, because as kids we all imagined a story happening in the game. We all told ourselves a story about these characters."

And until he said that I'd never really thought about it, but he's totally right. That's true. The *Clue* comic before mine is just a different interpretation of these characters and locations. Each time, it's a new interpretation and a new mystery that gets solved, based on that deck of people, places, and things. That's appealing to me. Like I said, I read a bunch of these other *Clue* things, but I didn't really want to think about how mine would fit in before or after. Every time the series comes out it's a totally new approach.

I didn't realize IDW did a *Clue* series before this one. It's cool to imagine all these different *Clue* series that don't have to be beholden to one another. They really can give it to a creator, and say, "Do whatever you want."

Another thing that I like about it is that, as far as board games go, it feels pretty gender neutral. There's an equal number of male and female characters.

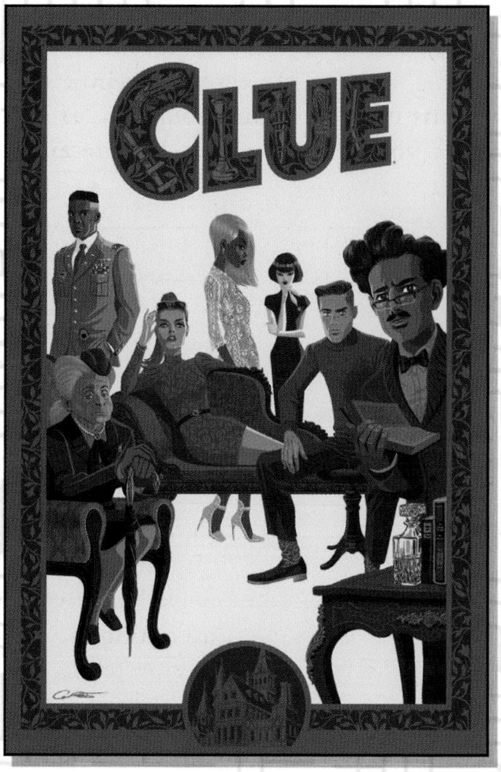
CLUE

Right, there's room for characters to be queer or not white. You start out with Professor Plum, who's a Black male character, and he's the central character until you get into the house. Then the narrative naturally comes loose and follows other characters, because now you're in the house so you can follow other people.

Yeah, the IDW comic before mine had people of color in the comic, so that had already happened. With mine, I thought it would be really lame of me to roll it back from what they did.

You've always put thought into controlling the motion and speed at which the audience reads your comics. *Clue* has some interesting puzzles that keep the reader on the page. Then there are pages that are highly symbolic, but not detailed. You could fly past them, like, "ball, dice, plum." But since they're abstract, they still slowed me down and made me consider what the ball represented.

Why a cross made of dice? It's meaningful, it makes the reader slow down, and it's a simple drawing. This seems like an accomplishment, as I've seen you move towards less detail in your drawings.

A BALL WANTS TO BOUNCE.
A DIE WANTS TO CHOOSE FATE.

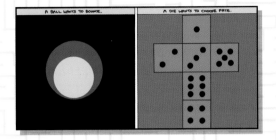

I think it's a combination of things. I grew up reading a lot of Japanese comics. I liked how those could move. There could be twenty pages of conversation, broken down. That decompressed storytelling was my main mode when I did *Bottomless Belly Button* and *Body World.*

Tom Scioli and *Go-Bots* went completely the other way, very compressed. In a single page, the Earth explodes. It all happens in one page full of 20 panels, very dense. For me, I feel like the space you give something in a comic—the literal size, scale—lends it importance. If you have someone die, you have to give it a page. If you give it one panel out of 20 on that page, you're saying it's not that important.

Regarding the simplicity of the drawing—I don't know. I wonder why I like certain things. I'm as confused—I think I'm more confused than most people about what a good drawing is. The kind of comics I like are Pete Morisi, things that look like clipart. Static. Kind of cliché imagery. Romance comics.

As soon as I read the comic, I was excited to see a lot of text. A lot of story generally connotes value to me.

I knew each issue would have 24 pages of comic, so I tried to make sure that enough happened in that 24 pages where it's a good read. But I also wanted to have it be decompressed enough to where it wouldn't just be a dump of information.

There are three comics in the series and this interview will appear at the end.

Right, I'm finishing up the second comic right now.

So, at this point, they're undrawn?

Yeah.

But you have the plot mapped out?

Yeah, but there's space in it. For me, part of the fun is pretending to be—or for a brief time being—an actual monthly comic book artist. Part of the experiment was that each issue is taking me a month to write and draw it. I didn't take a year drawing them and then stagger the releases. I have an outline, but this is an actual monthly book.

So many of the comics that I grew up loving—daily comics, pamphlet comics—were done on a schedule. They were done at this rate. I really wanted to do that. I think it's been good for my creative life to give myself this challenge.

When I was saying there's a simple symbology to it, there's also these really wonderful little bits that are drawn in a style that makes them feel like they're dashed off. There's hierarchy to it. There are detailed, arranged panels. And then you have sparse panels that are full of meaning and these little comic strip-y funny gags, like when someone meets Saint Peter or there's a Pig-Pen reference. Maybe that's more controlling the pace, controlling the tone. It's compelling, but it's also funny in some places.

Clue is kind of realistic because it's a murder mystery, but it also has that dry

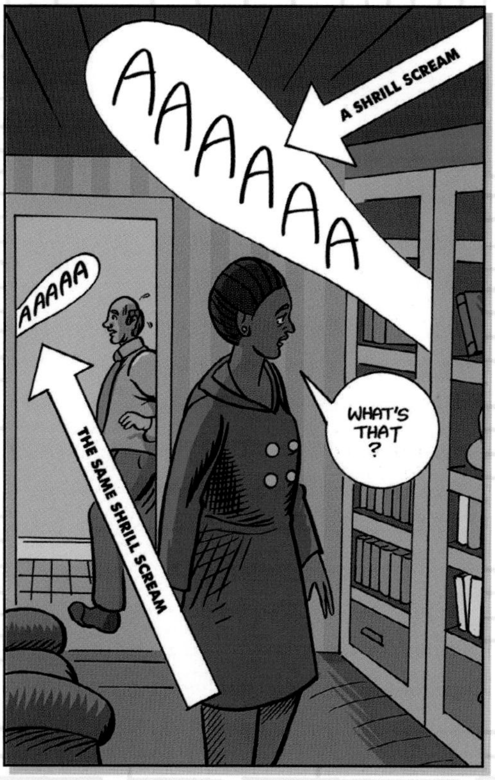
AAAAAA
A SHRILL SCREAM
AAAAA
THE SAME SHRILL SCREAM
WHAT'S THAT ?

New Yorker gag humor comedy, so I wanted it to be drawn in a space that could move between those things. And that it would be interesting and funny that those things are occupying the same story.

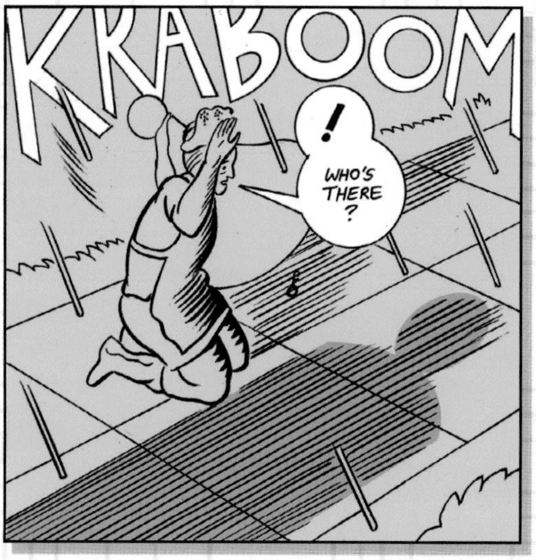
KRABOOM
!
WHO'S THERE ?

The way sound happens in this comic seems important. Sometimes there's a "boom" written across the page and sometimes there are arrows, pointing at a person screaming, denoting "a shrill scream. "There's a lot of stuff that works for me both as a person who appreciates comics and as a person who appreciates design and page layout.

A lot of that is based on intuition. I know I really want an arrow there on the page, so I'll write "a shrill scream" inside an arrow and it'll be more appealing to me than writing "Aaaaaa," a bunch of letters that also mean a scream. You're pointing out all of these things that are probably strange decisions but are just what I thought would be a better thing to do on that page.

Professor Plum has a Sherlock Holmes elementary approach to problem solving. Later we find out that Colonel Mustard has paranoid-ish thoughts, and he's trying to figure out everyone's motives. I was wondering if we're going to end up seeing the internality of all the characters over the course of the series? (The ones that haven't died.)

I hope by the end of issue three we'll check in with everybody. Issue two is mostly Scarlet, ninety-five percent Scarlet. It felt like Scarlet deserved her own issue. She goes first, famously, and I think she's most people's favorite character.

You've told me you have a bad memory, but then throughout you've been drawing down all these names of people I've never researched. You have a really precise memory for stuff like friends, collaborators, and influences. You always remember where you get stuff from.

I just have a bad memory of my life. I think it's because I spent my whole life drawing comics.

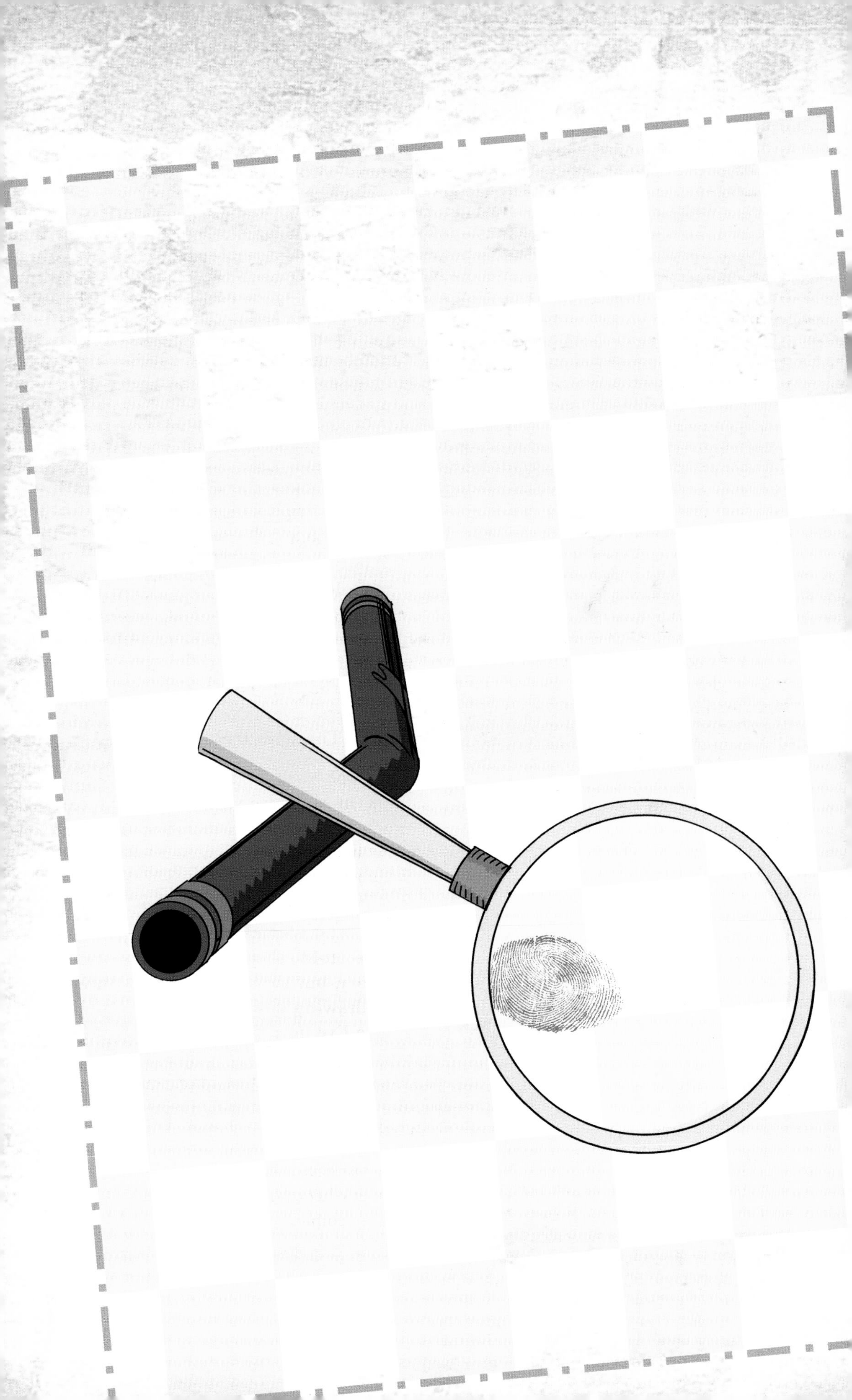

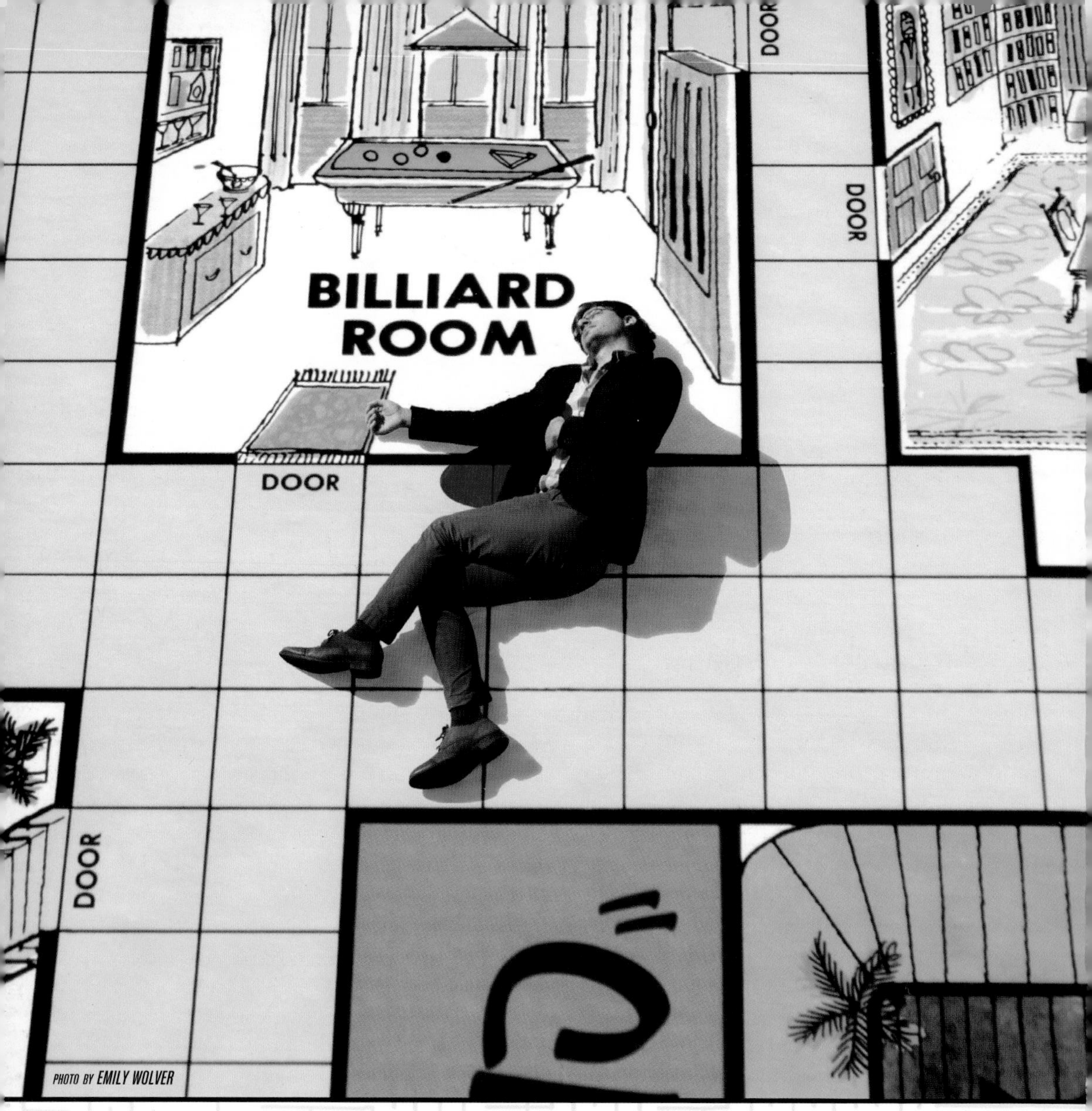
BILLIARD ROOM
DOOR
DOOR
DOOR
DOOR
PHOTO BY EMILY WOLVER

Shaw is the cartoonist of many graphic novels, such as *Doctors*, *Bottomless Belly Button*, *BodyWorld*, *New School*, and *Cosplayers*. He also wrote and directed the animated feature "My Entire High School Sinking into the Sea" (starring the voice talents of Jason Schwartzman, Lena Dunham, Reggie Watts, Maya Rudolph, and Susan Sarandon), which premiered in the 2016 New York Film Festival main slate and the Toronto International Film Festival. It continued to play film festivals throughout the world, and had a U.S. theatrical release in 2017. It's currently available on Netflix streaming in North America. It was one of ArtForum Amy Taubin's "Best Films of the Year."

He's directed a music video for Sigur Ros and animated sections for documentaries and television, such as for the second season of *13 Reasons Why*. His comic short stories recently appeared in the Fantagraphics anthology series *Now*. He lives in Richmond, Virginia.